# THE *Sweetest* REVENGE

## CHERYL BARTON

*All Preorders Available at www.cherylbarton.net*

### *Sensual. Stimulating. Suggestive.*

Those words and so many more wicked, sexy thoughts and salacious images ignited an irresistible, fiery flame of desirous passion in Delaney's recurring erotic dream. Her deepest hidden desires sounded embarrassing at her age. That kept her from telling even her closest friends about the mystery man who seduced her night after night, leaving her in a hazy, exhaustive state of out of this world satisfaction. All of this occurred when the world was sleeping peacefully without tossing and turning in heat; except for her. The truth was, she yearned for her fantasy to become her reality. Her body craved it daily, especially at night. If she could snap her fingers like a genie and turn her dream into reality, she would be snapping away, even while asleep.

In her dream, Delaney consciously knew it was a dream. She didn't know how it was possible, nor did she care. Her one and only desire was for it to keep happening.

A scandalous, sizzling sensation surged through her the moment her tall, muscular stranger dropped the towel from all of his gorgeousness. The sight of him gave her visuals of strength and power by way of the mountainous ranges of his perfectly physically fit body.

Gazing at his nakedness from behind, since he stood with his back to her, she admired that nothing about him ever disappointed. Her eyes traveled up and down his body from his broad shoulders to the massive, brawny, well sculptured back muscles that nature had blessed him with. Delaney felt and heard the shaky breaths from her mouth, not sure if she should inhale or exhale. She thought that any movement on her part, even turning to shift her legs over the side of the bed, would cause this man, who possessed perfect symmetry and

1

an aura of beauty she'd never experienced before, to disappear. Still, she was close enough to him from her vantage point under her satin comforter covered king sized bed, that a slight lift of her manicured fingers could result in her skin touching his. Temptation was so great that she couldn't resist not doing so for another moment.

Triumphantly, her hand out. She could feel the heat radiating from his body. It was still coated with wet pellets from the steamy, hot shower he'd just taken. She could see his wet footprints on the bedroom floor where his feet had made a path from the shower to her bed. She didn't care about the water residue on the floor. She cared about the way his body glistened and teased her eyes. Delaney's tongue was already doing a happy dance at the ideas floating through her head of what they could be doing next. There had been so many nights where he'd brought her raging body to a deliciously, blissful release. With anticipation, she tried to will the stranger, with her mind, to turn around in order to give her the full experience from the kind of man she'd only read about in romance novels.

For years, she'd kept her desires for untamed, uninhibited, wild, racy intimacy locked away, hidden from a husband she knew did not share her thoughts or desires when it came to more expressive ways to connect in their loving. She had settled for a more missionary type sex life for many years. Now, as a single woman, no more did she want to do that. Her dreams were showing her how to manifest what she wanted. The new, single Delaney owed it to the previously sheltered and married Delaney.

"Are you ready for me?"

Was she? She still didn't know.

Her mystery man spoke gruffly to her over his shoulder. His husky, baritone voice sliced through her resolve; her body shivered with need.

She gulped through the lump that landed and stayed put in her throat; her anxiety was on five-thousand.

"I want to be," she stuttered out.

"You are. Go ahead; touch me. I'm your entry into a life of no boundaries in the bedroom. My aim is to please you."

"Am I really ready for this much?" she asked on a whisper.

"What? You're not up for a little sexy revenge?"

"I've always been told that the best revenge is no revenge because it could backfire."

"Sweetness, the greatest revenge against who you were for someone else is to be who you want to be for you."

With his back still to her, Delaney heard his suggestive laugh as his head fell back and his body moved as laughter overtook him.

"Laughter?"

"Yes, because that kind of talk is for amateurs. I'm not talking about revenge against another person; I'm speaking of revenge against the *old* you by the she-devil you've held captive inside for far too long. That old Delaney has made you believe that you don't deserve the kind of loving *I* can give you – the kind that keeps you up at night, pleasuring yourself, waiting for the real thing; *ME!* I think you're ready. No more wet dreams for you. You've been waiting and wanting more for too long without successfully getting it. The time is now to treat that sexy body of yours right."

Delaney heard the words and saw the man. All she had to do was say yes. She needed to be willing to get out of life what she wanted and needed.

Moving her body, she slid from the bed, allowing her feet to touch the warmth of the wood floor. She reached for his body as he turned around to face her. Her brain screamed *yes*. She allowed her eyes to gaze down his body until they settled on that part of him that had been a mystery to her eyes. She'd only felt him in her body, in her dreams. If she were being real and honest with herself, she needed to literally feel it to know that it was real. Her purpose was to know that the long, strong, thick part of him could bring her the kind of pleasure she desired at this point in her life.

She was no longer afraid. Touching him was her step into making this more of a reality than ever before. No longer was everything about him a part of the unknown. Her eyes darted up to where his eyes should be, but his face wouldn't come into focus. Her hand reached down as her body moved down. He was right. She was more than ready for him; *all of him.*

Just when she was ready to take the leap, she sighed when she was suddenly shocked into reality. A piercing sound over her shoulder drew her attention away from another night of enraptured hedonism. She snapped out of her dream and sat straight up in bed. This was the real. She was again alone. She must have chosen the wrong pill when it as offered to her; the red or the blue. She needed the real.

There was no man in front of her, no wet foot prints on the floor and that part of him that she had reached for was no longer there.

Delaney shook off the disappointment of her greatest desire that was again out of her reach. She also remembered that her fantasy man had no face. Who was he? He made her feel the sweetest stirrings in every part of her body; a body that was ready to be awakened and ready to take intimacy by the reigns. She wanted that ride to ecstasy. Her mystery man was all-in. Was she?

Looking around her bedroom, she chuckled out loud, winking at the old, self-denying Delaney she imagined was standing at the foot of the bed shaking her finger to dissuade her. She was tired of her. She blinked her eyes like a genie actually would and the old Delaney disappeared. This Delaney who was now woke was more than ready to say yes!

# 1

A beautiful, sunny Thursday morning turned out to be the perfect day for driving on the I-10 out of Tampa, Florida headed toward Tallahassee, Florida. Delaney Monroe silently celebrated the person who had the incredible idea to create convertible cars like the magnificent one she was driving. Her new white, two-seater, soft top convertible Audi S5 had been her dream car. Affording the car had never been the hold back, but the life she lived had. These days, she was experiencing the kind of freedom she didn't know existed. Freedom felt good. She knew it also looked good on her and in this car. That garnered her an even brighter smile as she quickly glanced at herself in the rearview mirror.

Staring back at her was a woman who was more than ready to discover a life meant for her and only her. With her eyes back on the road, she sped down the highway without a care in the world as cars breezed by her on the left and on the right. Until she purchased her pristine white car, she hadn't noticed the large number of cars the same color that traveled the roads each day. By now, she was usually already at her office. Not today. She had other plans on tap that excluded anything work related. To her that was synonymous with not getting a fresh new start on working on her, which is exactly what she had been seeking and found.

Delaney had always wanted a convertible, but having twins, Kyrie and Kennedy, who are now adults who were once little children, this was not the ideal car to trudge two kids around Tampa in. She couldn't, not with the need for a large space to first include a double stroller and everything little kiddies would need, to then having space for sports equipment for when the kids were older and racing from one athletic event to another. She and her ex-husband, Davis, made sure their kids were well-rounded. That meant catering to their desires to try out various activities. Again, not something a convertible could accommodate.

With the kids, now twenty-one and moving into the dorms at Florida A&M University in Tallahassee for their junior year and having their own cars and lives, it was her time to shine. She'd worked hard the past four years running her own company, *Bronmon Consulting*. Her firm was a rising star among many, but hers also stood out because it was a woman-owned, black-owned business, specializing in enterprise information technology. *Bronmon's* focus was on planning and management of healthcare programs.

Staying focused on her driving, Delaney switched to the fast lane. She was a happy, sexy, forty-seven-year-old divorcee whose life was finally coming full-circle. She had learned to go for what she wanted in life when it came to personal and business ventures. That's how life was for her and she was having no regrets. She couldn't because one of her many mantras in life was, *what was for her, would be for her*. She refused to question this time in her life. Nor would she live it according to any rules. That's why for the next few days of her vacation away from the company, she was going to focus on herself and leave work in the office where it belongs. No staff came close to the greatness in those she employed. She also trusted the decision-making of her leadership team.

The heat of the first week of August, with a slight breeze in the air, more so from her driving, had her reaching for her long hair to toss it back when she remembered she now wore it short and sassy. Those days of keeping it naturally long and flowing because that's how Davis liked it, were over. Short, with little maintenance, was the key for a business woman, while still maintaining her sexiness thanks to the countless number of hours she enjoyed working out and running each week.

Long hair is perfect for a convertible and luckily, her walk-in closet full of wigs could have her with long hair in mere seconds. Everything about her life was about flexibility. She loved all that hair could be, but she wasn't her hair. It was a small part of who she was. Today, she was a woman on the road to see her kids before an even longer weekend full of fun in New Orleans. Kyrie and Kennedy came first and she couldn't wait to see their new digs for the year. They were officially moving in to begin another semester.

Her plan was to get an early start, hoping to bypass any morning rush hour traffic. Afterall, it was a workday for everyone but her. Her first stop had been the car wash. As she waited, she'd sent texts to both kids letting them know she was getting on the road. They had left home the day before, driving in their own cars, something she was still a little hesitant about. In the prior two years, she felt better with them not having cars on campus, but her ex-husband had made a promise to them.

Delaney thought she would feel nostalgic about the kids not only turning twenty-one recently, but exerting more independence after getting their own cars for Christmas. That wouldn't have been her choice for them as Christmas gifts, but Davis, who enjoyed spoiling them, especially after their divorce was final three years ago, decided it was time the kids were able to get around more. He'd promised them cars if they maintained dean's list status for their first two years. Both did it with ease, so he came through on his promise to them. Keeping promises was not Davis's forte. She went with letting him make the call about the cars. Though the kids wanted sports cars, they settled for safer versions of the BMW car brand; a new SUV for Kennedy and a used, only by two years, five-series for Kyrie.

Once they were settled in, she could then head to New Orleans to join her best friend, Monica Newton, for the meet and greet for the bridal party for her wedding happening soon, two weeks after Halloween.

Her best friend and once cousin by marriage was getting married to the man of her dreams, or so she had been told. She didn't mean to question the love Monica had found, but she was a little hesitant at hearing that her bestie had met a man, James Engels, after her move to New Orleans back in January.

Monica, who for years had also lived in Tampa, had accepted a new position as a professor at a college where she would be teaching African American Studies. Three months ago, Monica called her all giddy and said she was engaged. That was followed by the news that the actual wedding would be held in West Palm Beach, Florida. Delaney thought her love and marriage were moving extremely fast, but she was nothing if she wasn't the best friend that Monica could ever ask for. That love for her friend had her taking a nine-hour road trip to New Orleans before the end of the day.

With her black and gold Chanel sunglasses protecting her eyes from the sun, she glanced at herself again before quickly changing lanes to speed along, this time behind a sexy black Porsche. What was the purpose of having a fast sports car if the desire to go a little faster than usual didn't hit you?

She couldn't help it when her eyes strayed and landed on another sports car, a silver Mercedes two-seater with the roof down. The driver pulled up beside her, keeping up with her pace. Looking to her right, she spotted a handsome man, probably in his late fifties or early sixties. He removed his glasses and winked at her before blowing kisses her way. She smiled, knowing she still had it. She gave him a quick wave of her fingers and pushed her Audi a little harder, leaving the man in the dust. His quick flirting reminded her of what happened at the car wash earlier that morning.

As she sat waiting for the detail work to be done, a man walked over and sat on the bench near her. He started a conversation with her, which quickly turned to flirting. He was definitely handsome as he walked in her direction with a sexy, slight bow to his legs. He was wearing a sexy pair of denims and a crisp white t-shirt with his eyes covered in a flashy pair of designer shades. He had a way about him that spelled nothing but confidence; something she loved in a man. Because of that, she didn't mind a little flirting back and forth with him. The man seemed nice enough, but she wasn't interested. She knew he would ask for her number when her car was ready. When her car was called and she stood, she thanked him for the conversation while also letting him down easy.

As she walked to her car, he continued the flirting, letting her know that she was the most beautiful woman he'd ever set eyes on. She thanked him, got in her car and drove off. He waved as she pulled out of the water covered lot. Not being rude, she waved back, but kept moving. She loved the attention. She didn't focus on it too much when she was married. Now? She enjoyed it.

Delaney was relaxed as she drove, knowing the kids would be okay until she arrived. The day before, with their father driving the U-Haul truck with their belongings, they had set off for school. Arriving a day early, they had checked into a hotel the night before. Kennedy told her that Davis had taken them out for steak dinners once they made it to Tallahassee. He had arrived in town from his home in Miami, where he'd moved after the divorce. Divorced or not, and even with him living hours away, they each made the kids their priority. Part of that was his enjoyment of lugging them and all of their belongings back to campus each year. The kids were arriving earlier than most of the kids who would be arriving for school soon.

Kennedy was moving in as a resident director of her dorm floor. That meant she needed to be settled in before the other students arrived. Kyrie, who played football, had been at school for the latter part of the summer, but was now moving into the dorm where most of the players who played sports lived.

Together, they had all packed the truck and had hit the road later in the afternoon. She would miss driving them herself with Davis following in a U-Haul. Their lives were changing in so many ways. There was no room to complain because both had always made her proud.

She thought back to that day when the kids were seniors in high school and had come home declaring that they'd made their choice of where they would attend college. Both chose Florida A&M, her alma mater and the place where she'd met Davis back when she was a student there.

Back then, at twenty-two and a senior, Davis had been eight years older than her and like many of the other twenty-two-year-old college seniors, she'd fallen hard for him the moment she saw him. He was handsome and carried himself like a man on a mission. She was a cheerleader and he was a handsome professor. Knowing their connection was powerful, before the end of the semester and before he asked her out on their first date, he had resigned his position and joined his best friend, Stanley, in starting a major technology company. That move ended up being the best decision he could have ever made. Their company was one of the largest on the east coast, which made Davis and their family well off, financially. Stanley's father, a powerhouse on Wall Street, provided them with the capital to start the company. It quickly took off, making a huge profit in its third year. The following year, she and Davis were married and the twins came soon after.

When their marriage eventually ended after a year of separation and three years of back and forth in court, she used the money from the settlement, which was in the seven-figure range, to start her own firm. Since then, she never looked back.

She and Davis were cordial but not always friendly to each other. The divorce proceedings had become contentious when he thought he would be able to walk away with his only obligation being to the kids. A judge gave him a dose of reality. In the end, she got a large financial settlement with the purpose of it being to allow her to start her own business. She'd worked for his company on a part-time basis for over ten years, working most of the time from home. That allowed her to still be a stay-at-home mother, exactly what Davis wanted, while she still got the chance to be a part of the business world. She didn't have an undergraduate and graduate degree in information technology for nothing.

After the divorce, she wanted and needed to branch away from his company and felt she deserved the chance to have her own. The judge agreed with the case her lawyer made. In the end, she got the financial settlement along with the kids' private high school and college tuitions paid by him, a substantial trust fund set up for the kids, the home they shared in Tampa and an additional cabin in the mountains, on the water that they owned in Georgia. That cabin meant a lot to her. It was where they spent a lot of summers and spring breaks as a family. Davis wasn't hurting even after that. He left their marriage with millions and with more to be made from his profitable company. He also kept their Miami home, which he moved into full-time to run his company's Miami office once Stanley took over their other location in San Francisco. Their smaller office in Tampa which Davis had built and ran for years, was now run by another vice president in his company. Along with that home in Miami, he retained a condo in New York City, where he often traveled for business.

Reaching to change the station on her Sirius XM radio, Monica's name appeared on the large five by seven navigational system screen. She had been expecting the call.

Leave it to Monica to call at this ungodly early morning hour just to make sure she was still making the trip to New Orleans.

She accepted the call and waited.

"Delaney, I've been calling you for an hour. Are you on the road yet?"

Exhaling, Delaney continued humming a Mary J. Blige song as she happily drove along. She had heard the million times that her phone rang and knew who it would be.

"Monica, you know I'm on the road. This is check-in day for the kids, something I told you about last night when you called. You know how I get when it's time for them to go back to school. It was bad enough that I barely saw them this summer between them working summer jobs, Kyrie away at football camp and then spending any spare time they had with their friends."

"And you're coming to New Orleans right after, right?"

"Really? You're asking me if I'm going to miss celebrating being the maid of honor at my best friend's wedding?" Delaney asked with playful intentions. "Have I ever let you down? Before you answer, don't bring up that time when I promised to make you my famous lasagna and things didn't quite turn out that way."

Monica's hearty laugh bounced off of the inner walls of the car, causing her to drift slightly to the right. When she waved to the man in the large truck in the lane next to her to apologize, he winked and blew her a kiss. She sped by him and steadied herself.

"You did let me down, though."

"Again, I still got it!" Delaney yelled.

"What?"

"Oh, sorry. This guy in a huge semi-truck just winked at me. I think he mouthed that I am beautiful or something like that. That's like the third time today. I think it's the car!" she belted out.

"Yeah, we know you still got it and it's not the car. It's your killer smile, gorgeous face and sexy body. Men know a strikingly beautiful woman when they see one, even when she's speeding down the highway. About my lasagna? You still owe me!"

"Woman, I've made so much lasagna for you over the years. I've paid you a million times over."

"True, but I want the one you were supposed to make that night. You owe me for that batch."

"I went into early labor with the twins, your godchildren. Remember them? The best things that ever happened to your life and mine?"

"You're not telling any lies, but still, I want my lasagna. Let's not forget the first best day of my life was the day my cousin Davis introduced you to our family. You and I became instant friends. I miss living in Tampa. I miss you. I miss my godchildren. As far as Davis? Not so much. He didn't know a good thing from all those years of having you. He is too much like his father was."

"Yeah, I know. Well, the marriage is over, done, buried and stinking it's so over."

"He's with the kids?"

"Yeah. They left early yesterday. They can't check-in until today, I think at ten. I'll be there soon and then I'm headed straight for you. Are we having dinner later tonight or does James have plans to have you all to himself?"

"Yes, we're having dinner. James loves the things I do to him when he gets me to himself, but tonight is about spending some time with you. I'm going to see him soon at the hotel to check on some last-minute things. His cousin, Nashall, is arriving today, I think or maybe it was last night."

"He's the guy paying for everything, right?"

"Yes, he is. He's covering this weekend and everything around the wedding in West Palm Beach. Wait until you see the hotel when you get here. It's amazing. James went all out. I can't wait for you to meet him in person. I know you're still salty that you haven't met him considering I'm going to marry him. Trust me when I tell you he is a wonderful man. After my first marriage and all I went through, I was finally ready and open for a man like James who only wants to love me. You'll love meeting Nashall. I've only talked to him, but James has only had great things to say about him. I still can't believe you didn't know who he was. Even though he's retired from professional basketball, he was the biggest star, even bigger than LeBron James. I know, you've heard the names but don't know much about them because you're not into sports other than when your kids play them. No need to tell me. Either way, this weekend is going to be memorable. I'm glad you're able to make it."

"Monica, where else would I be? I know you keep saying you were unsure of what would happen to our friendship after my divorce from Davis, but one had nothing to do with the other. Our friendship is forever. You are my bestie and I would never miss anything involving you. I can't wait to get there."

"That's why I love you and so will James. He knows everything about you. I'm going to let you get back to driving and flirting with men on the highway. Drive safe."

"How about I buy you a nice Italian dinner when I get to New Orleans tonight? I know we decided to have dinner but we didn't lay out where we would eat."

"I know the perfect place. I've discovered a lot of nice restaurants since moving here. Can I tell you again how excited I am about this weekend? The bridal party gets to meet each other tomorrow night and hang out some over the weekend. You already know my sister and my cousins who are in the wedding. You will get to meet some of James' family as well. There are so many fun things planned for the next three days. Wait until you see the suite that I reserved for you. You are going to feel like a queen in a castle. Get off of here so you can get here sooner. Love you, Laney."

"Love you too. I'll see you later today."

Four or so hours to the kids and then five hours to New Orleans, she would be exhausted, but time with them all would be well worth it.

## 2

Being back in New Orleans gave Nashall Patterson that feeling of home he needed whenever he traveled here. This was the place where his life began. This is where he developed his love for all things basketball, thanks to his favorite cousin, James from his mother's side of the family. Like James, he was raised by their grandmother, Ida Mae Engels, his mother's mother and James' father's mother. A lot of kids came and went through his grandmother's house. Her kids may not have turned out the way she hoped they would, but when they messed up, she was there to help with her grandchildren.

He somberly thought about his grandmother because she was no longer living. He was happy that she lived long enough to see him attain great success. She had even attended a few of his games as a professional basketball player for Miami. She wasn't a big fan of flying, especially as she got older, not caring for airplanes. Rare for a rookie player, but in his second year of playing at the age of nineteen, he would rent a private jet to bring his grandmother to any game she wanted to attend. He eventually bought his own plane to travel the world in. His year of playing college ball at Duke University where he led his team to the championship had paid off for him. He missed everything about his grandmother. Mostly, he missed the tight hugs he would get from her whenever he visited. Usually, her house would be his first stop. The weight of her loss impacted him every day, but more so when he returned to New Orleans knowing she wouldn't be there. No matter what he did in life or where he spent his time, this place would always be home for him.

After landing hours earlier after a business trip to Chicago from his home in Miami, he had de-planed with his security team in tow. His team consisted of Kilton Jacobs, the head of security and Cord Lomax, the only person outside of Kilton that he allowed to drive him around. Most times, he drove himself, but after traveling pretty much nonstop for the past two months, he was too exhausted to do so. Either way, Kilton and Cord were never far when he was out and about. The two of them led his full team with ease.

Though he loved the fame and fortune his pro-ball career and now his business acumen brought him, he hated that he had to have security to protect him from those who wouldn't think twice about doing harm to him. That was the life of a celebrity. Though he didn't like the attention, he dealt with it.

No longer playing ball, he was happy to be able to focus on his life and career after basketball. First and foremost, were his kids, his daughter, Yasmine, who at ten, carried his heart around in her pocket. He loved her more than life. Then there was his son, Ashton, who at six wanted to follow in his footsteps to play basketball professionally one day. Their mother, Zonnique, whom he met while on the road as a player earlier in his career, told him that after every visit he would make to them while on the road, Ashton would sleep with a basketball, dreaming about the day he could play ball like his daddy. He missed the kids when he had to be away from them.

Though he and Zonnique's relationship never flourished beyond friendship with benefits during his long stints of being on the road playing ball, they remained friends while co-parenting. When he retired a year ago, just before his thirty-sixth birthday, Zonnique moved from her home in Atlanta where she was close to her parents, to a house he bought for her and the kids in Miami. He wanted to be close to the kids and she didn't hesitate to say that she felt the same way.

Being within driving distance of them was perfect. Even after Zonnique had fallen in love with an A-list music artist, she remained in Miami. Zonnique's fiancé, Chopper, recently made Miami his home, as well, in order to be close to her. All-in-all, the setup worked for them. He was looking forward to getting back to Miami after the weekend in order to take the kids to school on Wednesday for their first day of the year.

His original plan was to head straight for the hotel to connect with James and then relax in his suite until later in the day. He tried to resist his usual ride down his grandmother's street, but nostalgia took over and the car, with Cord behind the wheel, was making the last turn onto the street where he grew up.

"Nash, we're coming up on the house," Cord noted, interrupting his thoughts. No one ever called him Nashall anymore. Since his childhood, he enjoyed the shortened version of his name.

Snapping out of his mental trip down memory lane, Nash lowered the window of the black Navigator truck with its dark tinted windows just as the house where he'd spent his childhood came into view. The house had both good and bad memories for him.

"I still can't get over the transformation you made to the property for your grandmother," Kilton noted from the front passenger seat, in front of where Nash sat. He nodded in agreement. Of those in his inner circle, only Kilton could understand where he'd come from. They had been childhood friends back when he was a scrawny kid in school flexing a chest that was all ribs and skin; no muscle, unlike now.

"I could never get her to move out of this house. She would not budge. It was a struggle to get her to let me refurbish it for her. I begged and pleaded for almost two years. When I got my first big check, I was still living in an apartment. I could have bought myself a house, but I wanted to pour my money into making sure she had the best of everything. It wasn't until her sister came to visit, one day, and I talked about all that I could have done to make life easier for my grandmother," he said.

"Like what?" Cord asked.

Though he and Kilton had been friends since childhood, Cord had joined the ranks as a friend over ten years ago. He had shared a lot with Cord over the years, but the things of his past that he and Kilton knew about, he would never tell another living soul. They must have taken the drive down this street hundreds of times, but not once have they really talked about what this house meant to him.

"I told her that I could renovate the entire house. I wanted to put her bedroom on the first floor so that she wouldn't have to walk up the stairs to get to her bedroom or the bathroom. There wasn't one on the first floor in the original floor plan. I wanted to redo her kitchen, giving her marble counters and the newest in kitchen appliances. Back then, I also purchased the house next door to hers. I told them that I could make all the rooms bigger by combining the two properties into one.

My grandmother wasn't walking well. Getting her a wheelchair would help her a lot. It took her sister to convince her to let me make the changes. I wanted to add an elevator to get her from one floor to the next. I knew she would love a large back deck and a large yard for her to plant her vegetables, fruits and flowers."

"What finally convinced her?" Cord asked.

"When my aunt told her that I was going to do some renovating at her house for her, my grandmother got jealous," Nash snickered at the remembrance.

Kilton laughed too.

"That'll do it," Cord joked.

"Yeah, that definitely did it. No way was my Nana going to let her sister outdo her. She went to stay with my aunt for six months while the work was being done. When she got back, she cried in my arms the moment she saw the house. I thought she was disappointed that the house she knew was pretty much gone. Instead of just the one small house, I combined the two properties together to make one large house with everything on one level. She had finally agreed to that. When she finished crying, she told me that she'd never seen a more beautiful home in her life. She loved this house. She got all new furniture. I even hired an interior designer to help her decorate it. I added three bedrooms and the combined houses had four bathrooms. She had live-in care and a cook, though they would tussle in the kitchen."

"Man, your grandmother sure could cook," Kilton noted.

"You go that right! She never wanted to stop making the dishes that her family loved so much. I got her enough help so that she could still be independent, but have someone around when she needed a helping hand. She lived out her last days in this house. When I was told she didn't have much longer, she had been in the hospital for about a week. I went to see her and the first thing she said was she wanted to go home to her house. I had her discharged that day and brought back here. I stayed the whole week with her. I was thankful we were in the off-season or I would have taken those fines like a champ for missing games. What I would never do was miss those last moments with her. I sat next to her bed on one side with James over on the other. She told me that I helped to make her life worth living. She was proud of me. I'm glad that she got the chance to meet my kids. They loved the ground she walked on. They were her life. After raising me, she was happy to see the next generation."

"I also remember her telling you that you need to get married and settle down, but not with Zonnique. Is it that she didn't like her?" Kilton asked.

Nash looked over as much of the house as his eyes could reach from the backseat of the truck. He hoped that the family, who eventually purchased the house from him after his grandmother passed away, were getting as much joy out of it as his grandmother had. He was happy that the family that bought the house had four young kids. From his vantage point, he could see a large swing set in the backyard. He loved that his grandmother's favorite front porch swing was still intact.

"It wasn't that she didn't like Zonnique. She liked her okay and loved her as the mother of my kids, but she didn't think love with Zonnique would ever happen or be everlasting. She wanted that for me; she wanted a love that would last a lifetime. I didn't then, nor do I believe now, that a love like that exists; at least not for me. Kilton here is whipped beyond being in love, so he gets a pass," Nash laughed.

"Yeah, whatever. Don't talk smack about me and my woman. The best day of my life was the day she said she'd marry me. I never looked back," Kilton admitted.

"And you shouldn't," Nash agreed.

"Your grandmother, a lot like my mother, didn't think that celebrities like you could ever find and have real, true love because before someone sees your heart, they see your money and status," Kilton shared.

"You know my story. You've been around since we were friends in grade school. You know the journey and the struggle," Nash admitted.

"Man, I know all of it. I still remember the time you had a game in Los Angeles against the Lakers. When you checked in, there was a fine-ass woman stretched out on the bed in your suite. The only piece of clothing she had on was a pair of skimpy little panties," Cord joked.

"Don't forget the stripper heels!" Kilton added.

"Man, I remember that. She kept screaming how much she loved me as the two of you called for a female security guard who kindly dragged her out of my room. Though she'd never met me before, she had convinced herself that we were going to be happily married. As she was being dragged out of my room, she was screaming about making me pay and how she would say that I took advantage of her. Thankfully, there were others in the hallway who saw what happened. I was close to firing both of you after that. I wouldn't have really done it, but I was mad enough that I had considered it. It was your job to check my room before I arrived. You know what kind of nut jobs were out there. She was never going to be a candidate for the love of my life. When it comes to Zonnique, I think we both realized that a deep, forever kind of love wasn't in the cards for us. I cared about her enough to have my kids with her. She provided a place of comfort; a safe place. She kept me from taking women up on their offers of sex with no complications."

"What you and Zonnique shared was odd, but like you said it work," Kilton assured them all.

Nash nodded in agreement.

"I met Zonnique about twelve years ago when I was about to be wild and crazy because of all the money that I was making. She was the woman I could have when I wanted to kick it with someone who was uncomplicated and had no problem with no strings. We quickly became friends. At first, outside of the bedroom, we didn't have a lot else in common. It was about the sex. She then became that friend I could confide in. Love just never happened."

"I can't even imagine the number of women you would have had running in and out of your bed if it wasn't for Zonnique being that person for you. You were best friends who had two children together," Cord said.

"My grandmother sensed that. I mean, she didn't come out and say she knew with Zonnique it was all about the sex, but I think she still knew. Let's go. I've seen enough."

As they were pulling away, Nash glimpsed back at the house one last time and saw a little girl in the front bay window. When she waved at him, he smiled and waved back. She made him think of how much he was missing his own kids right now. He would call them as soon as he got to the hotel to meet with James and his fiancé, Monica. They were meeting with the event planner and hotel representative about the events for the weekend. He had plenty of time to visit and revisit the places that meant so much to him. He had five days to winddown before flying home to Miami. He couldn't wait to make the best use of his time while being here. He would also make the time to stop by the house he'd built for himself, which is where he usually stayed when he was here. This time, he agreed to stay at the hotel with everyone else, giving into whatever James wanted him to do. He owed his cousin a lot. Seeing a big smile on James' face this weekend was his priority. He owed his older cousin everything. He was who he turned out to be because of James. He could never repay him for all that he'd done, though he'd tried to do that most of his adult life.

"You plan on staying single forever, man? I mean, since Mariah, you haven't taken a serious interest in anyone," Cord asked as they drove.

Nash dropped his head in playful shame. Hooking up with Mariah was pure mayhem. She was all drama.

"Yeah, look how that turned out. I found out Mariah was stealing from me. I let her get too close even when I knew she saw dollar signs every time she saw me. Plus, you know my story. I like older women. The few I dated never took me seriously. Hey, when I find the one, I'll know it. Until then, I'm good with the friends-with-benefits situations. I've got my kids and my work. Right now, that's all I can handle. I was thinking about visiting Callie for a few days. She called to tell me she was taking a break from the runway for a few weeks and was heading home to Barbados."

"Ah, the latest to wet your whistle. She is fine. I mean, she is *Rihanna* kind of fine," Kilton said with more excitement than Nash was used to hearing from him when it came to women other than his wife, Sheena.

Callie was hot and he loved spending time with her. Something about her accent did it for him. She had been someone he could pop in on at any time when he played ball. He would also fly her in to wherever he was. She didn't mind that she wasn't the only one he was seeing. He loved women, but something in him was signaling that he wanted and needed more. Going from woman to woman, even to only satisfy his sexual desires, wasn't as appealing as it once was. Callie also wasn't for any trickery when it came to trying to trap him. Their mutual desire for each other was equally satisfying. She got what she needed from him. Because of her beauty, men came at her with ulterior motives. She only wanted to have fun. He was down for that.

"Shall I call Sheena and tell her you said that? Wait, I forgot, there isn't a person on earth who doesn't know that you have a thing for Rihanna," Nash joked.

Kilton's wife was not to be played with. They joked about each other, but when it came to Sheena, none of them played with her. She was a ball-buster and Kilton worshiped the ground his wife walked on.

"She'd kill you first for exposing me to all these fine women. She knows I would never step out on her, so I'm safe!" Kilton exclaimed.

"Is she still flying in to New Orleans tonight?" Nash asked.

Kilton had mentioned that Sheena was missing him just as much as he was missing her. They hadn't seen each other in two weeks. They also made their home in Miami. With Nash's busy schedule, Kilton was gone from home a lot. Nash sometimes felt bad about that. He tried to get Kilton to have someone else travel with him, but that never worked. His friend took his job serious.

"Yeah, she'll be here tonight. I told her to remember that I'm working while here."

"Man, all the members of your team that you could have here to take your place for a few days could provide your woman with all the time she wants and needs with you. You even hired some temporary guys for this weekend. These are guys we have used often when I'm here. Don't have her mad at me for taking you away from her all the time!" Nash hollered and pushed on the back of Kilton's seat.

"What am I? Chopped liver? I got security covered while you're here. I told Kilton to take some time off with his lady. He also has family here too. Marvin and Leo, the guys from here that we use a lot are ready and waiting to be told where we need them," Cord added.

"I would kill for some uninterrupted time with my baby," Kilton uttered.

"Take it. You know how we roll. I admire what the two of you have. In fact, I can even admit I'm a little jealous. Have your time when she gets here. I won't need you until we get to Miami for that television interview after I drop the kids off at school that Friday," Nash said.

"I almost forgot about that. I hear the station has announced a few times that you would be there. I hear they are preparing for an onslaught of fans and women looking to get a piece of you."

Nash pushed Kilton's seat again.

"You got jokes. It's your job to make sure women aren't ripping my clothes of; at least not in public."

"What's after that? I know you have two west coast late night television appearances. You also have a New York appearance on the Tamron Hall show coming up. Whew, that woman is gorgeous – always has been," Kilton explained.

"There you go again. Sheena!" Nash shouted as if he was calling her.

"Whatever. She knows only she gets all of this. What's happening with the new office park?" Cord inserted. They had talked briefly about Nash's new venture on the plane to New Orleans but then the subject changed to baseball.

"Cord, I want you to personally pick the head of security for my new office park in Miami. Construction will begin soon. I want new team in place to monitor the site before and during the build besides just running things at the building once it opens. Kilton and I will be tied up with some other projects. You know I don't trust anyone with that task but you or him," Nashall explained.

"Hey, I got you. I'll make some calls during our downtime this weekend."

"You know how to reach me if you need me," Kilton offered.

"He won't need you. Sheena is your priority this weekend," Nash said.

"Cool. She'll love that."

"Great. I'm going to send a nice basket to your suite for her. I like to let her know that I appreciate her patience when you have to be away from your family because of me."

"Get you a woman like her and you'll never have another care in the world when it comes to your home and your heart. She has both on lock!" Kilton explained.

Nash looked out of the car window without responding. He was already hoping for the same one day for himself.

"Hey, I'm getting a text from Vi. Her plane just landed. I told her we're on our way to pick her up since we're still out. She's staying at the hotel where the action is happening all weekend. She wants to stop in at the sporting goods stores and the gyms to check things out," Nash said.

Vi, was short for Vivian Long, one of his executive assistants who helped keep him on track when it comes to checking up on how well or not well his businesses are doing. She traveled with him more than any other assistant he has. He and James are partners in a couple of his business ventures. In New Orleans, that was four sporting goods stores and twelve gyms. James oversaw them all since he lived in New Orleans year-round. The others were in various locations across the country.

"I swear that woman works as hard as you do. Are you sure the two of you have never...?" Cord asked.

"Nope, never. Her girlfriend might have something to say about that," Nash added.

"Nash, are you staying at your house any time while here or at the hotel with everyone else the whole weekend?" Kilton asked.

"I'm staying at the hotel. I know I said I would be staying at the house, but James asked me to stay where everyone else was staying and be a part of the festivities. I promised him I would."

"Cord? You got him, right?" Kilton questioned. He understood the importance of protecting Nash. There was never a time that they could let their guards down.

"Yeah, I'm good. With the extra guys here, we're good," Cord answered.

"If you need me, just call me and I'll be there before you blink," Kilton assured them.

"Cool, that works. I think things will be pretty quiet this weekend. I don't plan on being out much. Most of what's happening will be at the hotel and it's all private," Nash told them.

"Just let us know what you need. Cord and team will be discreet knowing how much you like your space," Kilton said.

"You guys have mastered the art of being invisible but on the ready if need be. This weekend is about my cousin and anything he wants and needs," Nash offered.

"Man, I know your schedule has been crazy with work. You're busier than you were when you played ball. I'm glad you were able to put that all to the side to be here for James. You rarely get any time off. I also hope that you try and have some fun while you're here. All business and no play...you know the rest," Kilton joked.

"Yeah, yeah. I hear you, but I do have two meetings by teleconference I need to take care. My attorneys and business managers have been going over an endorsement deal that I want to be a partner in. I'll tell you more about it when I can. I will say this, get your dollars together because you will want to invest. I've never steered you wrong and I won't this time. When I make good from an idea, we all make good from it," Nash explained.

"You know I'm all over it. You were the reason Sheena got into selling luxury homes in Florida. That's how I know she loves me because she definitely doesn't need or love me just for my money; she's got her own!" Kilton exclaimed.

"Y'all are a true power couple!" Nash cheered from the backseat.

"I keep telling you; that woman you think is out of reach to you or possibly doesn't exist actually does. She'll be the Ying to your Yang. When you find her, you won't be able to forget about her. The two of you will be the new power couple," Kilton added.

"If you say so," Nash uttered under his breath. He could imagine it happening. What he didn't know was, when.

# 3

Delaney found a parking spot on the lot near Kennedy's dorm. As she drove close to campus, she called to let the kids know that she had arrived. Kennedy told her that they were currently moving her stuff into her room with the help of Kennedy's boyfriend of two years, Griffin. They had met at FAMU and the senior pre-law student was someone she and Davis both liked.

Though Griffin lived in Maryland, he had come to Tampa to spend a week with Kennedy during the summer, taking up residence in their guestroom. Kennedy had flown to Maryland to spend a week at the start of the summer with Griffin and his family before she started working for *Bronmon Consulting* for the summer. Kyrie decided he liked his parttime job working as a lifeguard as both kids were expert swimmers. That allowed him the flexibility to work a few weeks before heading to football camp. She and Davis didn't care where the kids worked as long as they worked someplace that kept them busy and enriched their lives.

Walking toward the dorm, Delaney spotted Kyrie first. When he saw her, he put down the box he had in his arms and raced to her. When he reached her, he did his usual of picking her up in the air as if she didn't weigh anything at all. At six-feet tall, he towered over her by several inches. He was tall like Davis while Kennedy was her height at five-foot-seven.

"Mom!" he shouted in her ear before setting her back down on her feet.

"Hey, Kyrie! Did you get taller since yesterday?" she joked.

"Really, Mom? I'm glad you made it. You got here fast."

"Not really," she said. "I left pretty early. I had to go to the car wash before it got crowded since my resident car washer is back on campus," she kidded, making reference to him.

"Aww, I'll wash it when I come home for Thanksgiving."

"You're not coming home until November?" she asked as they walked.

"I'm interning with one of my professors this semester. I told you that. Between that and football, I don't have a lot of time to come home. I will squeeze in a day for my godmother's wedding, but I have to get right back to school the next day."

"I guess that means Kennedy won't be coming home either? I don't like the idea of her taking that four-hour drive by herself just yet," she said.

"I know. If she needs me to ride with her I will or Griffin will. You know he would do anything for her. Dad's going to fly us to West Palm Beach for the wedding so that neither of us has to drive."

"Mom!" Kennedy shouted and raced over to her.

"Hey, baby girl! Any problems driving here?" Delaney asked.

She didn't want to say that she had been on pins and needles the entire day before until she got that call that they had all arrived safely in Tallahassee. Though neither of the kids were new drivers, there were a few times that she had to get on Kennedy about being on her phone, even hands-free, when driving.

"No, I didn't talk on my phone the whole time other than when you called. I told you I was going to do better now that I have my own car. I'm glad you made it. How was it driving here by yourself?" Kennedy asked.

"Brutal, but I'll survive. I missed having you and your brother to talk to. How is the move-in going?"

"Dad, Kyrie and Griffin are moving me into the dorm in record time."

"Is Jill here yet?"

Jill Iverson was Kennedy's roommate and had been since they first met as roommates their freshmen year. Kennedy was originally scheduled to move in with a friend name Heather from Tampa, but at the last minute, she decided on another school.

"She hasn't arrived yet. I talked to her last night when we were at the hotel. She said she was moving in a few days late. I'll have the room to myself until then; I think at least until next Wednesday. Classes start on Monday. She'll miss a few days."

Delaney looked concerned.

"Is everything alright with her?" she asked.

"Oh, yeah. They are late coming back to the states from an overseas trip, is all. She's good. How long are you hanging around? You know dad has us covered if you want to make your way to New Orleans. I know godmommy is looking forward to seeing you. I can't believe she's getting married again. I'm happy for her. I talked to her a few days ago. She sounds so happy."

"I do believe she is finally happy. She's had it rough, but this man seems to make her smile. That's all that matters to me."

"Hi, Delaney."

Turning around once she and Kennedy reached the U-Haul truck, Delaney came face-to-face with Davis. He was dressed down in brown sweat suit, white Nike sneakers and an expensive pair of sunglasses covered his eyes. The dark suit looked good against his light complexion.

"Hey, Davis. How are you?" she asked.

"I'm good. Headed to New Orleans?" he asked.

"Yeah. The bridal party meet and greet is this weekend. It should be fun."

"Cool. I haven't talked to Monica in a minute. I guess you got her in the divorce," he joked.

Delaney let his dry humor roll off of her lack of patience. She knew that he loved reminding her that she met Monica through him and yet, she turned out to be a better friend to Delaney than she was a cousin to him.

"We're divorced. You can let that go now. She's your family and, she loves you. I know she's been busy. I've only seen her once since she moved to New Orleans. I miss her and I can't wait to see her."

"You look beautiful as usual. In fact, I can't remember the last time I've seen you glow like this. Am I overstepping if I say you are looking extra beautiful in those body-hugging jeans, sexy white top and fly white Adidas by Ivy Park? I can't believe you don't have on heels. I know you love them. The jeans, though. Whew! Sexy!"

When Davis whistled at her, he drew Kennedy's attention. She knows how much her daughter loves her father, but she still held a bit of anger toward him for the many arguments she heard between them, something Delaney regretted. His take on where a woman's role in a marriage should be shocking to her, but it wasn't. She and Kennedy had to have a lot of heart-to-heart chats about women being all they want to be without limitations placed on them by men; even one that was her father.

"Dad! Stop it. I'm standing right here. Stop flirting with mom right in front of me!" Kennedy demanded playfully before walking away.

Delaney turned from Kennedy back to him.

"Thank you, and of course, I have my heels in the trunk of my car."

"Ah, the new car. The kids told me about it. I didn't see it when I came by to pack up the kids' things in the truck yesterday."

"It was in the garage. I love it, especially the soft top."

"You've always wanted one. I guess with the great success of your company, you can afford any kind of car you want. You waited until we were divorced to get a ride like that."

"Very true and yes, I can and I did. We never saw eye to eye on my ability to drive a car like that with two kids. My days of driving a van or a truck are over, though I'm thinking about getting a Chevy Tahoe one day. I love the new body style. I do love my car with the roof down and my new short hair blowing in the wind as much as it can!" she declared.

Delaney whipped her head in his direction, enjoying the pleasure of the moment. She still couldn't believe that they would have arguments over her desire to cut her hair while he wanted her to keep it long and flowing. She hated that he loved for her to be arm candy for him in front of people he wanted to impress. Never again would she settle for anything that didn't please her. It wasn't that Davis meant any harm; he hadn't learned any better from the man who raised him.

"I meant to tell you yesterday that I love your new haircut. I guess you're a new woman now. You look amazing," he offered.

"Thank you. I'm the same woman. What you see is happiness," she shot back as a retort. He got it; she knew he did.

Delaney found something odd in the way Davis was looking at her. It didn't escape her that he was extremely complimentary every time they were around each other; more than when they were married. He did the same thing the day before at the house, though she wasn't in his presence long. He and the kids did all the work. While they did so, she retreated to her home office to take care of a few conference calls. The way he seemed to be looking at her lately reminded her of the gazes he would send her way when he was first interested in her back during her college days. It was fine and cute then, but now, not so much. Whatever was behind his compliments, she didn't want any part of.

"You're so damn beautiful. Even when you're trying to gut-punch me, I enjoy it."

Delaney felt creeped out when he licked his lips while gazing up and down her body. His extra-long gazing came with memories of what she'd settled for in their marriage. She also knew that the look he gave her, wasn't always reserved just for her when they were married.

"Thank you." She decided to change the subject. "Are you going to the wedding?" she asked as she checked the back of Kennedy's truck for anything she could help put in the large trolleys used for moving items into the dorms. Seeing boxes labeled as towels and toiletries, she focused on those.

"I am. Do you know a lot about this guy she's marrying? I understand not many in my family know him."

"Not really. I haven't met him yet. I'll meet him later today."

"I hear he's related to Nashall Patterson, one of the best to ever play professional basketball. I've followed his career for a lot of years. I was surprised when he retired last year. I guess if you're worth half a billion dollars, you don't really have to run up and down the court to make money anymore. He makes more from his endorsements, investments and businesses than just playing ball. It must be nice being related to that kind of money. Monica is marrying up this time," he asserted.

"She's not marrying this Nashall guy; she's marrying his cousin," she blurted out.

She hated that Davis was so critical of Monica. She knew it had a lot to do with the friendship they shared that once included him, but not since the divorce. Monica was still angry at him for messing up and for trying to fight her when it came to what he needed to dish out as a result of the divorce.

"I know that. Nash is like thirty-six. I hear his uncle is significantly older than that. Monica is forty-seven."

Delaney blew out an air of frustration at him. He was always so judgmental of everything and everybody, but not himself.

"What does that have to do with anything? Love doesn't have an age limit. I would support her if she loved someone James' age or someone Nashall's age. I hope you're not going to be critical of her at her wedding."

"Of course not. I love my cousin and I'm happy for her. I'm happy that she's found love after what she went through with her first husband. Everyone should have love, don't you think?" he asked.

Delaney kept moving things onto the trolley as she grinned over at Davis, nodding her head. She knew what was next.

"Kyrie, these other boxes are too heavy for me and your sister. Come get these out, please!" she yelled to him. He stood to the side greeting some of his friends.

"What about you?" Davis asked.

She knew it. They were no longer married, yet he seemed to be interested in her personal life since the divorce.

"What about me?" she asked, not making the conversation an easy one for him.

"Are you seeing anyone right now?"

"Why? Are you taking a survey?" she asked him.

When Davis doubled over in laughter, she couldn't help but laugh too. He never missed a chance to get in her business. She didn't have to ask him about his. He was married to his first love; his business life.

"No, I'm just curious. With me living in Miami since we separated prior to the divorce, I don't know much about what's going on with you these days."

"That's how it's supposed to be when two people get divorced. Each other's personal lives are no longer a point of discussion. Why would it be?"

Checking the truck after Kyrie and two of his friends grabbed the last couple of boxes, she realized she arrived when most of the work had already done.

"It doesn't have to be all black and white. We don't have to be strangers," he said.

"We will never be strangers, Davis. We have two kids. We are forever a part of each other's lives."

"You still didn't answer my question."

"I'm not going to because it's none of your business."

Delaney silently patted herself on the back. Her retort game was on fire.

"I would share about my life," he offered.

"I'm not asking you to do that. Trust me, I know enough about what your private life is like to last me a lifetime. You seeing someone is not my business. You didn't make it my business when we were married; now is not the time."

Davis leaned closer to her out of reach for anyone else to hear, namely, the kids.

"One time. Only one time in all of our years together," he whispered.

"That was still one time too many. See where that got you? Shall we talk about that right now and risk the kids hearing? You would have a lot of explaining to do. Look, let's not do this. We are in the here and now, not in the past. Smile and let's make this time all about the kids."

Delaney turned to walk away toward Kennedy's dorm. She felt Davis lightly touch her arm before she got too far. Her plan was to help Kennedy unpack some of her stuff before she left. Kyrie wouldn't need any help. She already knew that he didn't care about unpacking his room. He only cared about jumping back into campus life with his friends.

"Listen, after you get back from New Orleans, I was wondering if I could maybe buy you dinner and talk a little bit. I want to do away with any bad blood residuals."

This was new, she thought. Dinner? Together? Without the kids?

"What?"

Delaney didn't know what else to say.

"Dinner. You know that meal that comes after lunch but before dessert. Dinner. Not a date or anything. Just dinner to talk. I promise I won't ask if you're seeing anyone. I wouldn't dare put you in a position to tell me again that it's none of my business. It's just dinner. With the kids in school again and me handing over more responsibility to others at the company, I love having more free time. Remember, that was a big part of what tore us apart was the amount of time I spent away from you and the kids. I know we're not married anymore. I'm just asking if we could have a civil chat about anything and do it over dinner somewhere in Tampa. Look, just think about it and let me know. I've been going back and forth between the Tampa office and the Miami office. The next time I'm in town, I'll see if you're free."

Delaney didn't answer because she still couldn't find the words to, first of all, say no and then to ask him why. She couldn't imagine that they would have anything to talk about that would cover the time it spent to eat dinner. For her, she didn't want to. Kennedy was walking toward her to gather her up so that they could go inside. Now wasn't the time to have a discussion about how she and Davis were not going to be having dinner.

"Mom, you ready?" Kennedy asked. "Dad, thanks for moving me in. Are you going right back home?" she asked.

"No. I'm going to check out a little of the campus. Kyrie wants to talk to me about moving off-campus next semester, so I'm sticking around for that talk. It should be good. Delaney, what did you say when he asked you?"

"I told him it was up to you and him," she said.

"I think he wants to pledge Omega Psi Phi fraternity and then move into the frat house," Kennedy said.

"How do you know that?" Davis asked, not surprised to hear that his son was interested in pledging the same fraternity that he'd pledged while in college.

"I heard him talking to Chante about it one night when we were all at the beach."

Chante was Kyrie's girlfriend of two years.

"What about you? Are you thinking of pledging this year?" Delaney asked Kennedy.

"I don't know. I might. Can we talk about it when we get to my room?" she asked.

Delaney was expecting that chat. Kennedy had shown interest in being a legacy of her sorority which she had, herself, pledged in her junior year at FAMU.

"We can talk about anything you want as long as it's not about you moving off campus for your senior year," she informed with a raise of her eyebrow.

"No way, not me. I love living in the dorm. Living off-campus is Kyrie's thing. You ready?" Kennedy asked again.

"I am. It was good to see you, Davis. If I don't see you before I head off to New Orleans, have a safe trip back to Miami," she said.

When Kennedy walked off, Davis moved in closer to her. Her first instinct was to move back when he came close but she didn't.

"I hope to see you soon," he said and then turned and walked away.

When Kennedy called after her again, she shook off any thoughts of Davis and raced to join her. She had two hours before she needed to get on the road and she didn't want to waste any of it on thoughts of what Davis' words and looks meant. He'd made mistakes in their marriage. There were some she could get over and forgive. There was one that she would never forgive or forget. He need not try to seek either.

# 4

As Kilton drove the truck through traffic on the way to the
Windsor Court Hotel in downtown, New Orleans, Nash sat in
the back with Cord on the left of him and Vi in the passenger
seat in front. He was going over invoices that she insisted he
look over, though he would never question any of the
amounts. He had given specific instructions to James and the
event planner, Paula, that money was no object. Whatever
James and his fiancé wanted is what they would get. He huffed
in frustration that he was even entertaining Vi's request. She'd
worked for him long enough that he found it best to just do
what she asked. She was very serious about her job and he
appreciated that she took great care in making sure his life was
in order. When it came to money being spent, every invoice
had to be signed by her or him. If she signed, she provided him
with a weekly rundown of everything she placed her signature
on, like the invoices that covered the weekend at the hotel for
all of the guests and each activity.

"Stop pouting like a baby. Don't forget I emailed you the
receipts for all the college tuitions you paid for this year. I've
heard back from all the schools and the students."

"Great. Can you set a reminder to be sure we reach out to specific HBCU's to cover outstanding bills for four hundred students."

"I've got some early numbers on that already. I'll send that to you for review by the end of the month. That's a hundred more than you paid for at the end of the last semester. I want to make sure you're good with what I came up with."

Nash looked at her in the mirror that she lowered in front of her to check her lipstick.

"It's like you think I'm going to say don't pay something. You know what James means to me. You also know my passion is helping college students succeed. Money should not be a crutch forever once they graduate. Whatever James wants, make sure he gets it and make sure it's paid for immediately. The accountants know not to question anything about this weekend including the cruise for Saturday evening," Nash said.

"The yacht Paula was able to rent is beautiful. I've never seen anything like it. Have you seen the pictures? That big yacht for twenty people," Vi exclaimed.

"I've rented it before. It's even more beautiful when you see it in person," Nash said.

"You really went out for James. I was looking over the information for the hotel. It has a spa, a rooftop pool, which is where the Sunday afternoon brunch will be. There is around-the-clock chauffeur service, which is great for those who like to drink. I know there are many other ride sharing companies but patrons of the hotel like to trust the services of the hotel over anything else. The room for tomorrow night's party has the top of the line in everything, food, drink, décor," Vi explained.

"Only the best for the man who gets just as much credit for my life as I get; if not more. It's all because of him and how he pushed me to be better than what I saw every day."

His parents, like James' parents had fallen prey to the seedy parts of New Orleans. None of them escaped the drugs and alcohol addiction that so many others that he knew succumbed to. James and his grandmother were his saving grace.

When he was nine years old, his father had already disappeared from his life, preferring life in the streets over one with him and his mother. His mother had asked a neighbor in their rundown apartment to look after him for a few hours. The next day, when she failed to return to pick him back up, the police had arrived and taken him to his grandmother's house. Everybody knew about Ida Mae. That wasn't the first time he'd been left with someone. For his grandmother, that would be the last. This time, when she took him in, she did it the right way by going to court and gaining custody of him just as she had done with James when he was a young boy.

James had been twenty-four and worked in the restaurant of the same hotel where they were preparing to celebrate his upcoming wedding. Ten years later when he was the number one draft pick, that same day, James had spent his last day working at the hotel at thirty-four years old. That was the day that he hired James to be a part of his management team to the dismay of the sports manager he had retained to look after his career. There wasn't anyone he trusted more than James. He knew his cousin would look out for him. He was new to professional sports and had come from nothing. He wasn't sure that those getting rich off of him would be looking out for his best interest. Having James in the mix saw to the safety of his choices.

He knew he'd made the right decision when James signed up for business classes at college so that he could learn what to look out for. In the sixteen years that he had played professional ball, James never missed even one game; not a one.

Three years before he retired, he confided in James that he wanted to retire and had been working toward his career after basketball. They had a late-night chat session one evening when he laid out his plan.

From the advice he'd gotten early in his career, Nash had invested well, getting in early on a new sports drink that really took off. His stake in that company was now worth over a hundred million dollars. He had also invested in a major sports training facility that now had locations in eighteen states. It's where professional athletes could go to train and have the best doctors and trainers in the country. When he invested in the company, there were only three locations. With his money and those of a few ball players, there wasn't a person in the world of sports in any field who wasn't using one of their facilities on a regular basis.

After leading his team as the star center to six wins over an eight-year span, he was able to secure deals for his own sneaker line, sports gear and gym wear. The year before he retired, he and James had gone into business together opening eight sporting goods stores and sixteen gyms. He happily split the profits, James sixty to his forty, looking to help set his cousin up for success for life. His latest investment into a healthy food chain of stores was his greatest accomplishment after retirement. Nash appreciated his net worth and his ability to surge after playing ball, but most of all, he got to spend more time with Yasmine and Ashton and that made retiring all worth it. When people wonder why he does so much for James, he tells them that he is who he is because of James. When he tells them the real story behind his career, people will then understand his reasons why.

He was currently working on what he and his agent knew would be a bestselling novel, his second, if so. He had already written a children's book that had been a number one bestseller. His second children's book, with Yasmine, he knew would also be a bestseller. There were big plans for that release and a few surprises. His plan to release his memoir was not to see it go public for a few years. He was enjoying writing down his memories and choosing what he would share that wouldn't tarnish anyone in his life, past or present.

Wanting to check in with the kids before his busy, long weekend, he dialed Zonnique's number. Yasmine answered on the first ring.

"Daddy! I've been waiting all day for you to call me," she said before he could get out a hello.

"Okay, hello to you too. What's going on? Did I miss a call earlier? I told your mom I would be calling around this time. I miss you. What are you doing?" he asked, grinning as if she could see him. He loved the sound of his daughter being happy to hear from him.

"I miss you too. When are you coming home? Mommy said Ash and I were going to your house."

"Honey, that's not this weekend, that's next week and the weekend. Remember I told you that there was a party for uncle James' wedding? I'm in New Orleans. I'll be back next week. I'm going to come right over and pick you and your brother up for your first day of school. You're going to stay with me through that week and the weekend until mommy gets back in town. Where is Ash?"

"He's sick. He's taking a nap."

"Sick? Did something happen?"

"He was coughing a lot. Mommy said he has a little fever or something like that. I hope he doesn't make me sick. I want to go swimming when you pick us up. Can Bindi come over and swim with me?"

Bindi was the daughter of his next-door neighbors in Miami. They played together a lot when he had the kids.

"Yes. I need to check with her mom and dad and then with Tracey to make sure she can come over to watch you and Bindi. You know the pool is off-limits if I'm not swimming with you or if Tracey isn't there. I'll call about her schedule."

Tracey was one of his life savers. He had several. Her super power was she was a certified lifeguard and expert swimmer. Between her and his two rotating nannies, Amelia and Ms. Susan, they helped him around the house. He made a note on his iPad to call Tracey before he returned home. Both of his kids were water babies. They loved being in the water. He'd started their lessons before they could even walk.

"Next week is a long time away, Daddy. Can you come home early and get us? Maybe Ash can't come because he's sick. Can you still come to get me?" she pleaded.

"I will try. Let me talk to your mother."

He waited as he listened to Yasmine scream for her mother over and over, racing about. He could hear her feet on the white marble floors of the living room that led into the kitchen area.

"Hey, Nash," Zonnique said into the phone.

"Ashton is sick?" he asked.

"He had a runny nose and a little fever, but he's fine. I gave him a little bit of cold medicine. He's been feeling better. I think it's a ploy to sleep in my bed. He's been asleep for about an hour."

"Okay, if that's all it is. If you need me, you know I'm a phone call and quick plane ride away."

"I know. Can you remind me of the colors for James' wedding? I want to note it so I know what I'm looking for when I get Yasmine's dress. I'm going to get slacks, dress shoes and a shirt for Ashton. I want the shirt to match Yasmine's dress."

"Gray and silver. I'll have Vivian send you a swatch from James' fiancé. Will that help?"

"Yes, that'll work. Are you sure you want the kids for the whole Thanksgiving week? I was planning on joining Chopper in Los Angeles for the holiday. I can also stay home. Perhaps you can have Thanksgiving with us at my house."

"I'm having my family and some close friends over. I told them to bring their kids after you said you'd be out of town."

"Oh, yeah. Don't worry about it. Chopper is excited to show me off to his family. Sounds like you may be having a bunch of people over. I can take the kids if you think that won't be a good time for you."

"Nique, I told you, I want them for Thanksgiving. A lot of my family will be in town. I have a lot planned and I want it to include them. I got them. You go and have a nice time with Chopper and his family. The kids and I will have a great time relaxing. I'm cutting all work out for a few days. They get all of my attention."

"I'm just checking because you're going to have them for three weeks for Christmas. Two for the break and one where you'll have to get them back and forth to school. They can be a handful. Though Chopper will be on a thirty-city tour, I want to be able to attend some of his shows that really pick up around that time."

"You act like I don't know what to do with my own kids. I got that covered. I will personally take them to school and pick them up. For Christmas, I think we're going to Boston to my house there. I'm hoping it will snow and they can really experience a white Christmas. If not, I'm going to have snow brought in to cover the property."

"I know, I know. I'm trying my best to get used to this new retired Nash who isn't flying in when he has a break between games in one part of the country or the other. You're a great dad, so don't think I'm questioning that. They will love Christmas in Boston. Snow? You'll win dad of the year with them. Co-parenting is going well, don't you think?"

"Yes, it's working."

"Speaking of co-parenting, I received the updated trust fund papers for the kids. You know you don't have to up the amount every time you make an additional million dollars. The kids have more money than they'll ever be able to spend one day."

"I don't want them to be spoiled by money, but I also want to make sure if anything happens to me that they'll be taken care of. Just file the papers away in the safety deposit box along with everything else, like the life insurance policies on me. They are my everything."

"Thank you. I don't want to seem ungrateful. You are a one in a million kind of guy. I appreciate you. It's too bad we couldn't make it work. I guess we are too much like friends, but weren't enough for a stable, long-lasting relationship. I think we would have been perfect as a couple."

"You wouldn't have met Chopper and fallen in love if I was in the way," he quipped.

"That's true too. Imagine if there was no Chopper," she said quickly.

Nash started to say something, but decided not to. There was something odd in the way she said it.

"What?"

He was giving her a chance to repeat herself so that he could clear up any confusion about their ever being or could have been a chance for them.

"Nothing. How are you handling being back in New Orleans?"

Nashall exhaled knowing that she was talking about his grandmother.

"I'm fine. I drove by the house like I always do. I was sad for a few minutes but then remembered that she left here happy, well taken care of and loved. That mattered. Thanks for asking. We're pulling up to where I'm meeting James. Kiss the kids for me. I'll call you when I get back. I may come get them earlier than Wednesday."

"No plans? Is Callie not going to be in town?" she asked.

"She went home to spend time with her family. You know that's not serious, right?"

"I know. One day you'll call me to tell me you've met someone and it's serious. I'm waiting for that day. Then again, you're not the commitment type, right? I mean, that's why you once told me things could never work out for us."

"Me? Serious about someone? Don't hold your breath. You and I have always been just friends who happen to have two kids together."

Nash didn't say more since he was in the car with three other people. He didn't want to open up a can of worms for them all to chime in on his personal life.

"Haha. Ever the elusive Nash," Zonnique laughed. "Kiss James for me and tell him I'm happy for him."

"I will."

Nash ended the call as Vi turned to him.

"Before you start trying to remember the dates you just talked about, I wrote down you're picking the kids up on Wednesday, maybe earlier, for school and for the whole week of Thanksgiving, starting with the Friday before. You'll also have them when they get out of school for the Christmas break until the week after the new year. Did I get everything?"

"You take great care of me."

"Good. I'll make sure there are no meetings or business calls interrupting your time with your kids. How's that for the perfect executive assistant?"

"You are the best."

Nash looked out of the car window just as they pulled up to the hotel where he was excited to meet up with James to be sure everything he wanted and needed for the weekend celebration with the bridal party was complete. Exiting the car, he stopped to exchange a few words with Vi when they were interrupted by a slight, soft voice behind him.

"Can I have your autograph?"

Nash heard those familiar words that were pretty much a permanent part of his existence. Kilton came rushing around to put space between him and an approaching fan. Nash waved Kilton off, knowing he was only trying to do his job. When he saw that the fan was a young boy, looking to be around ten or so, he turned and stooped down, lowering his six-foot-seven height to not be intimidating, yet friendly. He shook the kid's hand and looked up at the two men who were with him. He nodded to them as they stood proudly looking at him for taking the time.

"What's your name?" Nash asked him.

"Dwayne. This is my dad and my uncle," Dwayne pointed.

"Well, Dwayne, it's a pleasure meeting you, your dad and your uncle. Do you have anything for me to autograph?"

When the kid's bright smile turned down into a frown as he looked to the ground, Nash knew the answer was no.

"I...I...I don't have any paper. I was walking and I saw you get out and ran over. Dad?"

"I don't anything either, Dwayne. Sorry to have bothered you. Dwayne is a big fan of yours," his father said.

"Don't worry about that. Vi?"

She quickly handed a package to Kilton who then handed it to him. Opening it up, he pulled out the contents.

"Wow!" Dwayne exclaimed when he saw what was in Nash's hand.

"This is your lucky day, Dwayne. My assistant was just putting these packages together to send off to a local school. You're going to get the first one. Now, inside, there is a jersey with my number on it, which I'm about to sign. There's a wall poster that's rolled up. That's already autographed. There is a coupon for a free signed basketball that your father can order for you. Best of all, you can visit any of my sporting goods stores here in New Orleans and get a school backpack full of school supplies and other goodies. How is that?" Nash asked as he took the marker Kilton held out and signed the jersey.

"That's super! Can I really get all of that?" he asked.

With Dwayne now jumping up and down in place, Nash knew he'd hit the jackpot. This is what he likes to see; a happy kid.

"You sure can. Here's your jersey."

"Is it possible for us to get a picture with you?" Dwayne's father asked.

"No problem," Nash said as he stood, picked up Dwayne and posed for the picture.

"Thanks, Nash! I'm your biggest fan. I want to play professional basketball one day," Dwayne exclaimed.

"Keep those grades up and practice all the time and I believe you will," Nash exclaimed, setting Dwayne back down.

**

"I can't take you anywhere!"

As Dwayne rushed off, waving back at him, Nash chuckled hearing his cousin's voice behind him.

Pulling James in for a close hug, they stood like that for a few moments before James pulled back.

"It's good to see you!" Nash exclaimed.

"Let's get inside of the hotel before more fans roll up on you. If so, we'll never get through the final walkthrough. I'm glad to see you back in New Orleans even if it's because of my wedding party meet and greet that you're so graciously paying for. I keep telling you that you don't have to do that. Monica and I would have come up with a plan to host everyone," James said walking ahead of him as they walked inside greeted the event planner, Paula.

"You made it!" she said, walking up to greet him.

"Hey Paula! Do I need to apologize for my cousin? Has he been running you crazy the past few days?" Nash asked.

"Not at all. James has been wonderful and so has Monica."

"Let's go into the room where tomorrow's dinner party will take place. Monica is already in there," James said. "I can't believe I'm back here, not as a worker, but as a patron. The idea still amazes me," he added.

"You worked here?" Paula asked.

"I did full time. Nash worked here part time two summers in a row before he graduated high school."

"Ah, so this place is special?" she asked, her high heels clicking on the marble floors.

Nash didn't respond as they entered the room where people moved swiftly setting up decorations according to Monica's specifications. Nash smiled at Monica when she saw them enter and headed in their direction. He'd met her twice and loved how happy she made his cousin. Before he could answer Paula, Monica rushed up, pulling him into a tight hug.

"Um, can you hug me like that? You're marrying me!" James playfully exclaimed.

Everyone laughed when Monica swatted James on the shoulder right before pulling him into, not just a hug, but a sexy kiss.

"How's that?" she asked.

"Better," James blushed.

Nash couldn't remember a time when any woman made James respond in such a way. If he thought to question James' desire for a quickie wedding, he let it go. The two of them were clearly in love.

"Nash, you made it," Monica said turning back to him.

"I did. I promised James I'd try and get here early. I'm a whole day ahead. I wanted to make sure both of you were pleased."

"Pleased? I'm more than pleased. I had no idea Paula was this good. People have been running around making me happy all day. Doesn't this place look amazing?"

"All thanks to Nash," James said

"No thanks needed. I would do anything for you. I want to see you in love and happy.

Nash said walking further into the room. He turned when James tapped him on the arm, holding him back while others walked ahead.

"One day, I'll do the same for you. Being happy and in love isn't just for me," James explained.

"If you're talking about Callie, you know that's not serious. There isn't a love for me like you have."

"I beg to differ. We'll talk about that later over pool. We're still hanging, right?" James asked.

"I wouldn't miss it."

"Besides, wait until you see the women Monica has in the wedding. Trust me, you will have an enjoyable weekend."

"No, not going to happen. I'm here for you and Monica."

James chuckled.

"If you say so."

Nash did say so, though he knew what James was trying to say. He was no angel when it came to his life as a single bachelor, especially when it applied to women. Seeing his friends and family members in love, he respected that but didn't think it was in the cards for him. He was in town for James and that was it.

# 5

The second Delaney opened the door to her hotel suite and saw Monica standing on the other side, dual screams pierced the otherwise quiet hotel hallway. That sound was soon followed by two grown women jumping up and down, still not touching or hugging. The shock of seeing each other was so overwhelming, the idea of what to do other than scream and jump around didn't occur to either of them. When the door across the hall from them parted and an elderly woman poked her head out to test the now noisy environment, Delaney apologized.

"I'm sorry! This is my best friend!" she yelled and then finally, pulled Monica into a big hug. The woman across the hall gave her the thumbs up and closed her door back.

"I can't believe you're here!" Monica screamed.

As the two continued to jump around in a circle while holding tight to each other, more doors opened in the hallway.

"We better get inside before someone thinks I'm murdering you!" Delaney exclaimed and moved backwards, not thinking about letting Monica loose.

"We're going to kill each other trying to walk like this if you don't let me go!"

Delaney giggled and finally turned her loose.

"I can't help it. I'm so happy to see you. I get to lay my eyes on you and it's not through an electronic device."

Ever since Monica made the move to New Orleans to teach at Tulane University, they had only seen each over via electronic devices. When she lived in Tampa, they saw each other all the time. This new reality was hard, but today, that didn't matter. Her best friend was standing in front of her.

Realizing resistance was futile, Delaney pulled her back into another embrace. To her, the feeling was like all was finally right in the world.

"We can never let this much time go between seeing each other again," Monica said, stepping back as they looked each other over.

"You're telling this to me? I've been saying that for months. In a short period of time, you fell in love, got engaged and in a few months, will be marrying this man of your dreams that I need to see, again, without it being by way of an electronic device. Where is James?" Delaney asked.

"He's with his cousin. They're meeting up with some hometown friends and family. I wanted to have one evening with just you and me. The rest of the weekend will be crazy fun, but it will be with everyone in the wedding party. I needed some alone time with my bestie. I'm so glad you're here. I could hardly sleep last night knowing that I would finally get to see you today. I wanted to get by here earlier, but me and James had a lot to do today. It's Thursday and we have all evening to ourselves."

"Well, I'm here now and we're going to overstay our welcome at the restaurant because I want you to go back and relive this entire past year as if I don't know anything; most of it I don't."

Delaney moved about the room, gathering up her shoes from the floor, sitting on the plush sofa of the large one-bedroom suite that Monica and James reserved for her. When she first arrived to her room, she thought she had been escorted to the wrong suite. The amenities were crazy, from the separate bedroom, to the jacuzzi tub, to the magnificent view of downtown New Orleans.

"I can't wait to bring you up to speed."

"First, start with how you are able to afford this room. Is everyone getting this kind of treatment? A complimentary bottle of champagne, a large fruit basket, a spread of cheese, meet and crackers, a personal concierge and around the clock service of whatever I need. I won't even speak to this gorgeous top of the line suite."

"I told you who James' cousin was. I told him how important you were to me and so you get the best. James does have his own money, but this weekend is not compliments of me and James. His cousin, need I remind you, is Nashall Patterson, ex-NBA ballplayer, very well-off and, can I toss in there, very handsome. We call him Nash."

"Right, you told me that. James has been a father figure to him since Nash was a little boy."

"See, you get it. We could have covered all of this but he wanted to do this for James and for me. Love this suite, huh? All the guests are living large like this. Wait until you hear about the rest of the weekend. Did I fail to mention you look amazing? Not that you haven't always been at the top of the body, body game!" Monica kidded.

"Body, body? What kind of terminology is that? You've been spending too much time around those young college students of yours!"

"Laney, have you seen yourself? What kind of sorcery have you got going on where you don't age? Your body looks like it should be on a twenty-five-year-old. I'm going to get my body back in shape. I can't stop eating all of this good New Orleans food. I bet you're still a size twelve. I'm holding tight to this size eighteen frame and James loves it."

"Then why are you worried about changing anything? You look amazing just the way you are. You know we don't subscribe to the body image thing. I am still a fanatic about working out. With the business on a high and having more time to myself with the kids older and doing their own thing, I love going on long walks and spending time in the gym. I also have a home gym now that I turned Davis' old home office into a personal gym."

"I remember when you redid most of the house, especially the lower level."

"I've done a lot more. If you still lived in Tampa, we could work out together in my gym, but only if you were doing it for you and not for someone else. You know what I mean, right?"

Delaney looked Monica in the eyes and they communicated without saying the words. Besties knew how to do that. Monica had always been on the heavy side and for years, after they met, she suffered from self-esteem issues after being married to a man who chastised her almost daily about her body image. After their marriage ended, Monica had begun loving who she was inside and out. She didn't want to see her go back into a shell of herself to please another man.

"Yes, I know. I promise you, James loves all of me. He tells me that every day. If I decide to start working out again on a daily basis, it will be for me and not for any other reason. How is that for growth?" Monica cheered while spinning around and moving her hands around her body, smiling to show she was pleased with herself.

"That's all I need to hear. You look fabulous in all red. That wrap dress is doing your body good."

"I knew I had to have it when I saw it a few weeks ago. You, in this little royal blue dress is about to shock the men of New Orleans. I still think you've been lying about your age. You? Forty-seven? Gave birth to twins and hardly gained an ounce. I need to know how you've maintained this coke bottle figure all these years. I'm overjoyed that you're here."

Delaney stood after strapping up her heels for their girls' night out on the town.

"Me, too. Are we ready? I'm starving!"

Delaney grabbed her small silver and bling clutch bag that matched her shoes she decided to wear. Together, they headed for the door.

"Yes. We're right on schedule for our reservation. There's a car outside waiting for us which means, we can drink and not worry. Maybe even flirt a little. This life of a monk thing you have going on is making me twitch!" Monica chimed.

"How is my personal life impacting your ability to not twitch on demand? You've been a long time. You have no idea what I've been doing."

Delaney opened the door and waited for it to shut tight behind them as they then walked arm-in-arm to the elevator.

"Okay, I'll play along. Been doing anybody lately? If so, I want all the deets – don't you dare leave anything out."

Waiting until the elevator doors closed, Delaney waited to be sure another person wouldn't be joining them. Alone, she turned and faced Monica.

"I haven't been living a saintly life, if that's what you want to hear. Nothing too serious has happened. I've had a few guys who I've wet my single life whistle on. You know how busy I've been with the company."

"Girl, that company has been in the green for a long time. You don't even go in everyday anymore, choosing to work from home knowing you have the best team in place. Now that you have the business game on lock, it's time to work on that personal life."

"Oh, so you're all in love and now I'm minced meat?" Delaney joked.

"You know better than that. Every man who crosses your path loses if he doesn't make a play for your heart. You and Davis were married for a long time. I know what it's like to get back in the saddle of being in a relationship. It's not easy, but I also know that it's something you want; you told me that yourself."

"I've been dating and enjoying it. I'm good with that for now."

"Until someone rides in on a white horse, I love that you are enjoying dating. All I'm saying is when that white horse moment happens, I need to be the first to know."

They left the elevator and quickly exited the hotel. Just as they were about to get into their transportation for the night, Monica's name was called out in the early evening air. They turned and Delaney saw Monica rush into the arms of a tall, handsome man who she knew from photos and video chats that it was James. Then something strange happened that she had no words to describe.

As James picked Monica up into his arms and spun her around, there was an even taller, younger man standing next to him. Without moving her head, Delaney's eyes connected with his and the hooded gaze from him locked onto her. She was so mesmerized by his look that she couldn't look away. He looked at her in a way that made him seem and feel familiar, but she knew she'd never met him before. Her focus was no longer on Monica and James, but on the handsome man who made her world stop spinning just long enough for her to enjoy the moment they were sharing. Her eyes took in everything about him in what seemed like an hour, but was only a few seconds. He was more than worth her attention. She rarely took the time to appreciate men who were this clearly younger than her. She had no answer for the sizzling impact of his eyes.

This, she knew, had to be Nash, James' cousin. Finally moving her eyes away from his, she looked to Monica who extricated herself from publicly devouring James in front of the hotel.

"What are you doing here?" she asked James.

"I came by to snatch up Nash. We're meeting some friends to play pool and grab some drinks. It's a coincidence that we're out here at the same time. Delaney, you are even more beautiful in person. There is no technology between us anymore," James said.

Delaney extended her hand for a shake when she found herself being pulled into a tight hug by James.

"My two favorite people!" Monica said.

"I've been waiting an eternity to meet you. Monica says even at this point, if you didn't like me, she would call off the wedding. I've been practicing how to make a good impression on you!" James joked.

When a clearing of the throat happened next to him, all eyes, especially hers, turned back to Nash. A warmth from his eyes completely engulfed her. Delaney didn't know what she was experiencing, but it was a first for her.

"I'm Nash."

"Sorry about that," James exclaimed. "I should have done introductions all the way around."

"No, need. I got this," Nash said.

With his eyes never leaving hers and with his hand now holding hers in a solid shake, Delaney felt overwhelmed. There was a zing that fused through her body where they touched. The point of origin between her legs jumped with desire so piercingly strong, she wondered if anyone noticed when she slighted rubbed her thighs together to ease the keen, erotic feeling flowing from their connected hands straight to her womanhood. She didn't know what to say or do. Unexpected, her teeth grabbed onto the skin on the inside of her lip in her attempt to hide her obvious attraction to him. Her second thought after telling herself that his handsomeness was overpowering, was that he was young. She shouldn't have this kind of reaction to him. There was no way to fight it. Her body was going crazy with need.

"Delaney?"

Snapping out of an obvious trance, she heard Monica call her name. She finally looked away from Nash.

"Oh, I'm sorry. I'm being rude. I'm Delaney," she replied.

"I am exceptionally pleased to meet you."

Goodness, his voice enveloped her very being.

"Must be since you haven't let go of her hand yet. Set her free, Nash!" James yelled as he slapped Nash's hand away.

Delaney immediately missed the warmth of his hand and the heat of his gaze. She didn't know what was happening to her as she shyly looked away.

"Hey!" Nash exclaimed. "I was being charming and inviting to Monica's best friend."

"You'll have plenty of time to be charming and inviting. Delaney and I need to get going so that we can make our dinner reservation. I'll see you tonight?" Monica asked James.

"I'll be waiting in our suite with only a bowtie on," James said.

Nash faked like he was about to throw up and everyone laughed.

"I can do without that image," Nash shouted.

Delaney moved toward the car when Nash walked around her and extended his hand to help her get in. She looked up at him, smiled and again, placed her other hand in his since that was the one he reached for.

"Thank you," she said as she sat down on the brown leather seats in the back of the car.

She thought he was about to close the door when instead, he leaned down and stuck his head inside of the car.

"I hope I'm not being out of line when I say that you are a very beautiful woman. Before you think it's a line, it's not; it's a fact and when I said I was pleased to meet you, that was an understatement. I'm actually ecstatic," he said.

Delaney didn't know why he decided to make that point clear until he lifted her hand and kissed the back of it. Then he did something that shocked her. He kissed the ring finger of her left hand. When her eyes captured his again, she knew what the gesture meant. She wasn't wearing a wedding ring. He'd checked and now she knew. She wasn't the only one who experienced some type of recognition that doesn't usually occur. The words, *this is the beginning of something unexpected*, crossed her mind as he stood back up and closed the car door. She was then startled as the door on the other side opened and Monica hopped in. She assumed the big grin on her face was a result of being in James' arms. Then reality set in. She knew all of Monica's looks and what she saw had nothing to do with James at all.

"Giiiiiirrrrllllll! What the *hell* was that? You and Nash need to get a room. That moment of the two of you meeting was so hot and steamy! Wow! Again, what the hell did I just see happening between you?" Monica shouted and bounced around in her seat.

Delaney ignored her. She didn't have an answer because she didn't know. Forgetting about Monica for the moment, she turned her face back to the tinted car window. As the car pulled away from the curb, through the darkened glass, she watched Nash where he stood at the curb with his eyes still planted on her though she was sure he couldn't see her. She watched him until she could no longer see him.

That's when she turned to Monica.

"What the hell was that, indeed," she finally said.

Something was going on inside of her. Her heart was racing, her palms were sweating and the sweet area between her legs felt like it had just woken up from a long winter's nap. Even though the air was on in the car, she reached and rolled the window down a bit. The hot August air didn't cool her off. She hadn't expected it to. She needed more air to breathe.

She was hot, but not in a weather type of way. She was hot in a way that spoke to the hot as fire man she'd just encountered. At first look and first touch, she imagined kissing his sexy lips while his piercing eyes read every devious thought she was having about him. When Monica poked her arm, she turned around and reigned her thoughts back in.

"Damn!" Monica shouted.

Delaney didn't respond. She only smiled and left her thoughts in her head; for now.

# 6

Nash didn't know how to respond to the look on James' face. Every time he turned in his cousin's direction, there was a sinister look with a crooked smile. There was something on the man's mind and he was tired of wondering what it was. He took another large gulp of his beer and placed the bottle back on the table in private pool room in his old neighborhood. He and James had finally managed to pick up three of his childhood friends and headed straight to the pool hall. They were taking a break by venturing back to the wall enclosed lounge with its large black leather seating around a large round table in the center covered with bottles of top shelf alcohol and empty and full bottles of beer.

"Whatever is running through that crazy mind of yours is messing up your facial features. Just say it already, whatever it is," Nash jibed.

"Really? You want me to say what's on my mind?"

"James?"

Nash was losing patience.

"Alright, I hear you. Here it is. *Delaney*. That's it. That's the whole thought."

He knew it. Something told him whatever James was keeping in had something to do with Delaney. More specifically, it had to do with the reaction he had to Delaney's presence, something James must have noticed. Nash wasn't ready to reveal to anyone the instant attraction he felt for her. Never in his life had he come across a woman who smiled at him and made his heart skip a beat. He only had a few minutes in her presence and that spoke volumes.

As he sat at the table and thought back to his response to seeing her, he realized he must have looked like some kind of crazed stalker. Even when he tried to take his eyes from her and focus on either Monica or James who were speaking, he couldn't. After a minute or so, he realized he was making Delaney uncomfortable, but still, he didn't care. He couldn't tear his eyes away. He knew he only had moments to take in everything about her. He tried to get a picture-perfect image in his head that he could take with him the rest of the evening. His secret was out. If anyone knew him, it was definitely James.

"What about her?"

"You."

"Me, what James? Stop being cryptic."

"I'm being cryptic?"

"Yes."

"Nash, I saw you looking at her as if any minute, you were going to take her right there on the street. I've never seen you ogle a woman like that. I've never, ever seen you look at any woman like that. I've seen you around thousands of them. You're Nashall Patterson. Women flock to you like a moth to a flame. Usually you're the flame, but when you saw her, you became the moth. You were all over her. Don't you dare try to deny it either."

Nashall exhaled, lowered his head and shook it from side-to-side. He couldn't explain his reaction to her. Her beauty hit him like a ton of bricks. Her soft hands seem to smooth out all over him. He had been close to asking if he could join her and Monica for dinner. He needed more time with his eyes on her.

"Okay, tell me – do you think I creeped her out? I know what I did. When I think back on it, I'm pissed at myself over how I may have made her feel."

"She did look a little uncomfortable. What was up with you?"

"You know me. No one else in the world knows me better than you do. Like you said, you've never seen me react like that to a woman. I don't think I ever have. She is gorgeous. She smiled at me and I was done. I was puddy in her hands. Her eyes, that smile; she was a sensation that drew me in and wouldn't release me. Even now, she has me in her clutches. A woman I just met, spent maybe five minutes around and an hour later, I'm still thinking about her. What the hell is wrong with me?"

"I'd say you like her."

"I feel stupid saying this, so bear with me. I think it's more than that."

"First, you were in her presence for the first time for like, five minutes. Second, she's off limits, Nash. Do not come here this weekend to get with Delaney. She's Monica's best friend. There can't be any drama. We'll be like family."

"Yeah, but not family. I like her, James. I want her man."

Damn! Did he just say that out loud? James was right. He met the woman and in the first few seconds, he wished he was going wherever she was going. He didn't have enough time. He didn't know how to explain what he felt when he took Delaney's hand in his. There were no words to describe his body's reaction to a simple touch. In the seconds that he held her hand, he had seen a lifetime of passion beyond his belief; beyond anything he's experienced in his adult life. If James thought for a second that he wasn't going to test that immediate attraction to her as soon as he got the chance, he was mistaken.

"When you say *want*, what does that look like? I mean, I know you and how you are with women. You're a friend-with-benefits kind of guy. You're not known for having an interest in anything else. You're a self-proclaimed bachelor, according to you. That means you're what, looking for a notch on your bed post? Don't do that man. I'm begging you, find someone else. Delaney is off-limits."

"I can't promise you that. What I can promise is that I'm not looking at her as a notch. I want to get to know her. Plus, I'm walking down the aisle at your wedding with her. I should know more about her. First, you need to tell me everything you know."

"What? You mean like the fact that she's not married? I saw you check for a wedding ring."

"You caught that?" Nash chuckled. "I kissed that empty wedding ring finger. Man, I swear I'm toast."

"Yeah, I did. You looked like you were going to devour that woman right on the street. What was that? I thought Monica and I were bad. The difference is, we're engaged to be married."

"That was me meeting a beautiful woman and finding that we had an instant connection to each other. I saw it in her eyes. I know she saw it in mine. Tell me about her."

Nash didn't mean for his words to come out like a demand, but he felt like a desperate man. There was something about her. He couldn't even focus on his pool game. The memory of Delaney teased his heart; another first. She looked good, she smelled delightful and most of all, she shivered. He felt it in her touch. She shivered when they touched. She felt it. Reality set in for her just as it had for him. Something happened and it was beyond description. He had a weekend to find out and he would.

"She and Monica met when Delaney married Monica's cousin twenty or so years ago."

"Wait – she's married? I didn't see a ring."

"Well, if you would listen and not interrupt, you'll learn something."

"My bad. I was anxious," Nash admitted.

"Like a kid in a candy store."

"I'm not a kid and neither is she. This is grown man shit happening here."

James doubled over in laughter.

"Man, you are serious. You really did feel something with her."

"I did. Tell me more."

"She's divorced, not sure how long at this point. She's got twins who are in college at FAMU, I think."

"She's got grown kids? Really? Did she have them when she was ten? She's hot. That's all I have to say."

Nash heard James laughed under his breath. Nash growled at him and James threw his hands up in surrender.

"I'm just saying – I have never seen you like this when it comes to a woman. She's got you acting all weird."

"That should tell you that this isn't an ordinary interest."

"Okay, I hear you. She owns her own company and Monica says it's pretty profitable. It's a tech firm. I know that about six months ago, Monica sent her a large basket of fruit and other foods to celebrate her company winning a multi-million-dollar government contract. No, she wasn't ten when he had her kids. She and Monica are the same age, forty-seven."

Nash flipped him off.

"You're lying. That woman is not forty-seven. Okay, that's not to say that women her age are not generally as hot and sexy as she is because we both know that they are. I'm just saying I was blown away by her in mere seconds. You've never heard me say that about any woman, not even one that I simply wanted to hit the sheets with. I needed more time. She was walking perfection. That blue dress was fire, hugging all of her curves with expertise. The way she tilted her head and looked up at me was something out of a dream. I'm telling you, I felt something deep; it was a deeper connection than I've ever had with someone just from a handshake. I swear, I can still smell her and feel her hand as if it's still in mine."

James didn't comment, though Nash expected to hear something snide. When nothing came, he looked over to where he was relaxed back onto the black leather lounge chair. They were in a private room playing pool and the other guys were around the table playing and laughing. Nash was thankful for this moment with James.

"It was like that? She is beautiful. Don't you think she's out of your league?"

"Why? Because she's older? You know my thoughts about that. I once told you that if I ever settled into a relationship, it was probably going to be with an older woman. It can't be because of her business acumen. I think a serious business woman is the sexiest woman alive. She's clearly doing what she enjoys and that's important."

"She's over ten years older than you. I know you've kicked it with a few older women, but you mainly date younger or around your own age."

"Yeah? Well, that says a lot because I'm still single. I haven't found the right woman who is the full package."

"What? Are you trying to tell me that after a handshake and a quick word, she's the right woman? The full package?"

He sounded crazy. He knew it. Nash wasn't clueless to how he sounded but he was having a hard time finding the right words for what he felt. It was instantaneous; blowing him away with the level of desire he felt.

"James, look at me. You know me. I'm telling you that there is something about that woman that I can't let go of."

"What is that?"

"For the first time in my life, I think I just experienced love at first sight. It's real, James."

"Really? I didn't even have that with Monica. I mean, I fell for her hard, but it wasn't within the first few seconds."

"Then you know why I can't let this go. I held her hand in mine and I felt a tremor that led from her to me. I swear I looked into her eyes and they sparkled and winked at me. Before you say anything, I know how old she is and I don't care. If you think age would be an issue for me, then you don't really know me at all. Do you know what I saw when I looked into her eyes? Everything I've ever wanted in a woman. Yes, it happened just like that."

"I'm not saying age should be a defining factor. She's been married, has grown kids and may not be looking for a boy-toy," James explained.

"Cuz, I know you're not trying to be disrespectful with that comment because you and I have always been able to be open and honest in our chats. I lean to you and confide in you with everything going on in my life. I'm going to be like you and say, first, I'm no one's boy-toy, well, maybe that's not true, but I'm not looking to be that for Delaney. It was more than that and if no one else knows that, she does. Second, I'm old enough to know the different kind of attractions I have for women. This wasn't casual or sexual; it was more than that. It was a combination of everything."

"I know she went through a divorce and according to Monica, it wasn't pretty. Don't shake up her life unnecessarily if you're not ready for a woman like her. I'm saying this as your friend more than anything else. Do not mess over her. Don't play with her."

Nash paused and then leaned forward, placing his elbows on his knees and looked directly at James.

"Do you remember before Nana died and she said that one day there is going to be a woman who will knock my socks off? She told me that this woman would come along when I wasn't expecting it. She said we'd be successful and share in our success. She said that I would appreciate the value of the dollar but that it wouldn't make me crazy, stupid happy; that only love could and would do that. I played ball as long as it made me happy. I've acquired more money than I ever dreamed I'd ever make. I'm secure knowing that I've learned to not waste it on foolish trinkets and expensive toys that don't really interest me. She told me to never, ever walk away from wanting love with a good woman. You of all people know that I've been missing that in my life. I spent many years on the road living my dream. Now that life has slowed down for me, I want a woman in my life where there isn't a motive around money. That's hard to find with who I am. I think this woman saw me. She looked in my eyes and I believe she saw all of me. It's hard to know who to trust. I'm telling you I saw a lifetime in Delaney's eyes. I wouldn't lie about that just to get her in bed. I've never lacked in that department. It's much more than that."

"Hey, you fellas playing or are you just gonna sit there and talk like a bunch of girlies?" Tony, one of Nash's friends called out.

"I think I'm up," Nash said standing. He turned back when he felt James tap him on the arm as he stood.

"I saw it, Nash. I saw the way you looked at her and the way she looked at you. I didn't think much of it beyond the fact that you'd find her pretty, which she is. You've always been here for me. You've supported me without hesitation. I don't want you to think I would ever discount your feelings. Your response to her is taking me by surprise. I'm here for it though. Whatever you decide to do, don't mess it up."

"I hear that. Trust me, if what I'm feeling is real, I can't mess this up."

"Cool. Now, let's get to playing some pool so that I can take all of your money and your friends' money too!" James exclaimed as they walked over and joined the other guys.

Nash put off all thoughts of Delaney for the moment. He smiled knowing that he would see her again throughout the entire weekend. He was looking forward to every minute.

# 7

"I couldn't have chosen a more perfect place to eat. That had to be the best lasagna I've ever tasted."

Delaney pushed her empty plate to the center of the table and reached for her glass of wine. The meal was perfect and the company was even more perfect.

"I'm glad you enjoyed it. I knew you would. Now that we've eaten dinner and talked about everything that has gone on in my life over the past year, it's time to focus on you. Oh, did I forget to mention that I know more about my godchildren than I ever thought I would find out? To hear that Kennedy is still seeing the same boy is a shocker. She always declared she would never get serious about a guy until she was established in her career. I knew that Kyrie was going to edge his way into playing professional football. I talked to him the other day and I told him that I would try to make more of his games this year. I missed too many of them last year. No more talk about me or the kids. What's going on with you? Wait, first, are you ready to explain to me what was going on with you and Nash?"

Delaney exhaled. She's had an hour or so to think about what had passed between her and him. With the passage of time came reality. She didn't know what she thought she was doing swooning over him openly like that. She had reacted to him out of her usual character. He was definitely the prime example of being tall and handsome, but she also had to face reality that he was quite a bit younger than her. She had no business even being interested in him in any way. The way that her body reacted to him, she wished it understood how off-limits he was as much as her head knew.

"He's a kid." she explained, trying to convince herself as

She said that more to convince herself than convincing Monica.

"He doesn't look like any kid I know. That man was all over you. I couldn't see his eyes, but I could tell they were firmly planted on you. What did he say to you when you sat in the car and he knelt down?"

"That I was beautiful and he was pleased to have met me; actually, he said that he was ecstatic to meet me. What did that mean?"

She knew she sounded immature asking such a question as if a man had never made a pass at her before. There was something new about what she saw in his eyes.

"Men flirt with you all the time. I mean, we were here at the restaurant for a few minutes and a man had walked in, complimented you, asked if he could buy you a drink while also asking you out. He did all of that in the same sentence. Don't tell me that a man's reaction to you like that is new. You do know that we've been friends for what seems a lifetime. I've watched you fight them off with a figurative stick."

"This was different."

"Different how?"

Delaney looked across the table and then looked away. She's not one to talk so openly about her attraction to a man.

After being married to Davis for so long, getting back into the dating realm wasn't an easy fete for her, but she was working it out slowly.

"We shook hands," she said and stopped.

"Okay, and?"

"The feeling was odd; strange. I mean, it was like I could feel him in my soul. I felt drunk, like I was intoxicated. I've never been that attracted to any man that fast. It happened in an instant. Then he touched my hand again when he helped me in the car. If I thought the first time was a fluke, having it happen again wasn't; it couldn't have been. It was a tingle, or a vitality burst of energy. It was a vibe. And his eyes. The way he looked at me was penetrating; it was so intense."

"That was odd to you?"

"I've never felt like that before."

"Not even with Davis?"

"Not even him and I was married to him for a lot of years. There was a strong, powerful tug between us that grabbed onto me and held me in place. He looked at me and all I could think about was completion. I don't know what that means, but it was commanding. But, you know, I can't go there with him. You told me he's what, thirty-five?"

"Thirty-six, I believe."

"Well, there's that."

"There's what?"

Delaney sucked her teeth and picked up the dessert menu. She needed a reprieve as images of Nash's eyes came into focus as if he were standing right in front of her.

"You know I cannot go there with him. I'm years older than him. What would that look like? I don't even know why we're entertaining this conversation."

"He's an adult; you're an adult. There is no reason for you to doubt following a feeling you've experienced. If it was as you described, who walks away from that?"

"I can't get involved with him."

Delaney leaned back in her chair when Monica jokingly put her hand up in front of her face, stopping any other words of doubt that would come out of her mouth.

"Why not? Are you not entitled? What is the problem? His age? It's not like he's some kid out here still trying to figure out his life. Nash may be younger than you, but he's not young. You have a lot in common."

Delaney put the menu down and gave Monica all of her attention.

"Like what?"

"Well, you have two kids and he has two kids."

"He has kids? How old are they?" she asked.

"They're young. His daughter is ten and I think his son is six or seven."

"By how many women?"

"One. Before you ask, no they were not married. They are still very good friends. She's engaged to be married. I know that because James mentioned it when we were talking about our wedding. She's planning a destination wedding sometime next year. Nothing definitive yet."

"Sounds like they co-parent well."

"James said he's never seen anything like it. They were friends and pretty much sex buddies, which Nash was happy about. It kept him from being with all of the women who threw themselves at him throughout his career."

"Why didn't they marry?"

Why couldn't she stop herself from probing?

Delaney felt anxious as Monica laid Nash's life out for her. She wanted to know as much about him as she could without letting it be obvious that her attraction to him was off the charts.

"I don't know all of the details other than he never felt anything on that level for her. I think it was mutual. James said that they make amazing parents, though. He's not some fly-by-night father either. Once Nash left the game, he permanently settled in the Miami area and his kids' mother moved to that area so that the kids would be close to him. They are everything to him."

"So, he's not seeing anyone?"

Delaney knew she was asking too much. She couldn't help herself.

The question was out before she could pull it back. She tried to make Monica think that she wasn't interested, but here she was digging even deeper.

"I don't know that much. You know, you can ask him yourself. You'll see him the entire weekend. Look, it's okay to be attracted to him. I know you don't know much about sports, so believe me when I say, you are far from being the first woman of any age to have the hots for him. He's pretty selective. I've never heard anything in the gossip rags about his personal life. He's very lowkey. James said he always has been."

"I can't be attracted to him. What would people think? What would my kids think? What would..."

Delaney let the rest of the words trail off. The moment her eyes met Monica's, she knew she was about to protest too much. There goes her idea of not showing any interest in Nash when that's exactly what she was doing.

"Please tell me that you are not worried about what Davis thinks? I hope you are not planning your life out based on what he would say. He's no longer a factor. That was clear the day he turned his back on his family," Monica declared in a low enough tone that no one else could hear them.

"Of course not. Still, I am the mother of his children. Who I bring around them would be a topic of discussion with him."

"Why the hell would it? Your kids aren't three or four years old. They are grown adults. You know Kyrie is out here slinging it; I'm not sure about Kennedy."

Delaney laughed and covered her mouth when she got loud.

"You are not going to sit here and put my son's personal business out in the atmosphere."

"You were the one who told me about it. You don't have to be accountable for who you like. Davis certainly has no say; not after...nevermind. Speaking of him, you said he asked about seeing you when you got back to town. What's that about?"

Before she could answer, their waitress returned for their dessert order.

"I don't know if I can eat anything. I would love to take something back to the hotel since it all looks so nice," Delaney said.

"Let's share a big slice of strawberry cheesecake. Then you can also order something to take back with you."

"That works," Delaney acknowledged. "I'm going to take Tiramisu back to the hotel," she added.

While Monica ordered the cheesecake, Delaney thought about what Davis really wanted.

"So? Davis?"

"Oh, I don't know what he wants with me. Whatever it is, I'm not biting. You know what he did. He's been acting weird lately. I think he's actually been flirting with me."

"I get it, he misses you. He realized the grass wasn't greener on the other side. He cheated on you, more than once, wanted you to find out so that you would end the marriage, because he knew you would and then tried to fight you on what you were entitled to. My family is still pissed at him over that."

"The one thing you all know about him, just as I do, is that making more and more money is his priority; it always has been. I can't complain because he provided for me and the kids where we wanted for nothing. He claims he didn't cheat on me because of anything lacking at home. He said he was going through something."

"I'm going to ask this while also treading lightly – are you interested if he is, in fact, flirting with you or trying to get you back?"

"No. Still, it's complicated."

"No, it's not. You deserve to be happy and not fall back into something that would make you look over your shoulder, check his wallet and go over his shirts for lipstick stains. You know I love my cousin, but he was shady and you deserve more. You deserve to be happy. That man took you through hell. The best revenge would be for you to live your life and show him what he's missing out on. If that means having a little fun with Nash this weekend, then do that. No one said you had to fall in love. Just fall in bed with him if that's what you want to do. You are single and free to do whatever you want. If you're worried about his age, don't be. If you're worried about what the kids would say, don't tell them. It's a weekend. You're here until Monday. Go ahead and get your Stella on! I'm not mad at you. Don't you dare let thoughts of Davis possibly changing or Nash's age be a deterrent. It's time you lived for you and no one else."

The cheesecake and two forks were set in the center of the table. Delaney picked up a fork and sliced into it before she could think of an answer. She saw a light in Nash's eyes that she knew mirrored hers. She didn't know what could come out of their instant attraction to each other. She wasn't sure she could allow herself to go there. For now, she wanted to enjoy the dessert and girl talk.

# 8

Nash sat at the hotel bar and waited. His plan when they arrived back after playing pool was to head to his room and turn in for the night. He had been running into fans all day and was happy for the reprieve while hanging out with friends. Any time he came home, he could always count on his old neighborhood friends to protect his peace. The moment he returned, his security team was back in place watching his back. He wouldn't have needed them if he hadn't decided to head to the bar and wait with James.

On the ride back, James had been texting with Monica who told him that she was on her way back to the hotel. He decided to wait for her in the bar and walk with her to their room. Unable to control himself, Nash decided to wait so that he could get another chance to see Delaney. He had called Cord the moment he knew he wasn't going to head straight to his room.

"You know I can wait for Monica by myself. I'm a big boy," James joked.

"Yeah, real funny. You know why I'm here. If you're going to say anything about it, don't. I have to know," he said, looking toward the entrance just as Monica and Delaney walked through the doorway.

"You have to know what?" James asked.

"If my feeling of love at first sight will lead to love at second sight as well. Now that I see her again standing there looking like a beautiful angel, I already know. She's mine, James. I think my eyes have laid on my woman. If she felt anything like what I felt when we met, I look forward to the day when she claims me as hers."

Before James could respond or stand, Nash was up and heading toward the entrance to the bar. When he saw Cord appear to make a move from his vantage point at a table in the corner, he halted him with his index finger. Cord already knew that meant to standdown. Nash didn't need protection. He already knew his heart was on the line. Delaney didn't know it, but it already belonged to her. He walked right up to her.

"Hello again, Delaney."

"Hello, Nash.

"I hope you enjoyed your dinner."

"I enjoyed my dinner!" Monica interrupted, smiling from ear to ear.

Nash watched Delaney nudge her and Monica left them alone, racing over to James.

"I think I'm running a streak of being rude this evening. I don't know what's going on with me. I swear I'm not usually dismissive of people. I didn't mean to ignore her."

"She's fine. Don't worry about it. Yes, I did enjoy my dinner. I even brought dessert back with me for later."

"Are you headed to your room right now?" he asked.

"I was planning on it. Looks like Monica and James have disappeared."

Nash turned around and tried to find where his cousin had gone off to. He looked to Cord who pointed to a spot around the side of the bar where a few couples were dancing to slow music that filled the air from the speakers placed throughout.

"They're dancing on the other side of that wall beyond the bar."

"Is the guy who is staring at us with you?" Delaney asked looking toward Cord who was staring at them looking like he was ready to jump to his feet at any minute.

"He is pretty much a staple with me. He's part of my security detail. He tries to be discreet, but it's hard when you're almost seven feet tall and built like The Rock," Nash joked.

"I see that. Security huh?"

"They are usually unnoticeable about their presence, but I wanted you to know he's there. There's another guy at the other entrance to the bar. Does that bother you?" he asked.

"Not at all. I know who you are and why it's needed. It's better to safe than sorry, especially for celebrities like yourself. If I make a move toward you, are they going to tackle me to the ground?" she joked.

"I'll reserve that action for me," he quipped in response.

"I like that."

"Can I interest you in a night cap before you go to your room? I can tell you all about my security and anything else you'd like to know."

Nash extended his hand to her. The minute Delaney placed her small hand with purpled polished tips into his hand, there was that feeling again. There was a feeling that they belonged together.

"Sure," Delaney stuttered out.

Nash started to walk and then turned back to her.

"I need to say something. You feel it don't you? You felt it earlier just like I did and then just now, it happened again when I touched your hand."

Delaney looked up at him and searched his face. She was studying him with an awareness that said she understood. She was just as flabbergasted as he was.

Was this real? She didn't know what to think, but like Nash, she had felt something.

"It's like electricity – a shock to the system, but not in a bad way."

"Yes!" Nash acknowledged. "What is that? What is this?" he asked.

"I don't know. I've never had that feeling from someone holding my hand before."

"Never?" he questioned.

"Never."

"Can we sit and talk?" he asked. Nash was anxious to get into who she was and how he could become more than just the man who would be walking her down the aisle at the wedding in a few months.

Delaney had been exhausted after a long drive from home, to the kids' school and then to New Orleans. Then add in her night out with Monica. For the life of her, she couldn't understand why she wasn't asleep on her feet. She seemed to have more energy than she's ever had. She wouldn't dare admit that it was because of being in Nash's presence. She still didn't know. She couldn't resist finding out.

"Yes, I'd like that."

Taking her hand again and walking to a nearby table, he knew that he was already a lost cause. Something spoke silently to him saying that he never wanted to let her go.

He signaled for a waiter who quickly rushed in their direction.

"What would you like to drink?" Nash asked her.

"I think I'm just going to have a soda; Sprite, please," she said.

"She'll have a Sprite and you can bring me decaffeinated coffee, cream and sugar," Nash said, ordering for them.

"Coffee?" Delaney asked.

"It's late and it's been a long day."

"Are you sure you don't want to head to your room and rest? Monica and James have planned a busy weekend. You'll need your energy."

"I'm looking forward to everything they have planned now that I know I'll get to see you the whole time."

"Since we've been deserted by James and Monica, tell me who Delaney is."

"Well, I'm a business owner, a friend, a lover of life and best friend to Monica."

"How did the two of you meet?"

Delaney hesitated, hating to bring up any discussion around her being married, but that was how they met.

"She's the cousin of my ex-husband. We have been best friends from the first day he introduced me to his family when we were dating."

"And you've remained best friends even after the divorce?"

"Absolutely. Besides my two kids, she's another great thing that came out of my marriage."

"How old are your kids?"

"I have twins."

"Two and done, huh?"

"Yes. They were a handful. They are twenty-one and juniors at FAMU. Kennedy, is my daughter and Kyrie is my Monica mentioned that you have kids."

"I do. I have a daughter, Yasmine who is ten and a son, Ashton, who is six."

"You're no longer with the mother?"

"No. We were more like convenient friends. She's actually engaged to be married to a great guy. I'm quite single. Are you?"

Nash did his best to capture her eyes with his.

"I am. Um, I think I'm also a bit older than you if what you're doing is flirting," she offered.

"Does that matter? Our age differences?"

"I'm sorry. I don't know why I said that. I know you're just being nice."

"Am I? You think I'm just being nice to you and nothing else?"

"Is there something else?"

"Yes. Oh, yes there is. Like I said, you felt it. I've been waiting for you. In fact, even though I am bone tired, I refused to go up to my room once James mentioned he was going to wait on Monica. I knew you were together. I wanted to see you. It has nothing to do with just being nice to you. I like you."

"You're just learning about me."

"Are you saying you don't like me? I'm curious as to what you thought about the feelings our touching hands elicited."

"I'm older than you, Nash. Did you not capture that?"

"I don't care. I like you and I'm hoping there is some interest in me on your part. We're not getting married tonight, so we don't have to get really deep. I wanted you to know that I like you. I'd like to take you out on a date while we're here.

Is that okay with you? Dinner. Even thirty-six-year-old men like to eat dinner with a beautiful woman."

"Even one who is forty-seven?" Delaney asked.

"Yes, especially one who is as beautiful as you are. Can we put that age thing to the side now? I want to continue getting to know you, have you know me, and hopefully before we leave, you'll agree to have lunch or dinner with me. How is that?"

When Delaney looked away and then back at him, he saw a glimmer of hope in the brightness of her eyes and the way her perfectly sculpted lips turned into a smile.

"Okay, I can do that. Tell me how you and James became so close. Monica mentioned that the two of you are closer than a father and son."

"James saved my life."

"Oh? How?"

"James and I lived with our grandmother. I was a handful to her. My mother and father both walked away from me. I guess I rebelled when I realized I was never going back home. I arrived with the clothes on my back. My grandmother never went in search of them or my stuff at the small apartment I lived in with my mother. She just took care of me like it was the most natural thing in the world for her to do. She didn't know what to do with me. I kept waiting to be picked up by my mother. Day after day came and went and I was still there. I gave my grandmother a fit about it."

"Oh, wow. That's awful for a child so young," Delaney exclaimed.

Nash nodded and continued.

"James saw me getting into a lot of trouble and took me under his wing. By the time I got to high school he was the father figure I needed. One day some guys tried to bring me into the drug game. All I saw was money and I was sold. James found out about it and vowed to make sure I stayed off of the streets and kept my mind occupied. He was working here at this very hotel. When I got out of school, he would make me come here and sit anywhere, sometimes even in the closet, to do my homework. He kept me close. I didn't mind because when he wasn't working, he played basketball and baseball with me. He took me to concerts and local festivals. He kept me in fly gear and even got me a part-time job here. He told me he wanted me to have honest money in my pockets. In the tenth grade I decided to play basketball and went out for junior varsity. Who knew that playing basketball with James on the neighborhood court allowed me to develop skills that sent me straight to the varsity basketball team instead of playing junior varsity? After that, the sky was the limit. He would practice with me all the time. He made sure I had what I needed to play basketball, including taking me to college games to see their hustle. The summer after the tenth grade, he paid for me to go to a local basketball camp when my grandmother didn't have a lot of money. James put extra money in my pockets. He bought school clothes and school supplies. He did what a parent would do. I graduated, went to college on scholarship and after a year, I went out for the draft. Since I was nine years old, James never left my side. He was always there encouraging and pushing me. We only had one issue in all these years. At the end of my freshman year, I wanted to play pro-basketball. I graduated high school with crowds of professional basketball recruiters all over me. My height helped with that. The training James was able to pay for me did the trick. He pushed me to stay in college, saying that I could play ball after I graduated. I went against that and left school to play pro-ball. He was angry, but when I was selected as the first round, number one draft pick, he put his support behind me."

"Monica says you are amongst the best to ever play the game."

"According to the media, I guess I am. I don't take any of it for granted. Again, James is a big part of that. He was there for everything; leading and guiding. I was nineteen years old playing for the league. Over a year ago, when I decided enough was enough of ball playing, from day one to the last day, he was right there with me. There is absolutely no way I would have any of the things that I have in life or be where I am without him. When he told me he had met the most beautiful woman in the world, I set out to make this weekend and the wedding in West Palm Beach all about whatever the two of them want. It's not that James couldn't afford it. I wanted to do this for him."

"You have a kind heart. I can hear it in your voice. It's crystal clear in your eyes. That's both rare and admirable."

Delaney said the first words that came to mind. She wasn't lost on the fact that the entire time Nash was talking, he was holding her hand in the softest, kindest way. She was shocked that she felt this connected to him. His eyes were the brightest, most telling she'd ever seen.

And then there was silence. She felt as if she were under some kind of spell; unable to look away from his eager eyes. He looked at her as if he could see right through to her heart. Now she understood why she couldn't stop thinking about him over dinner with Monica. Not only was he amazingly handsome and built to please, but he was as unforgettable as anyone could be. She liked him; immediately.

Something about the moment had them moving closer to each other. Delaney shifted her body forward slowly as if she wasn't in control of it. Her eyes didn't leave Nash's even as he came closer and closer and then, even closer.

"Okay, kids. It's late. James and I came to walk Laney to her room. You ready?" Monica asked her.

Delaney sat straight up. She was no longer in a trance due to Monica's voice interrupting them. She didn't know what would have happened without the interruption, but something told her that it would have possibly been the hottest, sexiest kiss known to any woman. Nash has lips that were no doubt, made for kissing. She had been ready for it. Instead, she turned her head and smiled up at Monica. She tried to act as nonchalant as she could without giving away the fact that she was more than willing to lock lips with Nash. She didn't care that they were not alone or that they had just met a few hours ago.

"Late?" Nash asked. "It's not even eleven in the evening."

"We need our beauty rest," Monica giggled.

When Nash cleared his throat and faked a cough, she looked his way. His eyes told her that he wanted a little more time with her. She had to admit, she was feeling the same way.

"Um," Delaney uttered and looked between Nash and Monica, knowing her face displayed confusion.

"I can walk Delaney to her room on my way to mine, if that's okay with her?" Nash jumped in and said boldly.

"Laney?" Monica questioned.

"I'd like that."

Her words were not spoken to Monica, but to Nash. She was going with the mood of the moment. She wanted to stay.

"Okay, then we'll see you both later. Don't try any funny stuff, Nash. I'm watching you. She's my best friend!" Monica yelled as James pulled her away.

"I have to love her!" Delaney joked.

"I guess they walked up just in time," he said.

"You think so?"

"I know so. I was about to kiss you. I don't usually do that, but I couldn't help myself. You are so damn beautiful."

"Well, maybe there will be another chance."

"Only, maybe?"

Before she even thought of a quick quip to respond, she felt Nash before she saw him move. She didn't pull back when his hand moved to the side of her face. When a slight movement drew them closer together, she had no plans to resist and didn't. As much as the idea of kissing him seemed like this wasn't the time, she knew nothing was going to keep her from finding out if his lips were as tantalizing, demanding and yet as soft as they appeared to be.

Her stomach churned with longing as a need that surpassed any fused through her. Her eyes went from Nash's eyes to his lips. Without thinking, she licked her lips in anticipation. That move seemed to lure him even more. Perhaps her yearning was so strong that she was imagining that his eyes had changed from a light hazel to a dark smokey brown. There was no way she could miss what she saw as an erotic impact to the lustful moment they were sharing.

"Your lips. Can I taste your lips?" Nash asked her, just a whisper away from her mouth.

His voice was already deep. Did it just deepen even more? Her body sure thought so with the way she trembled.

She didn't speak, but nodded. Her words were stuck somewhere in the dream world waiting to be set free.

*Dream*. There was that word.

The moment she felt his lips, the kiss started out slow and seductive. Quickly the intensity changed to ravenous, due more on her part than his. His lips touched hers and sent her mind reeling with pent-up amatory sensual lust. She immediately wanted and needed more. He initiated it, but she joined him as an equal participant in both form and intensity.

Delaney moaned as she allowed her entire being to relax into the kiss, following along as it deepened while her mouth demanded even more. Her lips parted and the sensation of the soft pad of his tongue searching out hers sparked her brain's senses, bringing it even more to life. She switched between giving and taking while Nash's tongue damn near gave her an orgasm as it continued to stroke hers. The way he made love to her mouth made her womanhood jump with a running craving. Her heart thudded while her nipples tingled against the lace of her bra. She was on fire just as the kiss slowly ended and Nash pulled away from her.

"That was even better than I thought it would be. I need to walk you to your room. I need to find my way to mine and a very, very cold shower."

"Okay," Delaney uttered quietly. She didn't know if she should continue being overly excited or depressingly disappointed that he wanted to get to his room.

When he reached his hand out to her, she took it and stood with him. Before they moved, he held her gaze.

"I don't want there to be any misunderstanding about my desire for you. I also suggest you not look down where the evidence of that desire is quite evident."

They laughed together, taking all tension out of the moment. The sexual chemistry felt through the kiss was clear.

"I promise to not look. I will say that just because it's not as evident with me as it is with you doesn't mean it's not there."

Delaney shocked herself. When did she become this bold with her words. She also wondered who this man could be that she felt brazen enough to let him know her desire matched his.

Nash leaned over and whispered in her ear.

"I hope this is a to-be-continued moment for the right place and time. Me walking you to your room and then going straight to mine does not speak to how much I'm feeling you. I already know I'm attracted to you. What's foreign to me is how much. I want to slow this down just a bit. That cool with you?"

"Yes, it is."

Delaney looked behind them as they headed toward the doorway of the hotel bar. Nash's guys remained seated and waited for him to say if they should follow. She must have missed what that was because they walked alone to her room.

"Your guys are serious about protecting you," she said.

"That they are. They're my brothers, not by blood, but definitely by relationship."

"What happened to the guy from earlier?"

"Kilton? He's getting some quiet time with his wife. When I'm on the road, he's always there. He's the only one of my guys who's married. His team likes to give him as much time off as possible for family time. I told him if he didn't make sure

Sheena always kept a smile on her face, I'd fire him. He puts his family first," Nash explained.

"I understand that. I'm sure his wife appreciates that he makes that kind of time for her."

"I have no doubt that she does," Nash agreed. "Which way to your room? If that's what you want to do."

Delaney promised herself that she could learn to live a little more; take a few unfamiliar chances.

"I don't know. Is there another option? You did say it was barely eleven," she noted.

She grinned when Nash acted like he was thinking hard of another option. She agreed that they needed to slow down considering the hotness of the kiss. She still wasn't ready to turn in yet. It wasn't often she went out and enjoyed an evening that didn't involve work or the kids. She was in New Orleans. She wanted to do more than spend it in her hotel room.

"How would you like to go for ride to a place that plays the best music your ears have ever heard? I know an amazing place?"

"Music? I'd love that. I didn't come to New Orleans be in my room. You?" she asked.

"You want the truth? I was going to do that, along with get some business done. Now that I've met you, hell no I don't want to be in my room. Not when I can show a beautiful woman around the town where I grew up. I know all the sweet spots," he said as they walked.

"I bet you do."

The words came out without her thinking about them. She looked over at him shyly.

"Don't worry. I'll act like I didn't hear that so that all the images running through my head don't control the night. I will say I'd like to reserve my response to that for what I hope will be another time. Shall we?" he asked.

"Definitely.'"

"Cord, why don't you go ahead and do your own thing for the rest of the evening. I'm going to need the truck. You got transportation?" he asked.

"I'm good. We have two trucks. Kilton figured you may want some time to yourself. We were ready for your schedule."

Cord tossed him the keys and walked by them out of the hotel bar.

"I guess they know you better than you," Delaney quipped.

"That they do. Let's go find music where the night never ends."

Placing her hand in his, she was ready to go where the night was going to take them. She was living moment by moment. The current moment was better than any she'd experienced lately.

***

Sheena couldn't believe the suite Kilton had secured for them. She was taken by surprise that he wasn't running out for something with Nash. She knew what he was about when she met him years ago. He was head-of-security for one of the most recognizable celebrities in the world and no doubt, needed security around him. Kilton was also the best at what he does. Back then, he hadn't yet started his own security firm, but since then, they were able to find more time for each other as he continued to grow his business and his team. She loved that even when his schedule was crazy busy, he found time to surprise her with time like this.

After enjoying a quiet dinner before taking in a late-night movie, they'd arrived back at the hotel to find the suite had been decorated with lots of flameless candles placed throughout, including the bathroom around the large tub made for two people. There was a bottle of wine chilling on ice with a decorated tray of fresh fruit sitting on the table beside it. Soft music filled the room. She admired everything while Kilton went into the bathroom to draw them a bath. It was moments like this that she cherished the most. Though she missed their two babies back at home in Miami, this time with the love of her life was important.

"You like?" Kilton asked exiting the bathroom and joining her on the soft, plush couch that faced a window that covered the wall in front of them. The view of the night sky was magnificent.

"I love it. You outdid yourself, baby. I wasn't expecting you to have this much free time. I really have you to myself for the whole night?"

"Try the entire weekend which starts tonight for us. It will include tomorrow, Saturday and Sunday until I take you back to the airport that evening. By then, I know you'll be missing the kids like crazy."

Kilton smiled at her excitement.

"Seriously? Are you sure?"

"Yes, baby, I'm sure."

"Nash is good?" she asked.

"He's better than good."

"What happened to him and my girlfriend Eva? She said that Nash never called her for a second date."

"You know him. He's picky when it comes to women, even those he only has a physical attraction to. He went out with her because you introduced them. What did Eva say?"

He smiled, already knowing the answer.

"Nothing, really. She was hoping for more than a date. I can tell you she was beyond excited that I was introducing them. She asked me to find her another baller. I have a feeling she rubbed Nash the wrong way."

Kilton chuckled.

"That's the understatement of the year. You know what Eva is looking for. Her first priority is not a nice man; it's his wallet. Nash mentioned they went out to dinner and she spent the night talking about all the places in the world she wanted him to take her. They drove by some high-end store and she told him that she was happy that she finally met a man who could afford gifts from stores like that for her."

Sheena blew out a loud breath.

"Ugh. I need to apologize to Nash. I don't know what I was thinking trying to hook them up."

"Baby, Nash doesn't need to be hooked up. You have no idea the number of women who throw themselves at him every day. That's why my team sticks close. We don't want any groupies trying to find a way to make Nash some kind of cash cow. Anyway, I was checking in with Cord before we got back. He mentioned that Nash met someone."

"Really? When?"

"Today. I need to get more information. From what he says, he's never seen Nash like this about a woman before."

"Never?"

"Cord said never. That's saying a lot when it comes to Nash. You know reserved he is, especially in public. The word is he kissed this woman in public. Cord could barely describe it saying, he wanted to holler for them to get a room."

"Publicly? Nash and public kissing? You're right, you need to get me more information on that. No one has ever seen Nash even holding hands, let alone kissing a woman out in the open."

Kilton agreed.

"Who is this magical woman, is my first question."

"Nash is a legend when it comes to people trying to figure out his personal life because they can never catch him off-guard. There may be hope for him yet. I can't imagine a man as nice as him not finding and loving the woman of his dreams. I was talking to him a while back about that. He told me that he was ready to settle down with the right one. I should have known it wasn't Eva."

"Yeah, I don't know what you were thinking with her You know I stepped back from that to allow you to do your thing. Looks like you won't be doing that again. Nash has one-upped us all with this woman!" Kilton joked.

"I know you love him like a brother. I just wanted to see him as in love with someone as you are with me."

"You are my everything. I wanted to thank you for being patient with me. I know it's not easy being my wife. I want you to know how much I love and appreciate you."

Sheena raised her hand and caressed the side of his face, running her fingers through his soft, full beard.

"I ran into being in love with you with both eyes open. I know what you do. I'll always be okay with it. You love me and the kids and provide for us. That's all that matters. I will always understand and appreciate who you are and what you do. When you do things like this, I love you even more. I know the sacrifice you make being away from us. When you're home, I will always make sure you love the space you come home to."

"I'm all yours, baby! All yours!" he said and kissed her again.

Her giggling started when he swiftly removed every stitch of her clothing in record time. She tried to help, but Kilton pushed her hands away letting her know that stripping her naked was a task he never needed any help with. She watched in awe as he quickly removed his own clothing, starting with pants and shirts flying in different directions.

"I guess not seeing me in over a week has got you all in a frenzy!" she declared.

"You have no idea how much I've missed you."

Kilton stood. Sheena swooned, feeling herself being lifted up into his strong arms, straight up his tall frame until her legs were wrapped around his bare waist. She wiggled her hips when that long, strong part of his pressed intimately against her as if it were searching for the perfect place to enter.

She held on when he moved them to the closest wall., pressing her back against it; holding her tightly in placc.

Sheena delighted in the heat of the moment; her body's measured heat rising. They'd been kissing all night. This kiss being planted on her was demanding and full of hunger for the time that they were apart.

Kilton's mouth devoured has as the lower part of his body slid into hers. Their eyes met. The shimmering in his that sparkled and glowed was all she needed to see to join in their loving; using his embrace to move up and down on him. His groans moved her faster with purposed strokes, matching his.

They moved urgently together. The turbulent, stormy desire rose quickly. Her arms held Kilton tight. She found his ear as she leaned into him as his body pumped harder into hers.

"My love," she uttered.

Sheena wanted to say more, but couldn't find the words. The world around her crashed into a million little pieces the same way her body was doing. With their minds and bodies moving as one, she felt the moment Kilton surrendered to the feeling of how they fit perfectly together; how everything about a moment like this was more than sex; it was pure animalist love. They needed this. The best decision she made was to ask her sister to watch their kids so that she could fly to him to love him and to have him love her just like this.

# 9

Somewhere, someone was knocking on a door. Delaney was annoyed. Her bed felt like heaven. She snuggled deeper into the plush pillows hoping whoever was knocking would go away. Their timing was murder on her dream.

She'd been having another steamy, erotic novel worthy dream. She couldn't believe the sexiest moment was interrupted. All she needed was five more minutes. That's all it would take for the most powerful release she'd ever known. She felt it happening. Instead of basking in the perfect dream, she was startled awake by a second round of knocking. This wasn't a part of her dream. The knocking was happening in real time.

Sitting up in bed, her body was completely covered in sweat. The silver, silky two-piece pajama shorts and top she wore were completely soaked. She knew they would be because of how vested she was in the actions in her dream.

"I'm coming!" she shouted to the door, the words she had hoped to scream in the middle of her dream.

Looking around for her robe, she assumed it was Monica at her door. Who else would show up early in the morning without calling? Just then her cell phone vibrated on the table beside the bed. She looked between the door and the phone and decided to grab the phone as she headed to the door.

"Hello?"

"Hi, beautiful."

Delaney stopped walking. The voice on the phone was the exact same voice from her dream. She knew because her legs quaked hearing it hit her ears, stimulating her erogenous zones as they had before she woke.

"Nash? Hi."

"Did you change your mind about breakfast? I was worried when after a half hour, you hadn't shown up."

*Breakfast*, her head screamed. She forgot that she agreed to meet him for an early breakfast after he took her on a middle of the night tour of New Orleans. She may have crash landed in bed once he brought her back to the hotel around four in the morning, but while they were out, she was wide awake. Most of all, she enjoyed his company and his attention. They talked about everything, especially about his love for his hometown.

"I'm so sorry. I overslept and didn't set my alarm. Is that you at the door?"

"Yes, it's me. I'm sorry if I disturbed your sleep. I really wanted to see you. I was being truthful when I said I was worried. I know we got back here pretty late."

Exhaling, Delaney looked at herself in the large floor to ceiling mirror on the back of the bathroom door. She wanted to be sure everything was covered. Looking in the bathroom, she used a towel to quickly wipe the sweat from her face, happy that the robe covered up her soaked body. Feeling better about her appearance, she opened the door and lost the ability to breathe. Nash stood on the other side smiling and looking at her with his beautiful, piercing eyes. He looked amazing. She would find words, but none came to mind that were of an appropriate nature. He looked good now but what she was really seeing were the images in her dream of him naked, kissing her, covering her body with his and loving her hard, deep and wildly; exactly the way she yearned for. So far, she'd only been achieving that while asleep. Nash had filled her mind the whole night the way he filled the doorway of her room with his delectable presence.

He stood before her in a pair of blue denim jeans that hugged his muscled legs perfectly. His light blue short-sleeved shirt with the powerful arms appeared to be smiling right at her. When her eyes finally landed back on his eyes, she saw desire; heated, unabashed, unashamed craving.

"Delaney? Are you okay? You look strange."

Gathering herself, she disconnected the call since they were in front of each other.

"I'm sorry. Yes, I'm fine. I was asleep. I can't believe I forgot about breakfast. What time is it?"

"It's almost ten in the morning."

Her eyes widened in disbelief. She never sleeps this late; not even on her laziest days.

"Ten? I've been asleep all that time?"

"Well, it was almost morning when I walked you to your room. I wanted to check and make sure you were alright."

"How are you so bright and chipper after only a couple of hours of sleep?"

"Because I couldn't wait to see you again."

"I guess I screwed up breakfast, huh?"

Not her plan at all. Look at him, she thought.

If her disappointment didn't show on her face, she would be surprised.

"Not if you are interested in getting dressed and joining me for a late breakfast. I was also thinking about something fun before this evening's festivities begin with the bridal party."

"Fun? Like what?" she asked, definitely intrigued.

"I was thinking I could show you more of my town, but during the day. We have great places to sight-see and the best way to do it. First, we need to get you some sustenance. Are you interested or would you like to go back to bed for a little longer?"

With you? Hell yes! Had she said those words out loud?

"Um, yes, I still want to do breakfast. You didn't eat?"

Terrible play on words again. She was about to melt into a puddle on the floor. In her dream, Nash's head had been down between her legs with his tongue at work and eyes plastered on hers. She could almost feel his lips turn into a smile against her wet folds.

"No, I haven't eaten. I was waiting to do it with you; I mean to eat with you. Do you want to?"

"Definitely!"

"Should I wait for you? Or you can join me in the restaurant? I have a private table off to the side where we can eat and talk without being bothered. I know you have to get dressed. I want to do whatever works for you. What about my offer of taking you on a tour of this great city? Up for that?"

"That would be great. I wasn't planning on doing much other than taking in a few sights. With you being from here, you'll know what to show me."

"That I can do. I'll work on setting the tour up while you get dressed. We can still have our omelets."

"Give me about thirty minutes to shower and get dressed."

"Sounds good. I'll be waiting."

Delaney was about to close her door when Nash walked away but the temptation to watch him walk took over. Cautiously, in hopes that he wouldn't look back, she leaned forward to look beyond the doorway. Her eyes caught the most glorious sight. The man had a form that was worth every wet dream she could ever have. Most of all, he had that Will Smith walk, filled with confidence and oozing with sex. She was thankful for having more to add to her nighttime dream.

She'd just agreed to spend the day with him, just like that. She was already questioning her decision, completely forgetting that she was in town to spend time with Monica, not drooling over a man. Thinking about Monica, she moved away from the door and dialed her.

"Girl, you up?" she asked when Monica answered on the first ring.

"Of course, I'm up. Are you up? You sound a little sleepy."

"Yeah, I just woke up. I can't remember the last time I slept this late. Can you believe that?"

"You're just getting up? No, I don't believe it. Did you sleep alone last night? If not, I can understand why you would still sound a little ragged around the edges."

"Yes, I slept alone. Who the hell would I be sleeping with?"

"Don't make me tell you that. I saw you and Nash deep in conversation last night. How late did they let you and Nash stay there to talk?"

"We left after you did."

"Really?"

"Yeah. He took to a place to listen to some really good jazz music. We danced and had a good time. I got back here somewhere around four in the morning."

"That late? No wonder you're tired. You didn't invite Nash back to your room? He likes you. I already know you like him."

"Stop with all that."

"He likes you as much as you like him. Go ahead and get you some; you know you want to. I bet he wants to. I told you to have fun this weekend. The world is your oyster girl. What happens here can stay here. Only the three of us need to know about it," Monica chuckled.

"The three of us?"

"Yes. You, Nash and me. You know you're going to have to tell me. We never talked about your life with Davis because, that would be cruddy since I'm related to him. With Nash, I've heard the stories of his prowess. You'd be in for a real, *BIG* treat; if you know what I mean."

"Why are you like this?" Delaney said laughing uncontrollably.

"You're single, sexy and the way you turn heads, you can have any man you want. Don't even try acting like you don't want Nash. Do you know how many women would love to be the focus of his attention?"

"Women were eyeing him last night as if he were an expensive Burkin bag. His attention never wavered from me."

"I already know. As long as you're having a good time, I'm happy. We have scheduled events like the dinner tonight and the yacht party, but other than that, your time is your time. You're here to relax. What are you getting into today?"

She wanted to spend it with Nash, but Monica came first. This weekend is supposed to be about her.

"That's why I'm calling you. I didn't know if there was anything you needed me to do for tonight's dinner party. I'm here for whatever you need me to do."

"There is nothing to do. The event planner we hired has fixed my whole entire life this. All I have to do is show up. If I need anything else, she is a text away."

"Oh, okay. Well, did you have plans for us to hang out today?"

"Laney, do you have something you want to tell me? I hear the hesitancy in your voice. What's going on? I know you're here for me just as you always have been. We can have all the time in the world to be here for each other, but if you have plans you want to dive into, I want you to do that. I know you. You're calling me to see if I was planning something for you and me for the day and I'm not. Now, if you don't have anything to do, there is a lot to get into in New Orleans and yes, I can make some arrangements to do something fun before the dinner at seven tonight. What's going on?"

Delaney nibbled on her bottom lip as she tried to come up with a way to explain her plans.

"Well, Nash asked me to breakfast, which I'm late for. He then offered to show me around New Orleans some more. There are sights he wants to show me in the light of day. I said yes before I checked to see if you would need me or if you just wanted to hang out."

"Laney, do you. I'm just happy you're here. I know Nash is a surprised presence, but from what I see, that's a good thing."

"Can I be honest?"

"Always."

"What is your honest opinion about the age thing?"

"Stop that right now. I already told you – I don't care anything about that. I also said that you shouldn't either. It's not like you to be unsure of yourself. What is this hesitancy I keep getting from you when it comes to Nash? He's a man. He's a very good-looking man. Know what? He wants you. Don't think too hard on this. You act like you've never been on the other end of a younger man's interest before. I've seen how men of all ages look at you."

"You know what my problem is with this," she bemoaned. "I have a career, children."

"None of them are here. It's you and Nash. And stop with the damn age thing. Nobody cares. If they do, then it's their problem, not yours. Do you like him?"

"Monica, it's not that easy. People will call me a cougar. I don't like labels. "

"Since when do you care what anybody says about you? I'll ask you again; do you like him?"

Monica shouted the question at her this time causing her to tense up and pace incessantly.

"Yes."

"That's all you need. Go have you some fun. I will remind you one last time. Get you some if you want some. You're not marrying Nash. You're here for a weekend. He's here for a weekend. Make this weekend count. Make it matter. There is nothing wrong with slipping and sliding around on the bed with that man. I've seen the size of his shoes. Girl! Stop playing with me and get you some! I'm thinking about spending the day on my back under my fiancé. We've been so busy wedding and party planning that we are lacking in our personal, quiet time. My day will be busy, so do you. Let your short hair down. I love the new style, by the way. Put

110

something on that young buck. Show him what you're working with. No reservations. Now, whatever you do, don't you dare be late for dinner. James and I have a lot of fun stuff planned for the wedding party tonight."

"If you're sure you don't need me, I'm going to get dressed and have breakfast. I'll be out for most of the day, I think, depending on what Nash has planned. If you need me, call me. I better get moving before he thinks I'm not going to show up; again. I also need to call the kids."

"No, you don't. They're fine and they will be fine. You called them a million times yesterday after you saw them at school. You don't have to try and deny it because I know you. Be sexy Delaney Monroe. You share the last name of one of the sexiest, most sultry women who ever lived. She even sang a song to John F. Kennedy for his birthday. Channel her and sing Nash a song! Hell, put something on him that would have him singing you a song," Monica chuckled.

"Haha, real funny. Bye, girl."

Knowing she was late, Delaney grabbed what she needed for the day and raced to the shower. She had a man to get to.

## 10

While all eyes should have been focused on Monica and James, in truth, Nash couldn't take his eyes off of Delaney. She sat next to him around the table with twenty or so other members of the wedding party. He was trying to focus, but with Delaney looking and smelling like a goddess, he found it hard to concentrate on the task at hand.

The dinner party had begun about an hour ago with what turned out to be a five-course meal. It consisted of a one-bite hors d'oeuvre, individual plated appetizers, a salad, the main course, and dessert. They had just finished up the main course of blackened salmon, braised lamb chops, green beans and roasted potatoes on a bed of spinach. The dessert will be a large variety to choose from. Since they arrived, he had enjoyed the various games they played to get to know each other. When James clinked his glass with a spoon, he knew it was time for yet another one. When Delaney reached for her glass of Reisling white wine, he leaned in her direction, out of eat range of everyone else.

"I had a wonderful time with you today," he said as quiet as he could. When he turned to make sure he hadn't been heard, several women were giving him an evil eye. He'd seen those looks many times before over his career. He shook them off. It couldn't be that they heard him. Then he realized their looks were not focused on him, but on Delaney. This was a woman thing and he knew it.

He remembered times when he and Zonnique were out together years ago. She would get the same look from women. Like then, he ignored the ones around the table as well. He hoped Delaney would do the same. When she smiled and turned toward him, he didn't move. Staying that close to her put their lips mere inches apart. He wanted nothing more than to kiss her right here and right now. That would get him more glares. He didn't care. He would get to kiss her again like he'd been feigning to do since the dinner began.

"I did too. It was wonderful. I've never had a man pick me up in a horse-drawn carriage before. You really did that. Those white horses were so beautiful. The ride around New Orleans made my day. Today was a good day," Delaney said.

"We could have walked but I didn't want people who recognized me to mess up our vibe. Looks like not everyone can say that."

He looked around the table again, nodding for Delaney to see what he saw. Where the women should be filling out the cards and paying more attention to the person they should be writing the answers down from, they were staring at him and Delaney. The new game was to ask the person you were walking down the aisle with questions to find out more about them. They would then be read the answers aloud to everyone.

"That's because of you," Delaney laughed. She tried to hide her laughter with a cough.

"Okay, everybody, you have a few minutes left to get the answers from the person assigned to you," Monica exclaimed.

"You haven't written down anything," Nash said, as he pointed to the empty lines on Delaney's paper.

"I already know the answers."

"You do?" he asked.

"Yes. We shared a lot about ourselves yesterday and today. Listen to this."

"Oh, I can't wait to hear this," he said.

"The first question is your full name. It's Nashall Patterson. Next is, what's your favorite color? You have three. Red, black and yellow. You played for Miami, so that's a given. Next, what's your favorite vacation spot? You told me that today; it's the Maldives. You love to go there to escape where no one knows you or bothers you. What's your favorite dessert? While we were out today, we stopped at a bakery. You ate two slices of strawberry cheesecake. You talked about how much you love it. The list goes on for six more questions to ask you and trust me, I know them all."

He liked how proud of herself she was. She'd gotten each one of them correct.

"Well, you're not the only one. I know that your name is Delaney Monroe. Your favorite color is red because of your sorority. Your favorite vacation spot is a cabin you own in Georgia. It's your place of peace on a lake. I'd love to see it sometime. Your favorite dessert is lemon cake. You told me how when you were eight years old, you snuck into the kitchen and ate half of a lemon cake your mother made for Christmas day. They thought because it made you sick that you would never eat it again, but you loved it even more. I also know that your favorite book is *The Stand* by Stephen King. How am I doing so far?" he asked.

Before Delaney got the chance to respond, Monica stood and told them all that time was up. The wink he received from Delaney was all he needed. The woman did it for him. He wasn't sure she knew it yet, but he found a beautiful queen and hoped that their day out today wouldn't be their last.

As Monica gave instructions that they would start at the other end of the table and work their way up to the head of the table where he and Delaney sat, Nash leaned back in his chair and faked like he was paying attention to everyone. His thoughts turned back to the day he shared with Delaney. He couldn't get it off of his mind.

When she'd come down for breakfast, her beauty blew him away. He didn't know it was possible for a woman to get more beautiful with each passing day, each passing moment, but Delaney seemed to master that. Her casual outfit with sexy high black wedge heels had his tongue practically wagging like a dog in heat. He knew about the comfort of those shoes from a few of his cousins who often exclaimed about their ability to look hot and sexy while also being comfortable in heels.

Delaney had walked into the hotel restaurant with the flair and sass of a runway model. He hadn't let it escape him that when she opened her hotel door to him and he found her in a satin robe looking like she just rolled out of bed, he'd never been more attracted to a woman being that natural in his life.

After a tour of the French Quarter, he took her on a tour of the New Orleans Museum of Art. He smiled when her face showed her shock at his love of art. He loved shocking people with his knowledge. New Orleans was full of history. He loved learning everything about it as well as telling and showing others. They ended up back at the French Quarter where they ate traditional New Orleans food like gumbo and jambalaya.

He loved that she enjoyed trying new foods. There was a lot to be said about an adventurous woman who trusted his judgement and dove right in. A woman like Delaney was at the top on his list of what he wanted in a woman he chose to be involved with. Speaking of adventurous, he had tried to get a few women to go on an airboat ride to see the wild bayou country. When they found out about the speed of the boat, the water they would be on and the possibility of seeing live large animals in the water, they would freak out. Not Delaney. She couldn't wait to get to that boat. He sat back and watched her eyes light up every time the boat sped ahead. She held on to him with a vice grip, but still, he delighted in the fun she was having. He wanted to end their day out with a steamboat cruise, but they wouldn't have enough time until they had to return to the hotel to get ready for the dinner with the entire wedding party. They agreed to try and find time to get that boat ride in before the end of the weekend.

When it was his turn to share about Delaney, Nash stunned everyone by answering the questions that Monica posed to him without him having to read the paper. Everyone looked to her as he answered one question after another with the correct response. Monica, James and the other men around the table were perplexed. The women, on the other hand, showed their jealousy. There were a were a few who had been trying to flirt with him since the dinner party started. He appreciated their attention as he did with other women. He was in a new space. He was only interested in Delaney.

While out for the day, they had stolen several kisses from each other as if they had been in love for years and not two people who had met twenty-four hours ago.

After the last game, the desserts arrived. When Delaney excused herself, he took the time to stand from the table as well. Besides, he wanted to check out the options.

"Are you enjoying yourself?" he asked, walking up to her.

She turned to face him full on.

"I am loving every minute of being here. The women are hating on me right now, though. Am I the only person who feels that? It was getting hot at the table. I needed a quick break," she admitted.

"I noticed it too. Don't let it get to you."

"They want you. You get that, right?"

Nash reached for her hand and was happy that she didn't pull away.

"That may be the case. I'm also very flattered, but I'm not interested in any of them. I hadn't planned on being interested in anyone. I am, however, very interested in you. I hope you know that."

"I'm interested in you too. But..."

"Don't do that. Don't go back to the age thing. I get it; I know it. I'm hoping you can get to a point that it doesn't matter to you. When two people like each other and are grown ass people, they can like and enjoy whomever they choose. I'm choosing you. I want what makes you comfortable. You tell me what that is and that's what we'll be."

"Nash, are you talking about something other than a casual acquaintance?"

"I'm talking about dating beyond this weekend. I don't know what that will look like. Maybe we can find time between now and the time you leave to define what that is. Can you make a promise to yourself to live in this moment? From the way you kiss me, I know your moment matches mine. Let's just go with it. How's that?"

"I can do that. I don't know what I would want."

"Okay, I have a question for you. Let's focus on today, or rather tonight. This will be wrapping up soon. I'd like to spend some time with you if you're not too tired. What would you like to do? We can do anything you want to do."

"Anything?" she asked.

"It's your call."

"Can I see your house?"

"My house? Tonight?"

"Yes."

He wanted to ask more questions, but from the look in Delaney's eyes, he didn't need any more answers. He knew. She knew. They knew. The kisses throughout the day were hot and heavy at times. He wished he could slip away to someplace private and slide into her soft body. He couldn't deny how much he wanted to be with her. If he was nothing, he was patient when he encountered something he wanted. Right now, he only wanted her. He wanted her in any way she was open and willing to share.

"My house it is."

Nash turned back to the desserts and when his eyes turned back in her direction, she was still standing there with her eyes on him. She didn't walk away or reach for anything on the table.

"Since my divorce, I've done some dating. There hasn't been anyone that I've felt a real, live connection to until you. There is something about you that I can't shake."

"Do you want to?"

"No, I don't. I can't say where I think anything will go beyond enjoying each other's company, but if that's what it turns out to be, are you okay with that?" she asked.

He started to answer, but could only shake his head at the irony. She sounded like him. If he was correct, she was alluding to a casual affair. He was the king of that.

"Delaney, you are one amazing woman. You just made me see who I have been. It sounds like you're saying to me what I've said to women for a lot of years. Are you saying you'd be okay with something casual but not serious?" he questioned.

"I guess I am saying that. I was married for a long time. I'm not saying I want to spend years going from one man to the other. I am saying that I want to feel free to do whatever I want. I like you, but I have reservations and you know why. I can't just drop how I feel about that. I am okay with spending time together; alone and private. Is that okay with you?"

Nash took her hand, raised it to his lips and kissed the back of it.

"I'm perfectly fine with that. I'm really hoping this dinner is just about over. Kissing your hand made me realize I much I want to lick on and taste your lips. My house?" he asked, raising an eyebrow to relay exactly what was on his mind without saying it and risking being heard that he wanted her in the hottest, sexiest way.

"Your house."

Delaney winked at him and walked back to the table. The way she walked away, told him more than any of her words could. She was walking comfortably into what the night would hold for them. He heard her words. He was now accepting her challenge.

**\*\***

Stepping outside of the room where the meet and greet was being hosted, Delaney saw people through the glass panel of the door mingling with each other. After a few uncomfortable moments with a few of the women, their aggression toward her for stealing Nash's attention had dissipated and the night had actually turned out to be fun. James and Monica had rounded out the night by giving out gifts to everyone. She reminded everyone of a few more activities planned along with the arrangements in West Palm Beach for the rehearsal and the ceremony in a few months.

Ready to leave, she headed toward Nash when her phone rang. It was Kennedy. She excused herself and stepped out into the night heat.

"Mom? Can you hear me?" Kennedy shouted in the phone.

"Why are you yelling?"

"Because I asked you two questions and you didn't answer. I thought maybe you couldn't hear me."

"I hear you. How are things at school?"

"Great. I'm having a get-together with the students in my dorm that I'm the resident advisor for. I wanted to let you know about the charges you'll see on my credit card. I'm not going overboard, but I wanted to do something really nice. I didn't know if you wanted to know the amount before I went out spending money in the morning on the card you gave me for emergencies."

"Ken, you have money. You don't have to run everything by me, but thanks for checking. Just don't go overboard. You don't want all of the money you made over the summer to go toward your credit card bill. I know it's for school incidentals, so I will pay the bill; you don't have to worry about it."

"Thanks, mom. You told us to be more financially responsible now because it will carry over to our future lives. How's godmommy doing? Is she enjoying her party?"

"She is. She's so happy. I'm just as happy for her. James is a really good guy. I can tell that he loves Monica very much. You'll love him when you meet him at the wedding."

"I can't wait. I know she's been wanting a good man for a long time. What about you? Are you having a good time? Doing anything fun? Are you letting your new short hair down?" Kennedy joke.

"I'm having fun."

"No work?"

"Surprisingly, no. I'm shocked that I haven't even thought about calling the office to check in."

"Good. You needed this trip. Are there any good looking, sexy men in the wedding party?"

"Kennedy!"

"What? You used to ask me that before I met Griffin."

"Yeah, but I'm your mother. I don't want you asking me about sexy men. Besides, you have Griffin."

"I'm not talking about for me; I'm talking about for you."

Delaney pulled the phone away from her ear and looked at it before putting it back up to her ear.

"You think I'm on the hunt for a man?"

"No, I'm not saying that. You think I don't see, but I do. I see how men flirt with you right in front of me. I hope what happened with you and dad didn't tarnish your view of men. I hear divorce can do that."

"Not for me, it hasn't and it won't. You will be the first to know about anyone I'm interested in when I'm ready. How's that?"

"I love that we can talk about anything. Kiss godmommy for me and tell her I love her. I wanted to check on you and tell you about the charge before you see it on my card."

"The party sounds like a great idea. What's your brother up to?"

"He was just here. He took my car to fill up the gas tank. I forgot to do it earlier. When I said something about it, he showed up at my dorm to get the keys."

"Good. He knows to look out for you. I'll see you both during family weekend in two weeks. If you need anything from home, let me know before I drive there."

"I will. Um, dad asked about you when he called me earlier."

"I keep telling him that he need not be concerned about me."

"I think he's sweet on you again."

"It's not happening, Kennedy. Don't feed into that. I have to go and rejoin the dinner. Be careful and I love you."

"Love you, too. Remember, if you encounter a good looking, hot, sexy man, go ahead and be single!"

Delaney chuckled under her breath. She and her daughter were too much alike in being brutally and bluntly honest.

"Bye, Ken!"

Turning around to rejoin everyone, Delaney was pleasantly surprised to see Nash heading her way.

"Hey! Monica asked me to come get you. She didn't know if you had gone back to your room or not. Someone said they saw you go in this direction. I volunteered to come scoop you up. She's checking to see who is joining her for the girl's day at the spa and then for the Saturday night cruise on the private yacht tomorrow evening."

"Oh, I forgot about that. I'm planning on going to the spa and the cruise. You going on the cruise with the group?" she asked.

"You, possibly with that body in a bathing suit? Hell yes!" he celebrated.

"You are so bad!" she replied.

"My house; tonight. Shall we find out if I am? If we are together?"

The visual was too intoxicating to deny.

"With bells on!"

## 11

"Nice house. I didn't know there were houses this spectacular. It's all white and glass."

Walking through the full glass double front door of Nash's home, Delaney imagined herself in the middle of an episode of the rich and famous; which Nash was. She had no idea when he asked if she'd like to see where he lays his head when he's in town that this would be his version of a place where he loves to kick-back in. She was standing in the middle of a creamed colored marbled floor with staircases on the left and right of her. There were two gold and cream with glass topped tables on either side, in the alcove that made up the bottom part of the staircase. She could see that the marble extended all the way up the stairs with gold-like handrails.

"This is big," she exclaimed as her high heels clicked across the marble as she took in her first peek at a black, gold and white designed sitting room to the right beyond the stairs.

"Would you like a tour? I know it looks humongous, but it's not. I had always dreamed of an entryway like this. The rest is pretty much a mancave after the two rooms ahead, dining room to the left and living room to the right."

"I would like a tour, but first, the ocean. You said the ocean was your backyard?"

"Yes. There's an infinity pool and huge entertainment area out back. We're up high, so there is a long stairway that leads down to a man-made sand covered beach. Then, yes, there is water – lots of it. The view is amazing!"

"This way?" she asked, walking ahead of him.

"Yes. You can't miss it. In a minute, you'll see a wall of nothing but windows and glass doors that lead outside."

"I can't believe you live here."

"Not as often as I would like like, but when I'm here, yes, this is the one place I love to be."

"Can I open the door?"

"Do whatever you want."

Stepping out on the large paved patio, there was beautiful cushioned covered chairs, sitting and lounge with lots of tables for entertainment. In the middle of it all was a large enclosed lighted infinity pool. It was more beautiful than anything she'd ever seen in person.

From where she stood, she could see the water, flowing just beyond his house. Looking left and right, she saw a large private fence that prevented anyone from seeing his property. That didn't matter much because what she didn't see as they drove up was neighbors.

"You're out here all by yourself? Where are the neighbors?" she asked.

"Over a half a mile away. Before you ask, yes, I know them all very well. This place looks secluded, but it's not. It's close enough, yet far enough away that it offers the peace I like to have when I'm home."

"Is it always this put together; neat and magnificent? I know you said you live in Florida too."

"I do and yes, it is when I come to town. My groundskeepers are alerted when I'm arriving. Even if I don't stay here, the place is always ready to greet me just like this."

"Thank you for showing it to me. I feel special."

Hearing nothing from him after her lame attempt to engage him, she turned and found Nash smiling as he leaned against the frame of the sliding door. He was so strikingly handsome against the sexy moonlit night. She watched him push a button and the enclosure around the pool opened as the panels lowered into the ground surrounding it.

"How do you like the night air out here?"

"It's different. The night was humid on Bourbon Street. It's cooler and much more pleasant not being so hot. I love it. I feel wonderful."

"You look wonderful. You look beautiful."

"You're charming, Nash. I know you already know that. You're so calm, cool and well put together. I bet all of that works on women of all ages."

"At this moment, the only person I'm hoping it's working on is you. Any amount of charm resonating from me is genuine."

Nash moved toward her; his eyes focused on her.

"I feel that," she offered.

"Good. There is nothing wrong with us being attracted to each other."

"Why me? You just met me."

"Because there is already something going on between us. Yes, we just met, but I already have a feeling that you are a woman I need to have in my life. Besides, have you seen yourself? You are gorgeous; damn near irresistible."

Suddenly she laughed. It wasn't an outburst and most of the laugh was contained in her head. The thought of being at Nash's house had her thinking of the Jay-Z song, *"Do It Again"*. In it, he rapped about what he would do to a woman from twelve until seven in the morning. She wanted to be done like the woman in the rap song. She laughed about the fact that she knew the song and that she wanted to be done, but for longer than fifteen minutes.

"What's so funny?" Nash asked.

"Just something running through my head."

"That would be?"

Could she? Should she? Could she really be the type of woman to react to him with bold fervor?

"I've never done anything like this before," she blurted out nervously.

"Like what?"

Delaney exhaled trying to find the right words.

"I..."

She stopped.

Nash saw her hesitancy. He wanted her to know that what they talk about and share on any level is between the two of them only.

"This is a safe space. Whatever you're thinking about saying, do you; be you. There's no ridicule here; never with me. Whatever it is that you haven't done that you're thinking whether you can do it with me or not, just put it out there. You already know and feel what I'm thinking about you. I'm not a shy person. What made you laugh just now?" he asked again.

"A song."

"A song? What song?"

"*Do It Again*," by JAY-Z, Amil and Beanie Sigel. Crazy, right?" she asked.

"Not crazy at all. I love that song. In fact, I love every song *HOV* has ever put out. Suddenly thinking about the lyrics, it's now my most favorite song. I will make you a solid promise though," Nash offered.

"What?"

He leaned over with his face a whisper away from hers, his mouth right in-line with hers as he spoke.

"I will absolutely last more than fifteen minutes, for starters. Second, I will never, ever, ever kick you out in the morning at any hour! Trust that."

Delaney started to laugh, but her mouth was suddenly busy. The muscles in her stomach jumped. She was overpowered by an intoxicating feeling of hunger, of need. Nash was hypnotizing her with the potent way in which he was making love to her mouth. His lips were rubbing and teasing hers, coaxing her to join him for even more. She accepted the primal, lascivious, lustful kiss. There was nothing tame about it. Knowing she wanted more, she opened her mouth slightly, just enough to let him know that more was on the agenda. When their tongues found each other, his hands reached out and pulled her snug against his hard rock body, harder in that key place in the center of them, she grabbed onto his shirt and held on. She was giddy with joy over the exciting ride the kiss was taking her on.

She was hot; burning up even; just not from night's temperature. She was thirsty going at Nash's lips and mouth as if she'd never experienced an amazing kiss like this from a man before. Maybe she hadn't; definitely not this amorous.

When Nash lifted and pulled back, Delaney held tight to his shirt, afraid she would fall at his feet if she let go. Her brain was a mush-mess.

"Damn!" Nash said first.

"Wow!" Delaney replied. She couldn't think of another word. The world around her was still spinning.

"I've been waiting to do that since we left the hotel. Does the rest of you taste this good?" he slurred near her lips before kissing her again, this time softer and quicker. It was over way too soon.

"I..."

"Delaney, I don't want to frighten you, but I am a man who speaks what's on his mind. Right now, everything about you is on my mind. If it's too much, let me know."

Again, she was at a loss for words.

"I've never encountered such an open and honest man before. I'm not in any way bothered by it; it's more of being caught off-guard.

"Shy?" he asked.

"I don't know if I'd call myself shy. It's new and the feelings that pound within me when you look at me like you are right now, or speak so truthfully, just...just."

Again, she stopped.

"Safe place, Delaney. I speak from my feelings because I've learned holding my thoughts inside don't get me very far. I also never want anyone to have to guess what I'm thinking or trying to say. You say you've never met a man like me who speaks his truth. I hope that's a good thing."

Delaney moved the words that were caught behind her throat to put them in the atmosphere. She didn't want to mix Nash in with her past.

Nash coaxed her again to be open. She wanted to. This was all new to her.

"I've never expressed my feelings as openly as I want to right now. I thought I didn't know myself when I asked you to bring me here knowing that we could possibly end up in bed together."

"Only possibly?" Nash laughed.

She laughed in return.

"Okay, a little more than possibly. I don't know what to say that won't have me sounding like a wild woman."

"Wild? I can picture you like that."

"I'm not usually that."

Her shyness was sneaking out. She quickly pushed it back in.

"No? Why not?"

Delaney was finding it hard to breathe. As he spoke, Nash was moving his head back and forth across her face, kissing her cheek, then her chin before finding her lips. When she tried to speak, his lips would capture hers saucily again. He may not realize it, but his kisses were stealing her breath. She'd never been this aroused before. That, she was afraid to admit. What woman married as long as she had been would admit that a man she'd met hours ago had her in a state of practically begging for more like never before? Her dreams; her fantasies. She was realizing they, perhaps, were preparing her for this very moment. Trying to speak, her small purse fell to the brick patio. She was about to reach for it when Nash spoke.

"Leave it. You won't need it. I want to know what you want. I know neither of us planned this. We couldn't have. Before yesterday, we had not met. Before today, I didn't know

I could want a woman as much as I want you. As hot and tempting as you are, I could say it was about sex, but I believe it can be so much more, but nothing is about me. It's all about you. Why did that song come to your mind? Be real; be honest."

"You ever have fantasies?" she blurted out.

"I'm having about a hundred of them about you right now!" Nash exclaimed.

Delaney shook her head at him and smiled. This time when his lips came close, she initiated the kiss. She sipped at his lips before nipping the bottom one lightly with her teeth. When her tongue moved to open his lips, she loved how easily he did so, letting her seek out what she needed within the confines of his mouth. She closed her eyes tight and let her desire for Nash show him how much she wanted him. She loved leading and not just being led.

"Mmm, I like that. I love a woman who takes what she needs and wants."

"Do you give what she wants and needs?"

Feeling embolden because of the sultry, sinful thoughts running through her mind, all starring Nash, Delaney knew the night was just beginning.

"Tell me about a fantasy of yours."

Delaney looked around. She didn't know what for. Perhaps, there were others around.

"Umm."

"There is no one here but us."

"I can't seem to think straight," she admitted.

"Because of me?"

"Yes, but it's a good thing. I'm trying to pick my words."

"Why? Say what is on your mind – no thinking too hard about it."

"You've got me so damn turned on that I feel scatter brained. I've had these sexy dreams for a while. In them is a man who entices me into telling him my desires, my fantasies, much like you're doing now. It's overwhelming. It's erotic. It's outside of who I've always been. He satisfies everything that I didn't even know I needed or wanted sexually."

"Then feel free to be who you want to be, not who you have always been. Something tells me, and correct me if I'm wrong, but I get this feeling that things have been pretty, shall I say, vanilla for you?"

"All true. The fantasies are new for me; since my divorce."

"What's keeping you from having what you want?"

"Never having them fulfilled before."

"Never?"

"No. I was married a lot of years. He wasn't into anything beyond what would be considered the vanilla you just spoke of."

Nash reached for the bare skin in the area between Delaney's breasts and allowed his fingers to caress her there. He heard the hitch in her voice. There was someone hidden inside of her who was screaming to be set free. He couldn't wait to meet her.

He kept his eyes on her as his hand moved lower inside of her dress and bra until the tips of his fingers encountered her nipple, pebbling into a hard tip as he stroked her there. He made sure their eyes didn't wander from each other. She had fantasies and he wanted to find each and every one of them, satisfying each one slowly and seductively.

"Spend the night with me."

"Here at your house?" she asked.

"I'll have you back at the hotel before Monica knows you've spent the night here with me. Do you trust me?" he asked. "I know it asking a lot so soon, but do you?" he asked.

"Yes," she uttered, shocked at how soft the word came out. Her mind was focused on Nash's hand as her head was screaming for him to read it and not stop. In her dream, her fantasy man asked if she was ready. No doubt that with Nash, her answer was yes.

## 12

Nash took Delaney by the hand and led her to the large, double bed sized lounge chair on the edge of the infinity pool.

"Do you swim?" he asked.

"Yes. Why?"

"I want to swim with you. The night is beautiful. I love swimming, especially at night. The sky is lit up with stars, the sound of the water on the ocean is soothing and you will love the feel of the water on your skin up here on the hill."

"I don't have a suit. They're back at the hotel."

"I won't wear one if you won't. Does that frighten you? The idea of swimming naked with me?"

Hell no, is what she wanted to scream but didn't. Nothing in life would please her more than to see all of Nash in all of his glory. The minute the words left his mouth, she wanted to get her hands on his clothes to help him disrobe. She contained her excitement, not wanting to seem like some kind of wayward, unruly vixen. Honestly, it was exactly how she was feeling. The dryness in her mouth and the fact that her tongue felt heavy in it had her clearing her throat to stumble out her response.

"No, not at all."

"I'm going to grab us some towels and turn on some soft music. I like old school, so I'm thinking some Anita Baker, some old Barry White, or newer school Toni Braxton. That work for you? There are speakers all around here."

As much as he was ready to take Delaney and love her on the spot where she stood, he wanted to be sure the night was one she clearly has dreamt about. If she saw him as the man who could bring her fantasies to life, he was more than ready to oblige.

When Delaney nodded, he turned and walked back into the house. Usually there were fresh towels in the storage area next to the pool, but his appearance at the house was unexpected. When his housekeeper prepared his house, he stated he wouldn't have time to swim. She let him know that she would still leave towels on the lower level for him just in case. He would get them on his way back from his room. He raced up the stairs knowing that if he and Delaney went as far as he was planning, he would need protection which he kept only in his room.

Racing to his room and grabbing what he needed, after kicking off his shoes, he raced back down, grabbed the towels and turned on the house stereo system to play music in every room, including the outside pool area. Having everything he needed and having it in hand, he rushed through the house as the soft, soothing, sweet sounds of Anita Baker flooded the air. He couldn't wait to have something else in his hands; *Delaney.*

Tonight, he didn't need anything or anyone else; only her. If anyone could see into his head and his heart, they would be surprised that he was already contemplating feelings of love for her.

Nash slowed his steps at the idea of it. He'd gone his entire career, dating one woman after another, even having children with one, but not once, has he ever felt the kind of deep-rooted, heart-searing, body-determined kind of love that he was already feeling for Delaney. Any other time, he would run from those kinds of feelings. With Delaney, he wanted more of it. He loved talking to her, now kissing her and hopefully by the end of the night, loving her in so many ways, his mind would be exhausted coming up with new ways. Before heading to the pool, he grabbed a few bottles of cold water and soda, adding them to an ice chest he filled up. He took everything out to the pool. The moment he stepped through the doorway between the house and the pool area, he knew his world had just turned on an axis.

Nash couldn't move. His feet were stuck in place. His body hardened all over. Nothing else in the world existed, nor would it from this moment on. Without moving his head to check for the reality of the situation, in front of him stood Delaney in all of her naked glory. She was facing him with her hands on her bare hips, her eyes locked on him with the full moon illuminating every delicious curve he knew she'd been hiding under that sexy dress. No one had ever looked more beautiful in his minds-eye; never. Without words, she was calling to him. Nash held his composure to not drop everything he had in his hands so that he could divest himself of his own clothes to join her. He looked slightly to his left to find that Delaney had placed all of her clothes at the foot of one of the lounge chairs. He was surprised and extremely happy.

"Well, damn. Can a brother have a heart attack at this age just from gazing upon the most beautiful sight in his life? If so, I hope you know CPR! Just, damn. You are downright delicious."

"As you can see, the little bit of shyness I may have had and said I didn't have is pretty much gone. I figured I would get a head start on swimming. Care to join me?" she asked.

Before he could answer, he watched her turn and do a perfect dive into the pool, with little splashing. He couldn't move. His feet felt like lead. He watched her body move angelically to the end of the pool before rising at the other end to turn and smile at him.

"Damn."

Nash didn't know how many times he'd said the word, but his mind was on lock. His vocabulary seemed to get smaller and smaller.

"What?" she called to him before swimming back in his direction.

"How's the water?" he asked, setting everything down and quickly undressing. Before heading to the pool, he made sure to have a special something in his hand to leave on the side of the pool, just in case.

He reached the edge just as Delaney reached him. Silence lived between them. His gaze watched her eyes take in all of him. One thing he wasn't, was shy, especially not around a woman he desired as much as he desired her. No doubt, she saw his longing for her staring hard and strong, pointing in her direction. He felt himself stiffen the moment her eyes moved up and down before landing and staying on his hardness.

"Come inside and find out. Feel free to take that as a double-entendre," she slurred out.

Nash was nothing if he wasn't someone who followed instructions especially from a sexy, naked woman.

He dove into the water away from her to not splash her, then swimming up to her. He moved close, pulling her into his arms, taking a moment to wipe water from her face.

"You can never, ever question my attraction to you ever again. Beauty inside and out, intelligent, sweet, sexy and all around got it going on. Never, ever. You get that we're naked, right?"

Delaney didn't wait for an invitation to what their nakedness could mean. She was way beyond doubting herself or how much having Nash inside of her meant to her ability to continue breathing.

"That's a mutual suggestion. Now that we're naked, do I get to say what's next?" she asked.

Moving back toward the edge of the pool, lifting herself and bracing her body on her elbows, she smiled when Nash wasted no time joining her, pressing her lightly into the concrete back of the pool. The minute his body melded against hers, she opened her legs, circling them around his taut hips, where his hardness settled between her legs.

Nash leaned even further into her, his face brushing against the side of hers as he first kissed her cheek and then her ear. Her elbows quivered on the edge of the pool when his tongue caressed every part of her ear before kissing and licking the small diamond piercing. Delaney moaned against his face. She let go of the last vestiges of nervousness she started out with. Nash moved his face soft and slowly against her face while his hands moved along her body from her legs, up her hips to her waist. She grew anxious for him to discover something he may not have seen when he first saw her naked next to the pool.

"You know, as vivacious as you are, I can't believe you told me that you haven't been getting what you want and need when it comes to intimacy."

"I'm changing that. I can't blame anyone for that but me," she whispered on a soft breath.

Nash's hands moved higher up as his mouth moved down to her neck where he groaned sexily against her skin. The moment his hands moved further up her body to her sides and then around to her stomach, she held her breath for his hands to move a little higher. His mouth went to work on her neck moving slowly from one side to the other when she dropped her head back to give him all the access he wanted and needed. The moment his hands reached her full, heavy breasts, and then her nipples, she knew what he'd discovered when he stopped moving. She, on the other hand, moved her hips in a circular motion with a sneaky cat-like smile on her face. Nash leaned up and their eyes met.

"See, you keep shocking and amazing a brother. Nipple piercing? Damn. If only I had moved to this side when we were standing, I would have felt it. I promised I would have a much larger vocabulary, but again, damn! That's sexy as hell."

"I'm so glad you think so. It's a few months old."

"Mmm, sensitive to the touch and tongue?" he asked.

Delaney couldn't speak when he slightly tweaked the tip between his fingers. The feeling was so wonderful that she almost jumped out of the pool. She'd played with her own tips since getting the piercing, but the feeling of someone else doing it drove her wild.

"Yes," she whispered.

"More?" he asked against her lips.

"Yes!" she screamed that time before her mouth was taken in a kiss that caused her hips to glide back and forth against his manhood. She delighted in the feel of Nash sliding back and forth against her womanhood, slippery to the touch, she was sure, even in the water.

How could she have waited until this age to be this turned on. She didn't know what to do when Nash moved slightly until his mouth covered her breast, his tongue flicking away at the small ring he found there. Her body was on fire. As much as she wanted to prolong this seductive moment, she wasn't sure her own heart would be able to stand it. His masterful mouth worked her nipple so well that she felt her body already heading for a powerful orgasm; something she'd never experienced from nipple play. What was he doing to her? Her mind was wild and foggy. Her body was screaming for release. She wanted to tamper it down to allow the moment to last longer. She felt herself losing the battle. She looked and his eyes were locked on hers as her breathing increased. The sight of his head swirling around her breast had her moving so feverishly, that the water around them sloshed about.

Delaney tried to catch her breath, but her mouth would only form a delightful circle of enjoyment. She was barely able to contain herself when she felt Nash's finger slide down over her womanhood, caressing her lightly. The double pleasuring was breath stealing. She didn't know which feeling to focus on more. Before she could prioritize which part of her body felt the best, her body jerked as a mind-penetrating released slammed into her the moment first one, then two of Nash's fingers entered her body, easily sliding in and out with a third finger planted against her hardened nub, sending her over the edge so deliciously hard that her hips rode his fingers harder than a jockey would ride a horse. She couldn't control herself and so she allowed her world to spin on its own. He merely followed the lead her body set.

"Oh god," she yelled. Her eyes slammed shut as blinding lights seared across them. Her arms flailed about until she found his muscular arms and she clawed at them. She dug in hard, feeling as if her brain was liquified. His mouth, his fingers – she was done for; she had reached a place of no return. She was experiencing her fantasy kind of orgasm.

When Nash moved his body haphazardly up hers, kissing his way to every place that was now over sensitized, Delaney struggled to contain her breath. She'd never lost control in this manner before.

"That was so hot!" Nash exclaimed in the night air. "More?" he asked her.

Delaney could only nod her head. She didn't care what he had in mind. From the small slit of the opening of her eyes, she saw him reach behind her head and heard the tear. She knew what was next and could barely contain her jubilance. She was more than ready. She'd seen Nash before he dove in the pool. A man with his girth, length and steely hardness had to be a dangerous weapon. She'd dreamed about being loved by a man that large. From the nervous way in which he moved to put the condom on, she was about to have her wish granted; her fantasy fulfilled.

Nash pulled her down further into the pool, gripping her behind in his big masculine hands, holding her snug against him as he kissed her senselessly, zapping everything out of her while giving her every part of him.

"Oh, baby!" Nash murmured when her arms went around his neck.

"Please," she begged quietly against his lips.

After setting something wild and full of desire within her free, she had no shame in pleading for more of what he'd just given her. She'd be crazy to not want that feeling all over again.

Nash didn't make either of them wait any longer. He entered Delaney in one long, sexy, smooth stroke. He filled her before pulling out until only the tip of him lay inside of her. She was tight, but so ready. When she cried out in delight, he slid back in, this time burying himself to the hilt. He had to bite down on his bottom lip to keep from yelling like a wild animal. He was feeling possessive as Delaney joined his strokes, circling and writhing her hips about frenziedly. He loved a wild woman. He thought the pace would be slow and methodical, but that quickly changed with each pass into her supple body.

His feet on the bottom of the pool braced them while his one hand gripped the pool edge. He needed to protect Delaney's back from scraping against the side of it. They were riding each other wildly. He felt himself pulse inside of her. The water made huge waves around their movements. He withdrew again and again and surged back in, filling her with all of him. They moved like that, calling each other's names, begging and calling out for more. He plunged again and again before pulling all the way out. He saw Delaney about to protest when he quickly maneuvered them around until her back was to him. He placed her hands up on the edge of the pool and moved in quickly behind her, not wasting any time entering her from behind.

"Oh, yes, yes, yes!" she yelled the minute he entered her with a hard, deep plunge.

"Hold on tight, sweetness."

Nash knew the ride would be a bumpy yet gratifying one in this position, one of his favorites.

Holding to her hips he rode her, enjoying the sound of their bodies slamming together in the water. With precise strokes and piston-like movements, Nash looked down to where their bodies were joined. The sensations his body experienced were incredible as Delaney moved her hips back toward him, rocking against the hard length of his erection. When she screamed that her release was coming and for him to not stop, he didn't. He surged forward harder, hearing his own grunts of pleasure. He felt her body lasciviously give in as her orgasm seized her and then gripped him. Together they rode the cloud of ecstasy as the most amazing wicked vibrations caused his legs to tremble, his own orgasm taking his breath away. Still, he didn't stop moving because he couldn't; he never wanted to. A muscle jerked in his chin. His neck stiffened, but his body kept going, getting and giving everything to the moment.

Finally coming down from the high, Nash felt Delaney's body slouch down into the water as she lay her head on the concrete ledge, her body still struggling to maintain a steady breath.

"You out here making fantasies come true! In your words, damn!" she said. Able to speak, but barely, she had to say something.

Nash laughed out loud against her back, still connected to her intimately.

"I aim to please. You asked and I answered the call. Besides, have you seen yourself? Especially in the heat of pleasure? I've never been this turned on. That is not a lie or a line; it's all fact. I was driven mad by the way your body responded to me. I loved every minute of it," he replied and kissed every piece of exposed skin he could find.

Delaney was about to acknowledge her own pleasure but then words escaped her when she felt him getting hard inside of her again. She turned her head around, gazing in his eyes with disbelief.

"I feel you. You know that right? All that work you just put in and I feel you rising to the occasion again. Are you serious right now?" she laughed, shaking her head.

"I'm telling you that it's not me; it's you. What do you say, we step out of the pool and relax. I don't want you to think I'm some sex crazed guy who can't control his desire for you. I might be, but let's not acknowledged that," he joked.

Moving back from her, he leaped up on the edge of the pool, removed the condom and helped her out.

"That was amazing."

"The night is still young. Why don't we grab something light to snack on from the kitchen and head upstairs to the bedroom. I would delight in amazing you some more before I have to get you back to your hotel in a few hours like Cinderella. I would love to have you in my arms all night and the next day, but I understand."

"Then I say, let's make the most of the moment."

When Delaney walked in front of Nash and he lightly smacked her behind, she winked at him.

"Oh, you like that," he nudged at her.

"I do now," she replied.

## 13

Delaney pulled onto one of the two carports in front of her garage. She usually parked inside but this was the first chance she was going to get to reorganize some of the clutter inside later on. Her car would only get in the way. The kids had so many boxes stacked up that until they went off to school, she didn't know how much would be left. She was happy to have the time to do something other than work. She'd been focused on that since returning a week ago from New Orleans. After a late start and early exit at the office today, being home a little earlier than usual meant she would have a little extra time to herself to also relax. Work was getting so crazy that it had taken her the entire week and the weekend to get herself up to speed.

Exiting her car, she turned when her neighbor across the street, Ms. Sylvie, called her name. That was followed by her usual full body waving from left to right with her hand flapping high in the air. With the extreme heat of the day, Delaney thought that her neighbor would be inside soaking up as much cool air as she could.

She returned the greeting and the wave right before she was summoned across the street.

"I have a delivery for you," Sylvie screamed.

"Delivery?" Delaney questioned herself.

Leaving her purse and briefcase in the front seat of her car, she hurried across the street.

"How are you today, Ms. Sylvie?"

"Hi, dear. I'm wonderful. You look beautiful in yellow. You should wear that color all the time. I used to dress my Sara in yellow when she was little. She hates the color now."

Delaney nodded at Ms. Sylvie's reference to her daughter whom she lives with along with her son-in-law, Tim and their children, Timmy and Spencer. Both are teenagers in high school. Kennedy had actually tutored Spencer a few times in the past year when he fell short in Algebra.

"Thank you. I happen to love yellow a lot. In fact, I love all bright colors. You said you have a delivery for me?"

Delaney didn't want to seem like she was rushing the conversation along, but she was anxious to get out of the heat.

"Oh, yes. A delivery man was going to leave two beautiful bouquets of flowers sitting on your porch. I know we live in a safe neighborhood, but I wanted to make sure nothing happened to them. Spencer! Bring those flowers out to Ms. Delaney," Sylvie yelled through their front door.

Within seconds, Delaney was pleasantly surprised when Spencer exited the house with two of the largest and most beautiful floral arrangements she'd ever seen. She could only see the tops of them because the rest, including the bases were covered in paper in two large white boxes.

"Wow! Those are huge!" she exclaimed. "What a wonderful surprise."

"Is it your birthday or something? Spencer, take them across the street for her."

"Thank you, Spencer. No, not my birthday or any other special occasion. I wonder who they're from? Maybe from my best friend. I visited her last week."

"Maybe they're from a man; an admirer even."

Ms. Sylvie just planted a seed. What she didn't know was how happy the thought was that it could be from an admirer – one in particular. She then dismissed the idea. She was pretty sure what she shared with Nash in New Orleans was a weekend fling, even if they talked about it being more. The notion of it not being more only lived in her head. She didn't know how she could still question what was happening between them. Since her return home, they spoke or texted every single day; mainly at night. She was anxious to get to the arrangements to see if there was a card.

"Perhaps so. Thank you for taking them in for me."

"They may be from your ex-husband. He sure drives through here a lot. If you ask me, I think he wants you to take him back."

"Davis? You see Davis around here?"

"Oh, yes. Not just when your children are home. Just the other day, when you returned home from your trip, I saw him pull up right in front of your house. It was pretty late. I couldn't sleep and decided to make a warm cup of milk. He sat in his car just watching your house. He was there for about ten minutes. Then he just pulled off fast down the street."

"You've seen him do that before?"

Delaney was intrigued but also a little freaked out. What was Davis doing? He told her he wanted to talk to her when she returned from New Orleans, but to know he had driven anywhere near her house, sat out front without calling her before doing so, was strange. She didn't like it. She made a

147

mental note to ask Davis what he was doing at her house late in the evening.

"Yes, a few times over the past few months."

Delaney nodded. She wasn't willing to show how uncomfortable she felt over the idea of him slithering by her house all the way from Miami where he lived.

"Well, I doubt if the flowers are from him. You better get inside with this heat. I'm heading inside get in the pool for a bit."

"You be careful out here, okay?" Ms. Sylvie suggested.

"I will and thank you."

Hurrying back across the street, Delaney lifted one of the arrangements and carried it around to the garage, placing it inside before grabbing what she left in the car to take with her. Getting the other one, she took it with her straight into the kitchen and placed it on the center of the long, marble white counter. Locating the card, she opened the small white envelope and read.

*"I saw something beautiful and thought of someone beautiful; you. New Orleans meant more to me than something casual. Give me a chance. Oh, how I wish you would give us an opportunity at something special,*

*Nash."*

Delaney couldn't take her eyes off of the card. Nash had sent her flowers; not just any flowers, but an arrangement in shades of yellow, orange, purple and red. She removed the paper and lifted the large pink vase from the box. She raced out to get the other one. Removing the paper, she smiled at the large arrangement of red roses, perhaps three dozen of them.

"Absolutely beautiful."

Breaking her focus, the phone on the wall next to the garage door rang and she reached for it.

"Mom!" Kennedy gleefully yelled.

"Hey!"

"I thought you were going to call me when you got home last night from the gym."

"I sent you a text. It was pretty late in the evening. I didn't want to call at that hour. How are you?"

"I'm good. The question is how are you? Did you have a good time? I know how obsessive you can be about working out. You know you already look amazing. Girls my age wished they had your curves."

"I don't think I'm obsessive, but I do enjoy working out every day. Besides, I needed that workout. I'm still trying to lose the weight I gained from all that good eating a week ago in New Orleans. Speaking of New Orleans, I talked to your godmother today and she said she was going to call you after we got off the phone."

"I just talked to her. She wants to come and visit me at school in a few weeks before the wedding. I talked her into joining you in a few weeks for family weekend. I can't wait to see her. She said the weekend with you was great."

"It really was. I'm back to reality and bone tired. I should have worked from home this week."

"I tell you that all the time. You own the company, mom. You don't have to go there every single day. The way of the world these days is to work from home. I can't wait to hear more about your whole weekend with her. When I asked her what kind of fun things you did together, she told me to ask you. What's that all about? You must have been having a lot of fun. Did you meet anyone new? A man?"

"Stop digging. I've told you and your brother that if I meet a man that I like, you would be the first to know about him. You don't have to ask me every time we talk. We can talk about my trip when you come home this weekend."

"Uh, that's why I'm calling, actually. Is it okay if we reschedule? Griffin is going into Pensacola to visit a friend who is leaving for the Navy in a few weeks. He asked me to go with him for the weekend. I know it's short notice. It's just for the weekend. I know we had plans, but I'm hoping we can do it another weekend."

"Kennedy Noel Monroe! I thought you were coming home this weekend, not off in a hotel with your boyfriend. You've only been back on campus for two weeks and you're already away for the weekend? What about your job?"

"Mom? Why are you yelling? I mentioned that I might come home this weekend, but something came up. Besides, I thought you were going to be working. You said you were expecting to hear back about a new contract. Something about some things you wanted to sort out with your team at some kind of working retreat or something on Saturday. I'm off duty this weekend. I share the responsibility with three other advisors, so I'm good. We've already worked out our plan to cover each other so that we all get time away."

Delaney knew she wasn't being fair. Kennedy's time was her own. She had been looking forward to a little mother/daughter time before Kennedy's school work really kicked in. Going away with Griffin to visit a friend was more than just a road trip.

"Are you being sexually responsible? I am not ready to be a grandmother and, well, you know better – at least I'm hoping you do."

"Mom!"

Delaney could hear her own chastising tone this time. She felt bad knowing this was not how they communicated.

"Wait, I'm sorry for that. I didn't mean for my words to come out like that. You're an adult and so is Griffin. I just want to be sure you're looking out for what you want with no slipups along the way. I didn't mean to yell," she admitted.

"It's okay. I know you didn't mean to scream. You've educated me well about birth control and condoms. I'm being responsible. Griffin and I both know better than to take any risks. I do want to be married before I have any children. You have been cautioning me and Kyrie about sex and responsibility ever since we hit puberty. I listened. I came to you last year when I had sex for the first time and we talked. Trust me all of our talks sink in; I hear you."

"I know and I do trust you. I was looking forward to seeing you. I thought we would pig out on pizza and get manicures and pedicures this weekend. I miss you is all."

"I know and I'm sorry."

"No, I'm sorry. I've had a stressful day. The gym was good, but didn't really do the job of relaxing me like I had hoped. Let's plan something fun while I'm there for family weekend. Are you driving or is Griffin driving?"

"We're taking his car. It's only two hours away from school. We're leaving around five this evening. I'll be back on Sunday."

"Okay, do you need any money? Don't forget to take your credit card with you for emergencies."

"I won't forget. No, I don't need any money. Dad put money in our accounts a few days ago. Do you forgive me for bailing out on you this weekend?"

151

"Of course, I do. I love you. I still expect my daily text letting me know you're okay. That's all I ask."

"I know. If you don't hear from me by text daily, you will know something is wrong. I got it. I'm going to plan some fun stuff when you come visit me. You now have the weekend to have some fun. I hope you don't work. Get out more, mom."

"I get out plenty. Have fun and be safe. I love you, Kennedy."

"I love you too, mom."

Delaney looked for her cell phone in her bag in order to call Nash and thank him for the flowers when the phone rang before she could call out. It was Nash. It was amazing the way they were always in sync with each other.

"Nash."

"Hi, Delaney. I was hoping you're weren't busy."

"I *was* busy. I was busy admiring two beautiful flower arrangements I received today. They are so pretty. I love, love flowers!" she exclaimed.

"I know. I remember."

"Right, because you remember everything."

"I remember our time in New Orleans. I remember everything about you. How was your day?"

"Busy. My firm acquired some new contracts. My teams are busy at work preparing for the transition to those new projects."

"Business is good. I love it. You are doing the damn thing!"

"I never could have imagined how business has been going since I decided to take that leap. I'm going to be busy working with my team to get new hires and new subcontracts. There's a lot going on. How is your business trip going?"

"Better than I expected. I was presented with the opportunity to invest in athletic equipment. The return on my investment will be major; bigger than expected. I'll be replacing all of the equipment in my gyms. The plan is to open forty more gyms over the next few years."

"Yes! That is amazing. I'm happy for you. I'm not the only one doing it big."

"I'm leaving a legacy for my kids as well as for other kids. I've accomplished a lot over this past week. I'll tell you about that later. Work aside, I called to see if you've given any more thought to going out to dinner with me."

"A date?" she asked.

"Yes, a date. I miss you. I was hoping the feeling was mutual. I want to see you."

"Are you back home in Miami?" she asked, hopeful.

"No, but I'm flying back tomorrow. I was hoping, to instead, fly into Tampa to see you; that is if you would like to see me as much as I want and need to see you."

Delaney exhaled with excitement. His voice lulled her into giving him anything he wanted. She wasn't sure she should even be this excited about the possibility of being in his arms again. With Kennedy not coming home for the weekend, perhaps she could make better use of her free time. Why was she fighting being with him so hard when all she wanted to do was touch, kiss and feel all of him.

"I'd like that."

"Great. I've been thinking about you while I was away. Talking to you every day is like talking to my best friend. We have fun talking about everything. You're still giving me push back on getting more involved. I want a relationship with you."

"Nash, it's not that I don't want to. There is a lot at stake."

"Not the age thing again. I want us to get past that. There is more to me than how old I am. I need to jet to get into this meeting. I'll see you tomorrow evening. I'll make some reservations for a nice quiet dinner and maybe some dancing. I love holding you in my arms," he whispered.

"I love how you sing in my ear when we're dancing."

"Then that's a date. Anything I can do to make you smile, I'm all for. I'll call you later tonight?"

"I look forward to it."

Delaney stood, sniffed her flowers again. She was already counting down the hours until Nash would be at her door. She couldn't wait.

## 14

Nash pulled his rented Range Rover into the space in front of Delaney's house. He grabbed what was on the seat next to him, a gift for her, right before making his way toward the house, taking in its beauty. It was as gorgeous as its owner. The excitement that flowed through is body didn't compare to the woman his eyes finally laid on the moment she opened the door before he had the chance to ring the bell.

Delaney anxiously opened the door and was greeted by another large bouquet of flowers. This time they were all white roses.

"Nice truck you drove up in. That's my daughter's dream truck," she said.

"It's a rental. Wait until she sees the one that I own, a Range Rover Holland in emerald green. It's my favorite of any car ever made."

"I don't think she'll ever stop begging her father and I for one."

They were standing in her doorway making small talk. She was nervous. She hoped it didn't show. This was the first time she was entertaining a man in her house. She usually dated away from here. This was Nash. He was already special to her. He was definitely worthy of being at her home.

"Shall I drop these flowers and kiss you right here on your front porch or would you like to invite me inside?"

She moved to the side and took the flowers from his hands. After a quick inhale to smell the beauty of the arrangement, she gazed up at Nash and knew what was next. She was more than ready.

His head lowered toward hers. His eyes were wide open. Like her, he didn't want to miss anything until their lips touched. An immediate electric spark snapped. She could almost hear it crackle in her head.

With flowers in her hands, she couldn't wrap her arms around him the way she wanted to. The idea didn't seem to matter to Nash and she couldn't let it matter to her either.

The kiss was shameless and impassioned. She felt him in every part of her body. His lips parted hers. His tongue reacquainted itself with hers. Delaney knew he was telling her, through the kiss, they too many days had gone by since he'd last kissed her that last day in New Orleans. She had been packed and ready to go. Nash walked her to her car. He kissed her like he was going off to war. In a sense, he was. They were going back to their lives.

"Do you have any idea how I have waited to kiss you like that? Thank you for letting me come here to see you. I wasn't sure you would."

Delaney reached and locked the front door, putting all of the flowers in one arm. Taking his hand in her other one she led him into the kitchen. She wanted to add this new bouquet of flowers to a vase.

"You've been on my mind too. I've been contemplating what next looks like. You asked me that in New Orleans and I didn't have an answer."

Nash took a seat at the island with his long legs curved out, unable to comfortably fit them under the counter.

"You look beautiful. Let me start with that."

"Thank you and thank you for these beautiful flowers; all of them. They have already brightened up my kitchen."

"I have something else for you."

Delaney tilted her head, looking at him questionably. It was then that she realized he'd been holding one hand behind his back. When he showed her the small red gift bag, she wondered how she had missed that when he first arrived. She was so focused on the flowers and on seeing his handsome face again that she didn't think about anything else.

Taking the bag from him, she looked inside. She chortled when she saw what was inside. How could he have known that little things like this meant the world to her? How did he know these were her favorites?

"How did you know I love Hawaiian pineapple gummies?"

Not many people outside of her family knew how much she loved them.

Nash leaned close to her lips. Kissed her quickly and then leaned back.

"I pay attention. Monica had a big bowl of them at the meet and greet dinner. You kept visiting that bowl. You also snuck a few from your purse when we were out together on that Sunday."

"Well, thank you for them and thank you for being that observant."

"Sweetheart, I pay attention to what matters to me. Now, for the answer to my question about what's next for us. What are you thinking? Did I pass the test? Am I any of the things on your check list for a man you would consider being in your life? I know it sounds crazy, but I really missed you. Before you tell me that what we shared was only a weekend, it was an amazing weekend to me. I came here because I want to know if there is any chance for us to have more than just that weekend."

"Yes."

Delaney surprised herself with how fast the words came out of her mouth.

"Come with me. I saw a room with a sofa when we came into the kitchen."

"It's the room I call my 'Queen's Quarters'. It's my comfy space that the kids aren't allowed to lounge in. They have a separate family room," she explained, putting her hand in his and following him.

"Can I enter?" he kidded.

"Absolutely."

Nash sat and she took the seat next to him, turning slightly in his direction.

"So, you said yes. Just like that? I thought I was going to have some serious work to do convincing you. I had this whole speech rehearsed about not letting anything keep us from each other if that's what we want."

Delaney let out the breath she'd been holding in.

"I've tossed back and forth between what was going on between us. I admit that I was flattered by your attention."

"You aren't used to attention from men? If you tell me no, I have to say I don't believe you," Nash quipped.

"No, I'm not saying that. I get my share, trust me. I don't know. I haven't had that someone who checks all my boxes."

"Me? I'm dying to know just how many of your boxes I have checked off. I brother's inquiring mind wants to know."

"You have checked all of them. That scares me. It's unexpected. I can be myself with you. You came along and I can't get you off of my mind. That whole weekend, you catered to me. It was special."

Nash reached for her, moving her to straddle his lap. Just looking into his eyes and the way his searched her with so much longing definitely gave a rise to what she was feeling for him. With his arms circling her waist and pulling her snug into his lap, she wrapped her arms around his neck and kissed him.

"That's because from day one, you were special. It was more than anyone would be able to comprehend if I attempted to tell them. You are a woman who captured my heart within seconds of meeting her."

"I think I can do this, but there is some concern about what some will think."

There; she said it again without actually saying it.

"Don't, Delaney."

"Nash, you aren't concerned about what people will think? I'm a mother of two grown children. You're..."

"What? I'm what? I'm a man who is holding the woman in his arms that he can't stop thinking about and wanting. That's who I am. That's all of who I am. That's the most important part of me. There is no rush to what's growing between us. Just don't turn away from it without seeing what this can be. I'm leaping here just like you are. I never want to stop leaping with you."

"I want that too," she uttered against his lips.

"I want to give you what you want."

"What about what I need?"

Delaney could hear the desperation in her own voice. It was a new, yet welcomed changed to her being reserved.

"You know how to do that so well."

"You remember that?"

"I remember everything about that weekend. In the pool."

Nash nipping at her neck with his teeth paused her words. She was finding it hard to concentrate on speaking when he was now licking that same area with the heated pad of his tongue.

"And?" he questioned.

Focus Delaney, she said in her head.

"Later that night in your big ass bed."

"Mmm, that reminds me how much I love you being on top of me. Then?"

"You behind me on the stairs."

"Let's not forget Monday morning," Nash reminded her.

Nash's tongue circling her nipple ring had her squirming. She looked down to where Nash was loving her chest. He somehow not only unbuttoned her shirt all the way, but he had also unsnapped her bra and she hadn't even realized it.

"Yes, Monday morning after you whisked me away in the middle of the night. You took me back to your house."

"Yes, sweetness, I did. That's where I discovered you have some strong knees."

"And I was finally able to find out just how good you tasted."

"I'm still working on how to thank you for that. Your mouth, your lips and of course that tongue of yours left me speechless. You left me drained."

"And you had a lot for me to enjoy."

"You're telling me that you were willing to second guess the good times we can have together? I'm talking in and out of the bed. Me and you? This isn't just about sex."

"I know it's not. When you touch me, it's beyond that."

Delaney was admitting all that she'd been holding back.

"And this?" he asked, placing a kiss in the space between her breasts, removing her top completely from her body.

"Yes," she moaned.

"How about this?"

The moment her bare breasts hit the cool air in the room, now moist from his mouth, the shiver that shot through her drenched her sex. His tongue loved one side before moving to the other. Delaney held his head in her hands, with her head dropping back to enjoy the feeling. The kisses he placed on her body were achingly tender, causing her toes to curl where they rested on each side of his powerful thighs. Between her legs she felt him harden. Her hips moved in a circular motion loving the grinding his hips were doing across her womanhood. She wanted to be naked.

"Am I going to always want you this much?"

"That's what I want; always and forever – when you're ready. I'm already there. Am I spending the night?"

Delaney giggled.

"A part of you I hope will be. That means all of you should stay."

"Are you sure?"

"Nash, I'm sure. Just as sure as I am about us. Let's go slow with the public part. I saw some Reels on Instagram of you being hounded. Can you imagine what that would be like for us being out and about?"

"Your wish, as usual, is my command. I would never subject you to anything you're not ready for. As long as you promise me it's not because on some level, you're not ready to be seen with me; to be scrutinized. It will happen."

"I promise you that you are nothing to be ashamed of when it comes to people knowing about us. This is all new for me. I just need a little time, okay?"

"Baby, I'm more than okay with it. You are pretty much naked on my lap except for these yoga pants. I want you completely naked. I would say later since we have all night. I hope you don't have a lot of plans for tomorrow because I do believe you're going to be tired."

"Sounds like I'm going to enjoy it all the way. We still need to eat."

"My plan was for us to go out, but since we're not, I'm sure there are a lot of places that deliver. What are you in the mood for?"

Delaney kissed his lips again to remind him what she was in the mood for most of all.

"A lot more of that."

"Oh, you know I got that," he quipped.

"Then for food, how about Italian?"

"I'll order it as soon as I finish."

*"Finish?"*

Before she got her answer, Delaney felt her body being easily lifted in the air until she was flat on her back on the sofa. Dinner, it seems would have to wait.

## 15

Delaney inhaled deeply when Nash lifted her hips. She let him do the work of sliding her pants down her legs and off of her body. The way his eyes took in her naked body, she'd never felt more beautiful."

"And no, my eyes never lie. I love everything I see," Nash said.

"How did you know what I was thinking?"

"Still, you doubt me? This thing with us is all real. Because it is, I love learning your looks. I enjoy discovering all the places on your body that make you moan the loudest. Most of all, I love seeing the glitter in your eyes. They tell me that you're happy."

"I am. I also see that slow, cocky smile you have. That means you're on a mission."

"Baby, I was on that mission before I even got here. It's definitely a sign that I'm about to finish what I've started."

Quickly removing his own shirt, Nash moved between her legs. Delaney knew his intention. She spread her legs until they formed the perfect "V" for easy access. She was also thankful for the warm, softness of the red leather sofa.

The atmosphere steamed around them.

"You know that you're the mystery man in my dreams, right? I told you about that."

"I do. Everything that you have ever imagined him doing to you and you doing to him doesn't have to live in the dream world. Can I have one of your hands?"

The huskiness in his voice led Delaney to give him anything he wanted. The muscles in his arms bulged. The long, thick muscle behind his zipper strained in her direction. Licking her lips seemed a natural movement.

"All night?" she pleaded.

"Your tongue?"

Nash looked between her eyes and that part of him that was painfully pushing against his zipper to get to her.

"Yes," she whispered.

"That too and yes, all night. My attention and focus are on you and what you need at this very moment."

"What about what you need?" she slurred out.

"What I need is all about what you need; trust that."

When Nash licked his lips, Delaney watched him prepare to finish what he started. He was attentive; she knew that. He could read her body and it seemed her mind. When his face dropped low, he began with a quick lick and kiss of her toes, his eyes staying on hers. She sizzled as his lips made their way up her inner leg to her inner thigh, going from one side to the other, so painstakingly slow and provocative.

With her hand still in his, she held her breath as Nash moved her had down to caress her own thighs; first one and then the other. When he moved their hands together to the spot between her legs, she knew what he wanted her to do. She'd never done that in the presence of a man before. The feeling of what she was about to experience was electrifying; it was invigorating. The idea of it had her ready to explode.

"Feel," he muttered against her leg; his eyes saying exactly what his words were saying. He removed his hand, leaving only hers between her own legs.

"Damn!" she moaned.

"I want to watch you."

"Nash..."

"I know, baby. This is me. I never want you to do anything you don't want. I can see in your eyes that you want to. Am I right?" he asked, kissing her thigh.

"Yes," she almost screamed out. She'd never wanted anything more than to be this woman that even Nash saw. What he saw; who he saw, is the Delaney she wants to be.

"You know your body. You know what it likes; what it loves."

"I've never..."

"I know. After tonight, you'll never say that again."

Delaney nodded and moved her fingers a little. Her hips bucked instantly at how sensitive she was down there; especially with Nash's eyes on her finger. She didn't know the feeling could be this powerful. She wasn't new to finding her own pleasure. She usually did it when she was alone. This was so much better.

Nash's eyes widen as they watched the movement of her finger. He winked at her when she added in the uncontrollable need to move her hips in tandem with her personal strokes.

She easily found her pleasure point and pressed into it. It was that part of her womanhood that made her brain scream for more. She moved her middle finger up and down and then around and around. The image of her doing this and Nash watching was fascinating. It was enthralling. She was already so close. She needed to go faster. Nash nipped at her thigh again, this time with his teeth adding a level of sexual lure she didn't know existed.

She could hear her loud moans bouncing off of the walls. Nash was encouraging her to let go. Even though her eyes were barely open, she could see Nash unzipping his pants, pulling himself out and stroking himself to the visual of her pleasuring herself. The moment was euphoric.

The electric spark in the moment matched with the admiration in his eyes and the sexy curve of his lips had her hips rising from the leather with slow, methodical thrusts. She was close. Nash's gaze never left hers. Watching him watch her was more than X-rated.

"Nash," she groaned again and again.

"I'm here with you baby. You look amazing in the throes of passion. I wish you could see how wet you are."

She could feel it. Because she could figure out why he was moving away, she knew. He'd removed his shirt. In one of her motions up from the seat, he slid the shirt under her hips protecting the surface from the explosion she felt coming and he'd anticipated. He then lifted her legs, placing them over his shoulders with her not missing a stroke against the solid pointed nub that screamed for release.

Nash knew she was ready. He wanted to share in the heady experience. Keeping her finger in place excited him. He leaned in and licked, then sucked on her feminine mound slick with her essence. His lips were as wet as her fingers. He knew the moment her body released the sexiest, power-filled orgasm when Delaney attempted to cover her mouth with her free hand. He reached for it quickly wanting to instead, hear her scream. There was no need for a silent release.

"No, baby. Don't hold it in. Scream as loud as you want. It's so freaking sexy watching you like this."

Delaney couldn't hold out any longer. She bucked wildly. Raw need took over her.

When Delaney screamed, her delight sung a sweet song to his ears. Before her body calmed, he removed her fingers and replaced them with his mouth. He feasted as Delaney's high captivated her while kicking his need for her into gear.

Her body jerked and lurched up to meet his mouth. She continued to flail about, basking in the glow of ecstasy. Her face was a plateau of love and satisfaction. Never had a woman looked more beautiful than her. It was at this moment that he knew their powerful joining could never be dismissed as casual.

Nash quickly removed his slacks and boxers and grabbed a condom from the pocket. With the speed of a madman he didn't know he could muster up, he donned protection, slid between her legs and entered her with a fierce surge forward, rocking their worlds together.

"Oh my god, yes, yes, yes!" Delaney yelped.

She splayed her legs open as wide as she could, grabbed tight to his shoulders. When Nash kissed her, for the second time, and only with him, she was able to taste her own juices from her own body on his lips. That along with his powerful strokes had her racing toward a second out of this world release.

She leaned forward and laved her tongue across the expanse of his chest, nipping from one side to the other. She kissed her way to his neck. The louder he groaned, the more furious her kisses became. Her lips found his and they loved and mated as if this were going to be their last time. She knew it wasn't. There was no way she wanted to think about not having him like this.

Just when she thought he was close, Nash changed her position, turning her to her side with one of his knees on the chair, his other foot on the floor, raising one of her legs high in the air. He entered her again and continued his wonderfully acrobatic strokes.

With her leg in the air, Nash slipped her toe in his mouth. Her body went straight for her next release, shattering her body once again. This time, they exploded together; breathing regularly was an impossible task.

Nash growled through his climax. He tried but was unable to stifle the loud roar that escaped his mouth. He was experiencing his own personal Shangri-la, his heaven on earth. The solid foundation of the world fell away and he flew, his body bucked and his head exploded with vibrating pulses.

Delaney's body began to calm even though Nash was still pumping hard into her. She encouraged him on, making sure his enjoyment matched, if not surpassed hers. Each time they were together like this, he was an attentive lover. She reaped the full benefit of that. She enjoyed seeing him in this moment of pure pleasure. She loved this for him.

As his body covered hers and she felt his lips cascading all over any exposed skin Nash could find, she held him close. Then reality hit her.

She was falling hard and fast for him. Even if she thought she could protect her heart, should wouldn't be able to. Nash has found his way to it. She embraced him being there just as she held him when he leaned into her while he worked to control his breathing. This moment with him was perfection.

**

Delaney stretched and felt the sun hit the side of her face that wasn't blocked by Nash's body. He held her close in his arms, pulling her closer.

"Good morning – or is it afternoon?" he asked.

"I think it's close to the afternoon, at this point. I don't think we found sleep until about three or four in the morning."

Nash chuckled to himself.

"You mean right before the last time you rolled over and hopped on top of me. Tell me that you've ridden horses at some point in your life. I need to know how you expertly mastered riding me like that. I felt the whole bed rocking!" he goaded.

"Funny!" she replied jokingly with a playful swat against his arm.

"I discovered that being on top is my new favorite position. You have a lot of them – all pleasurable. I wanted to let you lay back and enjoy the ride."

"I definitely did that. What are we going to do today?"

"I didn't know if you were planning to head home or not."

"Are you throwing me out?" he asked.

"No way. I know you have a lot to do."

"If you don't mind me handling a few business calls while I'm here, I want to wake up another morning with you just like this. I don't need to get to the kids until it's time to get them to school on Monday morning. I'm going to call my team and have someone drive here to pick me up Sunday evening if that works for you."

"Seriously? I love the idea of that. You will be here the whole weekend."

"Me too. Why don't you get some extra rest while I make us something good for breakfast. Do you have the makings for omelets? Or I can run out to the store."

Delaney leaned back and looked him up and down.

"You cook?"

"I'm a great cook. Omelets are my specialty along with southern grits. I'm from New Orleans. I can cook with the best of them thanks to a grandmother who made sure I would be able to feed myself. What will I find in your kitchen?"

After kissing her lips, Nash rose from the bed. She never missed a chance to see his glorious body. He was walking perfection; toned and buffed in all the right places.

"Eggs, cheese, breakfast meat and yes, I have grits in the pantry. There is also some fruit. I should have English muffins and bagels with chive and onion cream cheese, my favorite."

"I can work magic with all of that. And yes, I love English muffins and bagels. You relax. If I'm going to be here, I'm going to earn my stay."

"Baby, you have been doing that since you walked in the door last night. Oh, don't let me forget the second helping of you after we ate dinner. This is the second-best weekend ever!" she proclaimed. "You already know what weekend won first prize. I can't believe you're going to cook for me."

I'm multi-talented. Haven't you learned that yet?" he quipped.

"I've learned a lot. I like all of it; all of you."

Nash leaned over her on the bed.

"The feeling is definitely mutual. Promise you won't run away if that like turns into something more serious."

"I promise."

"Good. I'll be back shortly with something good to eat."

Delaney smiled and looked down his body.

"Can I have an after-breakfast treat; my very own dessert?" she purred and reached for the area between his legs that seem to understand the assignment. She saw him hardening right before her eyes.

"Dessert after breakfast is all you, baby! I got you."

"I think I'm turning into a sexual maniac; a sex addict; a sex fiend. I'm a villain for you!" she joked.

"Isn't that what you want? Haven't you craved being uninhibited when it comes to intimacy? We are perfect together in that way, in case you haven't noticed. You told me that you owed that to yourself. There is nothing wrong with that with the right person."

Delaney moved to sit half-way up on her elbow.

"It is. I've been calling it the sweetest revenge on the old me. This is my time to be and do what I want for me."

"Know this, if there is ever anything I can do for you and with you, don't be shy to spell it out for me. I love discovering what you love in and out of bed. Nothing is sexier to me than a woman who says what she wants or needs. Do you know what else I'm great at?" Nash asked.

Delaney clapped her hands like an excited child.

"Tell me!" she cheered.

"Massages. I know how to knock any stress or tension right out of the sexy body of yours. I'm talking, you and me naked, because that's the kind of massaging I do. Add in some soft, romantic music, some fresh fruit, good wine and most of all, these hands. I want to make a day of nothing but fun relaxed times together after a few work calls. I want to call and check on my kids. I'll do that while I'm cooking. And then, I'm all yours. Sound good?"

"Yes, sounds amazing. I'm ready for all of that."

"Cool. Let me get this day started with a quick shower. I would ask you to join me, but then we'd never get to breakfast. We have both worked up major appetites for food. I promise, we will shower together sometime today."

"Mmm, I love the sound of that."

When he entered the bathroom and closed the door, she twirled in bed, moving to the side where his cologne still lingered. This was heaven.

**

A strange truck. It was still there. He'd driven by early Saturday morning and it was there. Now, very early Sunday morning, the same truck was still in the same spot.

Davis sat in his car two houses away from Delaney's house. He could see the large red brick single-family home from where he sat. He missed living in it with her and his children. He'd made a lot of mistakes. Marrying Delaney wasn't one. He was hoping that with the passage of time, they could see that neither of them was perfect. He wanted nothing more than another chance to live out their lives together as they had planned when they got married years ago. What he didn't expect was the possibility that there was already someone in her life.

As he checked out the expensive Range Rover, he wondered who it belonged to. He'd never seen it parked in front of Delaney's house before. Perhaps it belonged to a neighbor who decided to park in front of her house. As much as he would like to believe that was the case, there was a chill that ran up his back that said the car belonged to a man; a man who had been with her the entire weekend.

"I guess spending the weekend at a hotel in hopes to catch her at home to talk or perhaps have dinner was a waste. He thought that he would catch her this morning about to head out to the gym. He figured she still loved doing that on Sunday mornings. It seems he was wrong. It appears that Delaney like doing other things or perhaps other men on Sunday mornings instead.

Pulling out of his parking spot, he sped by the house, deciding to not even look in that direction as he drove. The idea of her with a man at her house for the weekend hit him like a ton of bricks. Davis hated that this was his new reality.

As he drove, he thought about it again. Perhaps it didn't have to be. He convinced her once that he could be who she needed. Maybe he could again.

Davis found his way into traffic, heading back to Miami. He'd overstayed his visit in Tampa. He would try again another time when images of Delaney with another man didn't plague his mind.

# 16

As the main conference room emptied out at the offices of *Bronmon Consulting*, Delaney rose to head back to her office, but decided against it. She removed the black jacket that covered the black and white striped dress before forcefully flopping back against her seat at the head of the table. A few minutes ago, all eighteen seats had been filled with her team for their end of the week round-up meeting. This was their time to discuss major accomplishments as well as areas that needed to be improved before they headed into the next week.

Some team members would be working on Saturday, the next day, in order to begin the task of laying out the plan in the statement of work for the major military health services, information technology contract they had just won the bid for. The millions of dollars coming into the firm would require hiring and training more staff. To start that process, she knew it meant all hands-on deck for everyone, including her.

For the past week, work had taken up every hour of her day and night, not leaving time for much else. When they were notified that they had won the contract to overhaul the health services system, she had been ecstatic knowing all of the hard work she'd been doing for years had finally paid off. The reality was, she also knew the exhaustion that came along with sitting in the seat as the owner of her own firm.

The day before, she'd sent out an email to everyone to encourage them by reminding them that they were important to the team. She wanted them to know that she saw all of their sacrifices and appreciated each and every one of them.

Delaney exhaled loudly. She checked the time because the back-to-back meetings for a Friday were just beginning. Next up was her meeting with her senior executive staff, a closed-door meeting that didn't include everyone else. They were about to discuss the promotion of several team members, including her own assistant, Tara Bennett.

Tara had been with her from the first day that her firm started business. She had worked her way up from an office assistant to becoming her executive assistant. Tara was ready for much more after receiving her college degree while working at the same time. Her greatest days were always those where she could reward great, hard workers. Tapping her pen on the top of the glass table, she looked up when Tara cleared her throat. They locked eyes, and like always, no words needed to be spoken. Tara ushered out the last of the staff and closed the office door behind them.

"You can't continue with this kind of schedule, Delaney. You're going to kill yourself. You've slept here at the office for two nights straight, working through the night and the day. I know what this company means to you but it won't be any good if you're not here to love and appreciate all of your work. You're drained. I'm going to reschedule your board meeting with the leadership team."

"I don't know if that's possible. There is a lot to deal with now that we have this new contract. It's our fourth this year alone. There's so much to do and little time to do it all in."

"You have the best in leadership of any company, that's for sure. You pay them to lead and you should let them."

"I can't always ask others to work double and triple hard without seeing me jump in with both feet, too."

"Your feet carry some pretty big shoes. Tell me what you need? How can I help you more? I know it's only been a month since you've been back from vacation, but you know my story; that one week wasn't enough. You have worked hard to get here. Enjoy the fruits of your labor more. You're always encouraging me to take time off; a week here, two weeks there, yet you take a day or even a week and you still tap into work. I wish you would disconnect completely sometimes."

Delaney laughed out loud.

"Is that why you acted like there was a phone-line issue when I called you from New Orleans? I know that we have the best in telecommunications. There was nothing wrong with the office phones."

"True. And look what happened when I did my job of looking after you. The team still went just as hard without you being here. I promise, we got you. Now, this board meeting that you still have to have – how about I move a few other things around that are not as critical to you being there? I can then schedule the board meeting at the end of the day. Tonight, go home. Surely, the man who has sent you flowers three times this week would like your attention. Are you ever going to tell me who this mystery man is?"

An image of Nash sitting on the foot of her bed, naked, hard and ready for her flashed across her mind. She trembled with a delicious infusion of energy just remembering how he slid her onto his lap and loved her like no other had ever done, right there in that position. Smiling, she shifted in her chair. She missed seeing him. Nash understood the schedule she'd been on since returning from New Orleans. Still, he made sure she didn't forget about him or what they shared. They talked each day, even when he was out of town on business. They were two very busy people. This week proved just how busy. Tara making reference to the flowers he'd sent her that covered almost every surface in her office reminded her of just how close they had become in a few weeks.

"You're thinking about him now, aren't you?" Tara asked, stealing into her thoughts.

Delaney nodded.

"Yes, I am."

"It makes me happy to see you happy like this. It's been a minute."

"I know. With the kids off to school, my focus always shifts to business when they're gone."

"But now, there is new business to shift to. Why aren't you spending your nights with him instead of here in the office?"

"It's sort of complicated. I don't have an answer."

"I can tell he misses you, not because I read the notes on the flowers or listen in on your calls when he calls you. I can always tell when it's him on the line because your whole body relaxes. If I'm not mistaken, you beam with, shall I say it, love!"

*Love.* Delaney hadn't thought about what she and Nash were heading towards. She could call it love, but the idea of it frightened her. Her feelings for him were unexpected. There was also no way to avoid it. Nash was too close to the perfect man, the perfect lover, the perfect friend. How could she not fall in love with him. Whatever it was, she didn't know if the time was right to share it with anyone. It was all so new.

"I don't know if it's all that, but he's definitely someone very special."

She started to say more, but stopped. She smiled at Tara who sat in the chair closest to her and placed her head in both of her hands to show that she was paying close attention.

"Continue. I'm still trying to find my mister right or even one for right now, but I think you have found yours."

Tara took out her phone and paused her for a moment.

"Leslie, can you please cancel the leadership meeting that Delaney has coming up in fifteen minutes? I'll let you know when it will be rescheduled."

Tara didn't wait for an answer from one of the two scheduling assistants she worked with as a team.

"You love running my life!" Delaney cheered.

"You're sharing and that's much more important. Besides, I know when you need a moment. That whole taking off the suit jacket, on dress-down day, mind you, and the flopping back in the chair was my key. I know how to read a room," she joked. "Continue."

"Okay, he is the most incredible man I've ever met. I want to spend all of my time with him, but he's busy with business like I am; even more so. I wanted this business and I love everything about it. I never thought about how to balance this with the kind of non-work fun I have with him. There are a lot of people at this firm who count on our success. I have to be all here when I'm here, especially with all of the new work coming our way. Our procurement team are masterful at what they do."

"That doesn't mean you can't work a good man into that schedule. If he's as busy as you are, there shouldn't be a reason that the two of you can't make something work besides your business acumen. We all love what you're doing here. I know I'm happy to be along for the ride. I see you working to the bare knuckles. It's all good until it's not, like right now. You're overworked. You put a lot of time into getting this contract, along with everyone else. I'm not slighting anyone, but your name does go a long way because of the level of excellence you inspire and encourage in all of us. You've built it, so let it run. Please tell me you're going home tonight. Do not spend the night here. I'm going to put some nails in your comfy couch in your office. I knew it was a mistake when you first ordered that oversized sofa. I didn't think you would be spending nights on it even though it's as big as a bed."

"Trust me, neither did I. I promise to not spend the night tonight, but I will be here late. I hope everyone is taking advantage of the celebratory, no working late tonight notification I asked you to send out. I expect our offices to be empty by five this evening. For those who usually work later to handle any needs of our customers, they can take care of those things from mobile locations on their devices. Still, nothing late into the evening."

"Oh, they are all well aware. They're also grateful for the bonuses you gave out, both the bonuses on our checks for today and for the restaurant gift cards. Can I get you to get out of here and have some fun?"

Before Delaney could explain that she would try and probably fail in her attempt to live up to that request, her cell phone pinged. Grabbing it and hoping beyond hope that it was Nash, she beamed when his face appeared on the screen."

"Um..."

"I already know. I can see it on your face that it's your mystery man. I'll leave you to it. Know that you will be free for at least the next two hours. I'll email you your new meeting schedule for today."

With that, before Delaney could respond, Tara, with lightning speed, left the conference room, leaving her to focus all of her attention on Nash.

"Well, hello," she said, accepting his request to face time.

"Hello to you. I was thinking about you. I hope I'm not interrupting anything. I know what this week is like for you with your latest contract acquisition. Have I mentioned how happy for you I am and how proud of you I am? If not, I really am. Congratulations, baby!" Nash cheered.

"Thank you. I appreciate you staying up all night on the phone with me last week when I couldn't sleep as I waited to hear about the contract. This is my first military contract and it's a big one."

"That's because you're the best at what you do. I already know that you're brilliant along with being sexy as hell. You got a brother going through withdrawals not being able to hold you in my arms. When can we remedy that? I want to see you. I know your business comes first, but can you squeeze me in anywhere? I've got something for you," he slurred and winked at her.

"I know you do," she happily acknowledged.

"Yes, there is always that, but I also have something else for you, whenever you can make the time. As always, no pressure. You know how much I enjoy the boss lady, business woman you are, so I respect that boundary of letting you be all that you want to be. I will always support you in that arena.

You know I can meet you anytime, anywhere. I have that kind of flexibility."

"I'm sure you love having that now that you're retired from playing ball. You have to love that your schedule, when it comes to all of your business ventures, is your whenever and wherever."

"I do. I'm glad I had the best business managers and financial partners who showed me how to work on retiring early. I loved playing ball, but I never wanted to play until my knees barely stood the test of time. If so, I wouldn't be able to love all on you the way you enjoy."

"Oh, yes. Those knees are definitely made for lovemaking. Where are you now?"

"In the air flying back to Florida. I had a meeting in Chicago. The basketball camp for youth that I opened in New Orleans is so successful that the two new locations I told you about, in Chicago and in Memphis, are both under contract for the construction to begin. I locked in both warehouses which will be torn down and turned into camps for both girls and boys who are interested in playing ball. You know how I feel about futures for young people. I toured the Chicago location on the southside and it's going to be perfect. It's in the heart of a community that really need a place for the kids to go to keep them off the street. The only requirement for the kids will be that they take Saturday classes to improve their math, science and biology skills. With that, they get to attend the basketball academy for free."

Delaney gave Nash a thumbs-up on the phone screen.

"You are such an amazing man. You have a big heart of gold, especially for children. Your own kids are very lucky to be able to call you daddy."

"Thank you. I will forever give back and pull up as many children as I can. They deserve an honest opportunity to succeed. I want to do that before the streets get a hold of them."

"You're doing amazing work, Nash."

"So are you, Delaney. With all of this work, there has to be some fun in our lives too. About that thing I have for you, if you're free for a few days. It's the weekend. I know you like to work through it. I'm hoping I can convince you to take a break from work for a few days."

"You have a few days to spare? I thought you had a big meeting with the production studio about the movie shorts you want to do? Wasn't California your next destination?" she asked.

As much as Nash wanted to see her, she wanted to see him even more. What she never wanted to do was impede on his busy schedule either with work or with his children. She knew that both were his priority. He had a lot of plans now that he's retired from ball. She wanted to support him in whatever way he needed. Her company was already lining up to support one of his non-profit companies whose focus is on empowering school-aged girls by connecting them with powerful women in the business and media industry.

"It was until I realized how much I missed you and my kids. I talked to my daughter this morning. She told me she missed my hugs. That's all I needed to hear. I'm on my way to see them. It's actually great timing because Zonnique wants to take a quick trip. She knows I like either me or her to always be present for the kids. I was thinking about picking them up for the weekend and taking them with me to Los Angeles.

Then I realized, I would prefer to stay at home with them and hopefully with you."

"Me?"

"You haven't met them yet. I was hoping you wanted to. Zonnique, of course, knows about you, but I haven't told the kids anything about us. Mainly because I haven't been sure about how to introduce you. I don't introduce them to women I see. You already know that you're more than just someone I'm seeing. I don't want to push you into anything you're not ready for."

"I'm ready to meet them. I'm sorry for acting like we have to hide from the world. I hope you know it has nothing to do with you. I have never met a more amazing man."

"I know we've had several discussions about us. Is that still an issue for you, especially if we take our relationship beyond the bedroom?"

Delaney covered her mouth as her eyes widened. She has been doing that. She was so busy enjoying him and the way he made her feel that she never considered the hidden nature of their being together.

"I have been doing that haven't I? Nash, I'm so sorry. It seems that for the past month or so, when we see each other, we're tearing our clothes off. We are more than that and I know it. You coming into my life showed me how to live again. The fun we have, the talks we have, how we support each other and never miss a beat on connecting with each other. You give me space and still hold me near when I need and want it. You're more than just a secret lover. I hope you know that. What did Zonnique say when you told her about me?"

"She said it's about damn time!" he joked.

"What does that mean?"

"Zonnique knows me better than anyone. She always says that she can't wait for me to meet the woman who would eventually be able to claim me. That hasn't been an easy task for any woman. With you, it's as easy as boiling an egg. The minute I met you, I told you that there was something special. I'm not planning on losing you or that feeling, ever. I'm patiently waiting on you to feel as comfortable with what we have as I am. I told her that I wanted the kids to meet you and she is all for it. Not to hit you with too much, but I also have some friends who are from New York and currently visiting family in Miami. I want to have them over for dinner. I'd like you to join me. What do you say? Are you free this weekend?"

Delaney tapped her teeth nervously. Tara's words rang true. She needed to live a little more. She works hard. Her business is flourishing like she prayed for. Now, there was a man who looks at her as if she was the most precious thing in the world to him. It all felt real. Here she was being hesitant. Not anymore.

"Yes, I would love to."

"Seriously? Wow. I was actually expecting an uphill battle to get you out of the office for a few days."

"I'm at work and will be here a little late, especially if I'm going to be in Miami while my team works tomorrow. I have some things I need to do. I would say I can drive to Miami tonight, but that may be pushing it. I can make it tomorrow morning," she suggested.

"No way. I don't want you driving four hours after I know you've been working around the clock all week. I would be nervous thinking about you on the road, even in daylight. I'm going to reroute and in Tampa in a few hours. Why don't I meet you at your house. I'll rent a car and drive us to Miami tonight. You can even sleep in the car."

"Won't you be tired? You've had a busy week."

"I will never, ever be too tired to see you or to get us where we need to be safely. I'll see you in a few hours?" he asked.

"Yes. I'll meet you at my house, say eight? Is that too late?"

"Never. I'll see you then, baby. Pack light."

"Light?" she asked.

"Yes. You know – that sexy lingerie and panties you wear that I love. Of course, don't forget bathing suits. Wait until you see the infinity pool. It's even more magical than the one in New Orleans where you rocked my world!" Nash joked.

"Oh, that was a mutual rocking, believe that. I guess you have something for me, this weekend, and I will have something hot and sexy for you. I better get back to work so that I can get out of here by seven. Thanks for realizing I needed a break."

"I hear it in your voice. I can see it all over you. Anytime you need a break, all you have to do is whisper and your mystery man will always be there to swoop you up to make the craziness in the world disappear for you. I'll see you this evening."

Ending the call, Delaney rose with a new level of energy. She grabbed her jacket and the stack of papers and electronics in front of her and headed for her office. There was a lot to wrap up, but she had a new reason to get it all done. The man that she deserved was only an arm's length away. She was ready to grab life and let it take her where she was always meant to be. Happy, and to herself, she said, *"in love"*. She smiled and decided to let those words linger in the air. She loved the sound it made to her senses.

## 17

"Amelia! Amelia!" Zonnique hollered from her bedroom. She hated that she had to scream for the kids' nanny a million times when no one was in the house but the two of them. The kids were in school. Most of what Amelia had to do should have been done already. The time was near for the kids to get out of school. Her original plan was to pick them up herself, but after her call with Nash while he was on his way to the airport to head back to Florida, she didn't feel like moving. "Amelia!" she yelled again.

"Yes?"

Zonnique turned her head away from the television to find Amelia standing in the doorway with a basket full of laundry in her arms.

"Is this house really that big that you didn't hear me the first time?"

"I heard you. I was getting the kids' clothes from the dryer to put them away. Shouldn't you be up to pick them up? They're getting out soon. Mr. Nash is still out of town."

"I know where he is. He's probably on his way to see that woman he met. Have you met her yet? Have you seen her at his house?"

"No. I haven't seen a woman at the house. He asked me to work next week. He said something about you going out of town. I wasn't aware you were going someplace," Amelia said.

Zonnique sat straight up in bed. She was about to curse Amelia out if she uttered even a single word about her not really having any plans.

"What did you say to him? Did you tell him you didn't know about any plan for me to take a trip? You don't know everything I do. You know that. Your only job is to look after the kids; not worry about if I have plans or not. I could have plans."

"Yes, I know. I didn't say anything. He said he would need the babysitter who swims because the kids love the pool. He also said he had some friends from out of town who may be visiting. I told him I would make myself free to help him next week. That's all I said."

"What about this woman? There is something different about this woman. She's not like all the other women he hops in and out of bed with all the time. None of them mean anything to him. This new woman is different. He actually wants her to meet the kids. He's never done that before."

"I'm happy for him. He needs to have a good woman in his life."

Zonnique took offense to that. She exhaled and then smiled at Amelia. She didn't want to show her anger. The thought of Nash actually being seriously involved with a woman didn't sit well with her. She needed to find out more about this woman.

"What am I? Chopped, unwanted flesh?"

"No, but you are engaged to someone else. You have Mr. Chopper."

"So?"

"I just haven't seen him around. Mr. Nash said he thought you were going away with Mr. Chopper."

"That's not for you to worry about. I've been looking up this woman he told me about. She's some big-time business owner. She's pretty. She's older than him. She doesn't look like it though. I wonder what it is about her? Men would kill to have me. I'm gorgeous. I may not have the degrees and have a business like her, but I still have a lot to offer. All of a sudden, he's found some remarkable woman."

"Are you getting up?"

Amelia asked her about getting up again and this time, she did let out her frustration. It was more about her call with Nash than anything else. How dare he find some woman that he thinks he's falling for. Falling for? Him? Nash? He doesn't fall for women. He beds them and then moves on to the next.

"No, I'm not getting up. You go pick up the kids. I don't feel like it."

"You've been in bed all afternoon. Are you ill?"

"Do I look ill? Hell no, I'm not ill. I'm doing some thinking."

"You're acting really weird since that phone call with Mr. Nash. Are you sure everything is, okay?"

Zonnique knew that she had to be careful with her words. She'd been living so many lies for so long, that she didn't know whether she was coming or going. Things were coming to a head now. Nash had met a woman. She kept saying that over and over in her head and not once did the words appeal to her. She didn't like it one bit. She told Nash she was okay with it, but she wasn't. The idea of this woman who was still on her phone screen made her want to throw up. She had to save face with Nash. He wouldn't understand if she all of a sudden became perturbed about his dating life.

"I said I'm fine. I just need you to pick up the kids. I'm going to be going on a trip for a few days. I'm going to leave tomorrow. I think Nash is coming home either tonight or tomorrow. Either way, you should prepare to spend the night here until he returns. The other nanny, Chloe is won't be around until next week. Someone in her family is getting married or something like that this weekend. Can you make arrangements to stay?"

"Yes. You were supposed to take the kids to a birthday party tomorrow? Remember the invitation on the refrigerator? I emailed a picture of it to your phone. They're looking forward to that."

"Well, you'll have to take them. Also, can you pick up something expensive as a birthday gift? I forgot about that. I should have done that while they were in school today."

"You haven't left the bed."

"I said, I should have, Amelia. Are you not listening? Go ahead and pick up the kids. You don't want to be late. Take Ashton's temperature when they get home. He may have another fever."

"He didn't have a fever the last time. You gave him medicine and he wasn't sick."

Zonnique rolled her eyes. Amelia was too smart for her own good.

"As his mother, I felt like he was a little warm. I should know. Remember? I'm his mother. I would know. You're wasting time standing here talking to me."

"Okay. Will you be gone all week?"

"Yes. You should prepare to be at Nash's house all next week. Wait, on second thought, I'll be around to drop them off at his house. I think he's planning on bringing this woman this weekend. I want to meet her."

"Good. I better go."

Before she could say anything else to Amelia, the doorway was empty. She could hear Amelia rushing down the stairs.

Turning back to her phone, she looked at the picture of Delaney Monroe again.

"Her name sounds like a stripper name!" she declared.

She went back to reading about her on her company's website. Finding information on Nash's new woman was easy since she was a business woman. She hated her just on principle alone. She locked eyes with the woman on the screen. What did Nash find so irresistible? For one thing, he wouldn't have to worry about this woman being after his money. She had pulled up an article that talked about how successful her company had been in just a few short years. That was mostly due to business connections she'd already made years prior while working for her ex-husband's firm. She was able to also find out that Delaney had received a large settlement in her divorce from her ex. What she couldn't find was how much she'd received. She knew that Nash loved business women. He loved powerful women. She still couldn't believe that Nash described her as his *perfect* woman. She never thought she'd see the day that he even knew what that word meant when it came to women. He never called her that. In all the years they've known each other, not once has he called her that. Not even after giving him two children because he was ready to be a father. He told her he wanted someone uncomplicated. Is that who she was to him? Uncomplicated?

Should she have been complicated? Would things be different? Would she have ended up as his perfect woman?

Zonnique had one plan in mind. This woman was going to be meeting her children. There had to be more about her. She would find it or die trying. She was running out of time. For what? She didn't know. She just knew the walls appeared to be closing in on her. She hasn't felt this way since back in high school when Andre Masters didn't want her, kicking her to the side for a girl who wouldn't even put out for him like she did.

"Delaney Monroe – you're not special. You're not special enough for Nash.

**

Rushing to her office, Delaney stopped by Tara's office first. Before she could get a word out, Tara started clapping as if she were at a concert. The only thing missing was loud music and adoring fans.

"Well, look at you. You are glowing! What a change from when we were talking in the conference room. Good news?" she asked.

"The best news. Nash is coming to take me to Miami for a few days. Can you move the board meeting to four and cancel everything else that doesn't need me. Also, can you check my calendar for Monday through Wednesday to see what I can be on meetings remotely instead of in-person? Everything else will need to be rescheduled if it's here in the office. I'm on travel the following week, so if you can make sure that's all set, I would appreciate it. That meeting is in Colorado. Are you free to go with me that week?"

"Colorado? Seriously? Absolutely I can! I'll confirm all of those arrangements."

"Good. Let's take Albert with us too. Our product manager will be needed for that week-long conference."

"Anything else?" Tara asked, beaming from ear to ear.

"Yes, thanks for being more than just an assistant."

"That's never a problem."

Delaney turned to leave and again, Tara cleared her throat causing her to turn back around.

"I know you're not going to toss out a name and skip over it as if I didn't hear you say it. Nash?"

"Oh, you caught that?"

"Do you know why you keep me close and depend on me? It's because I never miss anything, especially you saying a name. Again, Nash?"

Delaney looked around and stepped all the way inside of Tara's office. She had a few minutes to spare.

"Nashall Patterson."

"What!" Tara yelled and then covered her own mouth.

Delaney waved at her to lower her voice.

"You heard me. Right now, only you know."

"You're involved with *THEE* Nashall Patterson? Really? We're talking about professional ballplayer turned business mogul and philanthropist, Nashall Patterson? How? When? *Where*?"

Tara was jumping up and down. She'd gone from concert clapping to church-like praising behavior, dancing all around.

"Calm down. Yes, that Nashall Patterson. I met him in New Orleans. Monica is marrying his uncle soon."

"I heard about him being in New Orleans. It was all over the news, but I had no idea the two of you had something going on."

"It was quiet. He's good at that."

"That's apparent. There were rumors that he was lip locking with a woman, but no one knew who. That brother sure knows how to be discreet."

"It just sort of happened. I have to say it's been amazing! Like, out of this world amazing."

"Why have you kept it a secret? It's a good secret too because with him being as high-profile as he is, I haven't seen any scoops about the two of you."

"He's good at shielding his life from the public when he wants to. I respect and love that. It's been a whirlwind romance. He has definitely reeled me in. You were right that I needed a break. He said the same thing. He's coming to pick me up later. I'm going to spend a few days with him in Miami."

Delaney wasn't prepared for Tara to race in her direction and pull her into a tight hug. Unlike some work relationships, she and Tara were not just boss and employee; she considered Tara one of her best friends.

Their friendship started back when they both worked for Davis' company. She watched Tara begin college in her early forties and while working full-time, secure two degrees, one in public relations with another in public health administration. Their friendship grew over the years.

"I'm so happy for you. Also, that man is fine! Do you know how many women have done all kinds of clown tricks to tame him to win his heart? Go for it! I'm loving all of it. Why don't you get out of here now? You can take that board meeting at home while you wait for him."

"He's on a plane, so I have some time. I want to wrap up a few things so that I don't have anything pressing while I'm gone. No calls from anyone other than you. Please make sure all requests are filtered through you before contacting me."

She loved the feeling of finally telling someone other than Monica about Nash. She was ready for everybody to know. One thing she knew for sure was that they were solid. The way he felt about her was exactly what she was feeling. They could be much more if only she allowed herself to let go and enjoy what they have.

Tara returned to her desk and started typing away.

"I have everything covered. Do you need me to stay a little late with you?" she asked.

"Not on your life. I don't plan to be here any later than six. For anyone who wants to work tomorrow, they can, but it's not mandatory. Just make sure you get overtime requests in by five today. You can add my approval to them all. I'll be in my office."

"Go, go, go!" Tara yelled and waved her off. "You know, you and Nashall Patterson - I can see that. Two amazing people who love life. I see how perfect you are for each other. He's one guy that my husband says has done his life right. Wait until I tell him. Can I tell him?" Tara asked, holding her hands up in a prayer stance.

"Yes, you can tell him, but only him. For now, swear him to secrecy."

"Done. Now, go. Get ready for your man!"

Delaney walked away with an extra pep in her step. She didn't have to get ready because for Nash, she stayed ready.

## 18

"Byron! It's Nash. How are you, buddy?"

"Nash! I'm good. Are we still meeting in LA? The studio execs are ready to sign on the dotted line to work on this movie shorts project with you."

"They haven't even seen the final yet."

The idea of one of the most powerful movie production studios wanting to partner with him was great, even if they haven't seen the final draft preview which was still being cleaned up for him to review.

"They know who you are and what you're about. They loved the original treatment for each movie short and they want in. You are rocking this post professional ball game like no one else has ever done. These movie shorts that show sports players how to be successful after retirement has been the talk of Hollywood for almost a year. You've done it and now you want to teach others how to do it. They find that admirable. You know sports teams admire it, but they don't want it. They want players to play on forever, getting every bit of juice out of them with the lure of money. They need to know that they can maintain a good livelihood without playing until their bodies and minds are worn down."

"Well, as one of my attorneys, I'm glad you've been working around the clock to broker this deal for me. About coming into LA - I'm going to push that meeting for a week. Do you think you can make that happen?"

Nash didn't want to tell all of his business, but right now, Delaney and his kids were the only priorities for the next few days. He was finally getting the chance to introduce the woman he's fallen in love with to his first true loves. His mind was already spinning with a weekend packed full of them all getting to know each other with Delaney as a part of the mix.

"I'm sure I can. Anything wrong that I can help with? You, okay?" Byron asked.

Nash smiled as one of the best Black multi-media attorneys in the country was not only his lawyer since his first endorsement deal when he played ball, but also a remarkable friend. He trusted him with everything.

"I met a woman."

"Okay."

The nonchalant way Byron said that one word meant that the way he said that he'd met a woman didn't provide the impact of what those words meant.

"Byron?"

"Yeah?"

"I *met* a woman," he said again.

This time there was silence. In that quiet, Nash knew that Byron understood.

"Oh, you *met* a woman. Well, damn. Really? You? I don't believe it. Some woman has come along and snatched you up? Snatched your soul? You're telling me such a woman exists to tame the untamable Nashall Patterson? I'm going to need to clone her! You are blowing my mind with this news. I'm happy for you," Byron said.

"Yeah, whatever. Call it whatever you want, but it's true. She's amazing, man. She's got me thinking about her and only her. Have you ever heard me say that?"

"Are you kidding me right now? Are you joking to get a rise out of me?"

"Man, you know me. When have I ever said that before. Listen to this – when have I ever said that I think I've fallen in love with the most incredible woman I've ever met. I wouldn't joke like that; you know me."

"Well, hot-damn! Who is this woman?"

"You'll meet her when the time is right. For now, I'm respecting her privacy. You know how the media can be. I don't want her getting any unwanted attention from the paparazzi. I know you wouldn't spill, but her privacy is very important to me. I signed up to have them following my every move, especially when it comes to my private life, but she didn't. I want to protect her from that until she's ready. She's a serious business woman. She's got everything going on from business to being sexy as hell. You know how I love a powerful woman; a woman who walks and lives in the confidence of who she was created to be. She runs a company that makes it look easy to show women running the world. There is also a non-profit that her company has to empower young women who are looking to start their own business. She's going to partner her company with one of my non-profits. There is nothing sexier than a woman doing the damn business! Besides that, yes, she has completely snatched a brother's soul. I'm all hers, bro."

"Where are you, Nash? Seriously, I need to send a doctor to check your mental health. Is this really you? I can't believe the words that are coming out of your mouth. I love hearing it. It's just a shock to my system. You know some women. You've always kept them at a certain distance with no one getting too close. What about..."

"Nope, not since I met my lady."

"Not even..."

"No, not her either. I'm not joking with you. I haven't seen any other woman since I met her. I admit it's not easy with she and I both having busy business lives, but she's worth giving up every other woman for. "

"You're serious, aren't you?"

Nash couldn't believe his own words, but if nothing else, they were true. He was in love with Delaney. What he didn't want to do was scare her off from a serious relationship with him. He remembered a few talks they had about her time in her marriage. She had spent a lot of years faking her way through being in love. She still had her reservations because she, more than anything, wanted to make sure she knew who she was before she got seriously involved with another man again. He'd had his own reservations for years of getting too close to the wrong woman. That woman wasn't Delaney. She was everything he wanted.

"I've never been more serious. I'm on my way to pick her up for some time together. She's been crazy busy with work. I need to remind her that in the midst of chasing dreams, there should be time for fun and quiet. I'm also missing my kids. I've been on the go for a week. I need to spend some time with them, taking them to school next week, cooking, swimming, just having family time. Business has to wait," he explained.

"Business will wait. The one thing I have always known about you is when it comes to your kids, nothing comes before them. I'll make the change in the meeting. These guys are so anxious to get this project under contract before someone else comes in with a better deal that they would have no problem waiting a little longer."

"Assure them that I have no intentions of going anywhere else. It's not too often that a brother owns his own movie studio. I know there are a few in Atlanta that are black-owned, but I've had my eye on this deal for a while. Our partnership will be one for the record books."

"I got you covered. Speaking of books, when is your next book coming out?"

Nash smiled at how successful his children's books have been. For his next one, his daughter expressed an interest in doing the audio part of the little girl. He couldn't be more excited to help her live out her dream of being an actress. At ten, Yasmine had spent the last two years with an acting coach. They had all come to the same conclusion – Yasmine was definitely ready. He wouldn't allow her to spend any time making videos for social media because he didn't want to subject her to the general public like that, knowing who he was. He would control the narrative when it came to his kids and what they were exposed to.

"The book is in the making. I'm writing this one with my daughter. I'll tell you more about it when we connect sometime next week."

"Cool. Did you get the proposal I sent you? One of the biggest sportswear companies in the world wants to partner with you to sponsor the kids and the uniforms for your basketball academies. I also let it slip that you want to open a science academy in Miami. They want to pitch you on how they can partner with you on that too."

"I got it. I'll take a look and get back to you on what I think. I have a call with my marketing team in a few minutes. My plane is landing in Tampa in about thirty minutes. I need to get to that call really quick. If we're good with rescheduling, send Vi my updated schedule and she'll work everything out."

"I'm finishing up the changes to the contract for the Chicago location today. I'll have those ready for you to sign next week. Look, I'm happy for you. It's been a long time coming that you find that woman who would turn your world upside down in a good way."

"She is definitely that. When she's ready, I can't wait for you to meet her."

"For this woman? I will be ready anytime she is. I need to meet the woman who has put a lock and key on the ultimate bachelor!"

"Yeah, yeah – whatever! I'll holler at you later."

"Thirty more minutes, Mr. Patterson," his pilot yelled back to him as they headed toward Tampa on his private jet.

"Got it."

Making a quick call to join his team, he had a lot to discuss in thirty minutes. After that, he was shutting off everything and everyone that had nothing to do with Delaney or Yasmine and Ashton. Being this focused on a woman was all new for him. He wouldn't have it any other way. Two months together and he'd fallen in love. His grandmother was right. He would know when it was right. With Delaney, things were more than just right; they were perfect.

**

Delaney checked the time again and cursed at herself for still being at the office. She needed to call Nash to tell him she was running behind. The office was quiet and empty except for the cleaning crew and the security team who worked in the three-story office building around the clock.

Her office sat at the far end of the top floor, only accessible by elevator with those who had a card-key and clearance by security. Being in the building alone wasn't new to her. She was simply disappointed that she was still here. She didn't want to be the woman who valued work more than the fun part of life. Her plan was to make sure she was up on everything so that she could focus on being with Nash for the next few days. She needed thirty minutes more and she would be done. She reached for the phone on her desk to call him. It was already eight in the evening and he was probably already at or near her house.

She waited nervously while his phone rang. When his face appeared, she smiled, hoping he wouldn't be upset.

"Tell me that is not your office I see in the background," Nash said jokingly.

"I know and I'm sorry. I am still here. I'm leaving shortly. Are you already at my house?"

"No."

"Oh, good. I don't want to keep you waiting. Where are you?"

"I'm in the lobby of your building. One of the security guys was just about to call to let you know I was here."

Delaney stood up so quick that her office chair fell over behind her.

"You're here?"

"Baby, don't hurt yourself. Are you alright?"

"Um, yes. I wasn't expecting to hear that you were here at my office. How did you know I would be here? I guess this is you knowing me again."

"Because we're kindred souls. I would be at my office closing things down also if I knew that I needed to lock it all down so that I could have uninterrupted time with you. I know you, Delaney. Can I come up?"

"Of course. Tell Phillip, I said you're good. He'll escort you up. Just tell him who you are," she said.

"He already knows who I am; they all do. I've signed eight autographs. How many security guys does your building have?" he quipped.

"Sixteen, so you have more to sign. I'll see you in a few."

Hanging up, she rushed to the bathroom in her office to quickly freshen up. She had to make sure she didn't look like a mad-woman whose been working like the devil since five in the morning.

Minutes later, she heard the elevator door ping. She rushed back into her office. Her heart thumped loudly in her chest. Her legs weakened watching his long, sexy, powerful strides head in her way. She was about to lose her mind seeing him in denims, dress shoes, a black casual suit jacket over a black t-shirt. The man was a walking god. Her heart could barely stand its continued pumping at the thought that he was all hers; Nashall Patterson in all of his sexiness was all hers. Every image of them locked intimately together played havoc on her senses. She couldn't wait to be in his arms. Luckily, she didn't have to wait too long.

"You, baby, are a sight for my waiting eyes," Nash said, picking her up in his arms the minute he reached her office door.

Delaney eyed the security guard walk back to the elevator as Nash kissed her with a zest that had her needy for more. She was thankful for the way her dress gave way for her to wrap her legs around his waist. Their mouths fed the hunger that not seeing each other for two weeks had unleashed on their desire for each other.

"Damn, I love how you say hello. I would say I should stay away longer just to come back to a greeting like that, but I don't know if that would have any real benefit at all. I couldn't get here to you fast enough," he chuckled against her lips.

In response, Delaney could only sigh her heated relief that they were together. With the stressful week she'd had, this is what she needed; Nash is who she needed. How could she not realize how much she just wanted him in her arms like this. Every time he held her, he felt like home.

She leaned back after kissing his lips softly, lingering there for a minute.

"Don't you dare. I knew I was missing having you hold me like this, but it wasn't until you actually pulled me into your arms that I realize how much I really missed you. Is that crazy? We met over a month ago; something like six weeks. My world was made so perfect the minute I saw you exit the elevator."

"No, it's not crazy because I missed you just as much. Nothing about what has happened between us since we met is crazy. This is what I call fate, baby."

"Okay, then are we both crazy for being this hungry for each other? I swear I could devour you right here in my office. The thoughts going through my mind at this very moment would have me going to hell fast and in a big hurry. Just damn sinful!" she declared. "I feel like we are moving fast, but I like it. Don't think that this is me being hesitant again. I thought I would say that before you assumed that's what I'm saying. What are you thinking?"

"I understand, but let me add that there is no such thing as moving too fast with us. I think we're on a perfectly good path once you allow us to come out of the closet."

"Well, I think the cat is out of the bag. Building security know that you're here to see me and Phillip, who brought you up, saw me practically devouring you as your lips claimed mine. Also..."

"Whatever you have to say that's giving you pause, I'm the one person you can always speak your mind to. We're lovers, yes, but most of all, we're friends. That combination is everything to me. What didn't you say?"

"I told my assistant about us. She's also one of my good girlfriends."

"Is that so? Ah, you're telling people about me. I like that. That means my mojo is working on you. You're stuck with me. Can I admit that I told one of my lawyers about you? Like your friend, Byron isn't just a lawyer on my team, but a very good friend. He can't believe you got me all hemmed up. I made it clear that whatever he wants to call it, I'm okay about it. Are we going to finally put the age thing to rest?"

"Yes. It's buried and stinking at this point. I don't know why I was so afraid. I think the idea that people and cameras follow you around was frightening to me. I want and need to protect my children."

"I understand that. You know how I am about my kids. Most people leave me alone, especially when they see Kilton and Cord along with others on my security team. I avail myself to interviews and photos and because of that, in general, other than fans, the media leaves me alone. I wouldn't let anyone cross a line that would interfere with your safety. I believe we'll be fine. After I landed, Kilton and Cord took the jet to Miami. I wanted time on the road with you alone; no security. It's possible for us to have a simple life together. If and when our relationship finally does hit the entertainment news, it will be big news for a lot of people who continue to peg me as the bachelor who still needs to be locked down. I'm still a bachelor but now, I have a bright, beautiful, powerful woman with me who I want the world to know about so that they can move on from it. I'm ready for us. The question is, are you sure?"

"Yes, I am."

"So, I can officially call you my woman, my girlfriend, my partner?"

"Was I already all of that?"

"Yes. That and then some," he answered swiftly.

"Are you still dating?"

Delaney had to know. Since they were talking, the best time to put it out there was now.

"You mean someone other than you?"

She didn't say the word she just shook her head. She wasn't seeing anyone else and had no plans to. She needed to know where they stood when it came to other people in their lives. She wasn't trying to be pushy. She only needed to know what to expect. She'd been married for a long time. The last thing she wanted to do was put what they have in some category that they both hadn't agreed on

"I'm not saying I expect you not to. I'm sure you had a dating life when we met. There can't be too many women out here who wouldn't kill to be in your arms like this. I think we should both be clear of what we are doing," she explained.

Nash placed her down on her feet but still held her close. His eyes perused every inch of her before their eyes met again.

"Baby, I have not even thought about seeing anyone else since the moment we met. That is the honest truth. Look, I don't want to smother you. Trust me, I'm not trying to put you in a corner. I have no interest in anyone but you. Was I seeing someone before I met you, yes. I was casually dating a few women. I enjoyed the friends-with-benefits situations for a long time because they worked for me. I hadn't met you yet," he winked. "I'm not seeing them anymore and, yes, I've shared that with them."

"Because of us?" she asked.

"Because of what I hope we can be. I want you, Delaney. That shouldn't be a secret to you or any kind of surprise. I'm not shy about how fast I've fallen for you. I don't want it to scare you away because I know what you've been through and your struggle to find you. I'm all for that. I'm here for you. I only ask that you allow me to be a part of your life in the way that you feel most comfortable with. I'm not seeing anyone else nor will I be. In saying that, I want you to have the room to do what you want. We talked about the freedom you felt with your divorce. I know you weren't ready for anything serious. Neither was I, but here I am. I also don't want you to think that not having you is an option. I don't want that. I enjoy everything about you and being with you. So that we can clear the air, what about you. Were you or are you seeing anyone? Do you want to?"

"No," she said quickly, leaving no room for doubt.

"Whew, I can breathe now," Nash joked.

"I wasn't seeing anyone when we met and since then, I've only been seeing you. I don't want to change that. I love who I am and have come to be. There is room for you in my path to being all I've ever wanted to be. You're all I want and need. I thought I would get a divorce and really get out there to do a lot of dating. I don't want that. I enjoy the idea of being secure in who I am even when I'm with someone; the right someone."

"It's me and you then."

Delaney didn't get a chance to respond. She felt herself being lifted up back into Nash's arms again. She went willingly.

"I love how easily you pick me up," she murmured against his lips when he moved to kiss her. The kiss quickly turned heated their lips going at each other for more and more.

"About that idea in your head of the sinful things you want to do to me right here and right now. Are there any cameras in here? Anywhere on this floor?"

Delaney smiled at how each word came out in the middle of each kiss to her lips.

"No," she replied softly.

"We're alone?"

"Me, you and these walls."

"And just how sturdy is your desk?"

"I have a comfortable sofa over there," she pointed.

It was clear Nash didn't care. He continued moving toward her desk. All she could do was hold on and prepare to have her hunger for him fed.

When he moved quickly back to the door and closed it, her head fell back knowing what he had in mind. If nothing else, their sex was adventurous. She loved the spontaneity.

"I really like your desk."

"The desk can hold me and you. Thank goodness for sturdy wood."

"Right now, I only need it to hold you," Nash asserted.

"I have an image in my head that I need to carry out."

In mere seconds, her body was lowered to her desk. Together, they moved all breakable items out of the way with a swift move of their hands.

"Our images are matching."

When Nash fumbled around, her eyes lit up with delight when he raised his hand and produced the gold package.

"I have come to realize that with you, I have to be ready, able and willing. I would say I can wait until we get to your house so that you can pack for the next few days, but I don't want to. How about you?"

Delaney didn't need to answer. She reached for the condom. Opening it, she shifted her hips around as Nash slid her red thong down her legs.

"I've been waiting what seems an eternity for this. You owe me!" she blurted out and then quieted when without any pretense, she felt Nash's finger at the entrance to her womanhood. She could feel her warm heat pooling around his fingers. He moved them around in the wetness he already found there.

"I see you're ready for me. You know what I want to do, right?"

"I do. We don't have time for that. This has to be a quickie, sweetheart. We are alone on this floor, but any minute, the cleaning crew may come through or one of the security guys who checks the floors hourly may check the floor."

Getting to what she really wanted, Delaney tried to get Nash's pants open, but chuckled when her hands moved hurriedly with no progress.

"You are the one who said this has to be a quickie. Undressing me is not that. This is," Nash exclaimed.

In a quick move, he unzipped his pants, leaving them in place, but pulled out that part of him that needed to be inside of her.

Neither of them had to wait long for what she'd been craving. With her hands braced securely on his shoulders, Nash held her hips in his hand. He slid her body forward and right onto that strained part of him that called her name with every delicious inch that entered her body. Never had she been this free when it came to sex. She was never the person who would have considered having sex in her office right on her desk, but this was her. This was the part of her that she always wanted to be. She wanted loving when and where she desired it.

"That man in your dreams that you told me about? Am I living up to the dream?"

Delaney wanted to answer; she really did, but her mind couldn't form a response with the way Nash's hips moved in and out of her body with precise precision, touching every part of her that was on fire for him.

When she moaned her pleasure, his mouth covered hers, taking in the sound. His tongue was hot, her need was at a point of desperation; her body screamed for release. She mewed into Nash's mouth as her climax did away with anything soft and gentle. That was replaced by a raw, animalistic like orgasm that had her hips meeting Nash's hips pump for pump.

"I love being inside of you. I can't seem to get enough of you!" he yelled, breaking off the kiss and resting his head on her shoulder. His own body spasmed on a blissful level.

He would give her anything she ever wanted in the world. He gave her what she needed most; he gave her, him.

# 19

The awkwardness Delaney thought she would experience meeting Nash's friends flew out of the window the minute his best friend, Calvin and his wife, Marisol, embraced her as if they were long-lost friends. For the past hour, over a table full of appetizers and drinks, they talked, laughed and shared as if they were catching up after having been apart for a long time. Everything about being in Nash's world turned out to be more than she ever expected. She wasn't a people person, but being around Nash cured that problem.

He and Calvin played for the same basketball team. Calvin was still on the team, though he was contemplating retiring himself. Nash's sports management group also managed Calvin. More than making money for team owners, Calvin had learned how to maximize on making money for himself to last well into retirement when he was ready.

Marisol was a stay-at-home mom. Outside of that, she was working on opening up her own dance studio. They had five children that ranged in age from three to thirteen. Her hands were definitely full. Delaney could only imagine the madness. She had her own hands full when it came to raising her own twins. Taking care of five has to be a challenge. Marisol loved it and smiled through it all while telling stories about them.

"Nash told me that in a matter of seconds, he knew you were the woman for him. Is he lying? Did you get that vibe too?" Calvin asked her.

"It's all true. The initial meeting was brief but very much a storytelling moment. A few hours later, I returned after dinner with my best friend and there he was again. It was as if he was waiting for me."

"I was. You had to come back and there was no way I was going to miss the chance to see you again," Nash explained.

"I've known this man for what seems like my *entire* adulthood. This is the first time that he's introduced anyone as his girlfriend. I couldn't wait to meet you," Calvin added.

"Well, I was excited to meet you also. Nash told me a lot about both of you on the ride here this morning."

"How long are you staying? He told us that you are a busy woman, but he had to whisk you away for some rest and relaxation. I guess he didn't mean today because we've interrupted your peace with all this eating and drinking!" Calvin cheered.

"We tried calling him last night thinking he would be in town. He said you decided to wait and drive to Miami this morning. You live in Tampa, right?" Marisol asked.

"Yes, with my kids, though both are away at college."

"Oh? Where?" Calvin asked.

"Both go to FAMU."

"Nice. An HBCU. I love that. Twins, right?"

"Yes. They're doing quite well in their junior year."

"Her son is a star football player. She showed me some footage of one of his games. The kid has the makings for

212

professional sports," Nash noted. "You should see her daughter on the volleyball court."

"Both kids are athletic? Our oldest daughter was going to play volleyball until she discovered cheerleading. That's now her life, well for the moment," Marisol said.

"Daddy!"

Everyone looked to the stairs that led up to the bedrooms on the second level. Seconds later, Yasmine and Ashton came down the stairs, both rubbing their eyes.

"Hey, Pumpkin. You should be asleep. What's wrong?" Nash asked rushing over to them.

"Ashton's machine that helps him sleep stopped working. He came into my room and woke me up."

"Okay, let me check it out. Guys, give me a minute," Nash said, lifting both kids up to take them back up the stairs.

Delaney watched him go and admired the love he had for them. When they first arrived earlier in the day, Zonnique and the kids had pulled up to the house at the same time as she and Nash did. As he took the kids inside to get them settled, she had a chance to talk with Zonnique.

They were silent, at first, choosing to smile back and forth. Delaney equated that to sizing each other up; at least on Zonnique's part. She welcomed it. After all, she would be spending a few days around her children. She wanted Zonnique to be comfortable with her. That passed and they began talking while they walked into Nash's house. Delaney was usually pretty good about reading people. Though Zonnique was nice, there was something off-kilter about their interaction. Though Zonnique expressed how happy she was that Nash had finally found someone that he felt he could have a real romantic relationship with, her eyes said something else. Delaney didn't know quite what. She let it go.

She shared that she and her fiancé were going away and that she understood the kind of connection between her and Nash. Delaney took the words and the sentiment at face value.

If nothing else, Zonnique was a beautiful woman. She had long, natural flowing locks, flawless skin and a killer body. She could see how she and Nash made naturally beautiful children. What she didn't see was an engagement ring on Zonnique's wedding finger. Perhaps she chose not to wear one. Considering how high-profile her fiancé was, she found that odd. Not many women would pass up on flashing a ring from Chopper. She'd heard her own kids playing some of his music around the house over the summer. Women swooned over him and his music. Brushing off any odd feelings, she enjoyed spending the day with Nash and his kids. Both loved reading. They spent a lot of time talking about their favorite books. They had gone for a walk in Nash's gated community. She could see why he didn't need security around him while he was at home. Everyone they walked by waved or hugged Nash. All in all, they left him to enjoy the peace of not being hounded. He said it was the reason he chose this on-the-water community for his home. Zonnique's home was a few miles away.

Earlier in the evening, after a day by the pool, she helped Nash get them ready for bed. When Jasmine asked her to read them a story, she leaped at the chance. She used to love doing that for Kyrie and Kennedy.

"Delaney, I hope you don't have any reservations about Nash. He is an amazing man and the greatest friend to Calvin and I. We love him with everything in us. We want the best for him. From what I can see, that is definitely you. He lights up at the thought of you," Marisol said when Nash had gone off, leaving the three of them around the table.

"I care very much for him. I had some second thoughts, but I don't anymore. My concerns were superficial. I see how great he is. Any woman would want to be with him. I'm lucky that he's chosen me."

"He's the lucky one. You've brought a light to his life that was missing. I know he's always wanted to find someone like you that he connects with on a deeper level than he's been able to find. Nothing against any other woman he's been involved with, but until now, none make him sit up and take stock in what he could have for more than a night here and there. Thanks for taking great care of his heart. He's like a brother. I want the best for him."

Delaney nodded at Marisol's words.

"Thank you for that."

"I'm going to step away and check on our kids. I promised I'd call them before bed," Marisol said, standing.

"I'm going to refill this fruit and veggie tray the chef left in the kitchen," Delaney said standing with her.

"Well, I guess that leaves me to fend for myself until Nash comes back," Calvin said.

"Find some good music while we're gone," Marisol told him.

Delaney smiled at their back and forth as she walked off into the kitchen with the empty tray. Finding what she needed in the fridge, she started filling the tray back up. The cold air sent a chill up her arms which were quickly warmed with memories of the night before that she and Nash spent together before driving to Miami this morning. Thinking about him always gives her great pleasure.

After incredible sex on her desk, Nash cleaned up in her bathroom while she shut down her computer. She looked forward to being away for a few days. When he was done, she did the same before they headed out to her house. They agreed that they were too tired to try and get on the road that late. Instead, they spent the night at her house. That way, they could have a lazy night in just relaxing; something they needed even if Nash didn't want to admit that he was as tired as she was.

After seeing her to her car in the private garage under the office building, Nash followed her to her house before continuing on to pick up the dinner they decided to order and eat in. Thankfully, he was able to make a few phone calls to friends who recommended a restaurant she didn't even know about in her own town. He ordered and the owner agreed to bring the order out to his car so that Nash wouldn't run into any fans.

What she hadn't told him was that shortly after he left, she thought he was returning because he'd left something after only a few minutes of her being in the house. She rushed back to the door and was surprised to see Davis when she looked through the peep hole. She opened the door quickly thinking something may have been wrong with one of the kids. To her joy, there wasn't, but to her dismay, he was there for a totally different reason.

When she asked why he was at her house at that time of the evening, he told her that he'd come by a few weeks before to see her so that they could talk. She told him that her neighbor said she'd seen him in the neighborhood a few times.

As they stood in the doorway with her not inviting him in, he admitted that he'd been around a few times trying to get up the nerve to have a heart-to-heart talk with her about them. She told him that there was no them other than when it applied to the kids. Without shame of appearing like some kind of stalker, Davis told her that he saw a man leaving her house one morning. That shocked her. She didn't understand why he was casually driving by her house, let alone making reference to anyone leaving her house. The kids were at school. He had no reason for being near her house for any reason. When he revealed his reason, she dismissed him immediately.

Sometime after their divorce, he discovered how amazing she had been all along. What he wanted was a second chance with her. She missed several words he'd spoken after that. She was too mad that he would have the nerve to think she would be interested. She divorced him for a reason.

When he started questioning her about the man he saw leaving her house, she waved him off letting him know it was none of his business. He mentioned how familiar the man looked but because of the angle of his view of him, he couldn't get a good look. After a little more banter, she told him he needed to leave and to only connect with her when it had to do with the kids. She also suggested with all of the extra time he has for visiting her neighborhood, he should take that time and instead, go visit their kids at school. She asked him to leave and he did. He didn't seem angry as he did so. Davis simply turned around and walked to his car.

When Nash finally arrived with their dinner, she decided to not dampen their night with ex-husband drama. All she wanted to do was get comfy. In the back of her mind, she wondered if Davis was somewhere nearby.

They showered together, changed into comfortable clothes and settled in her family room to eat and relax. In no time at all, Nash was carrying her sleeping body up to the bedroom. She had been fatigued. The movie they had planned to watch had actually watched her. She fell asleep in Nash's arms. The evening was perfect. She had also gotten the best night of sleep in a long time. She knew it was due to sleeping while wrapped in his arms. Not much could have been more seamless than the natural state of them being together.

They woke early the next morning and got on the road. That was the moment that she decided she was ready to tell her kids about her and Nash. No doubt they would be shocked. She also hoped that they would be supportive.

"Are you okay in here?"

Delaney leaned back when Nash came up behind her. She exhaled the moment he wrapped his arms around her.

"I was just refilling the tray. Are the kids alright?" she asked.

"You looked like you were a million miles away. Yes. Ashton loves the sound of waves when he falls asleep. I bought him this machine that he loves. It plays soft sounding waves and self turns off. The timing was off so it stopped playing sooner than usual. I fixed that and they're both sleeping peacefully. They'll be good until the morning. Are you having a good time?"

She turned around to face him.

"I'm having a wonderful time. This is exactly what I needed."

"Good. I'm glad you came here. Can I entice you to stay a few extra days? If you have work to tend to, you can use my home office."

"Well, I packed enough to last me through Wednesday. You have the kids you have to take to school and pick up. I can get a rental back to Tampa."

"No need. I will drop them off. The babysitter can pick them up and make sure they do homework until I return. I want to drive you back home."

"Are you sure?"

"Anything for you. I won't get the chance to spend time with you next weekend. You're visiting your kids for family weekend. I'm working out of my Miami office this week, so things could get busy. I need all of my Delaney time for the next few days."

"You're good to me, Nash. I want you to know that. You're also good for me. You didn't mind me invading your space for a few extra days."

"Babe, you are welcome to come here anytime you want. My house is your house. You can either drive here or I'll come get you. For the rest of the time that you're here, all I want you to do is relax. I want to order a masseuse for you. You can swim, go for a walk, listen to music, just about anything that's not work related until at least Monday. Are you good with that?"

"I'm perfect with that. A massage sounds wonderful. I haven't forgotten my last massage from you. Are you sure? What are you and the kids going to do?"

"We're going to get out of your hair during the day. In the evening, I'm all yours."

"Your kids are amazing and smart. Both can read at levels way above their ages."

"That's because I read to them all the time. When I'm not, they have tons of books to read themselves."

"They have a wonderful father."

"I have wonderful kids along with an exceptional woman."

Just when their lips were about to connect, Calvin tapped on the refrigerator to announce his presence.

"Uh, can I get some grapes? Also, can the two of you get a room?"

"Whatever, dude," Nash said, waving him off.

"It's fine. The tray is filled back up. I added lots of grapes just for you, Calvin. I saw you eat all of them earlier."

"You're the best, Delaney. I'm telling you, she's a keeper, Nash," Calvin exclaimed.

"Man, tell me something I don't know. You sure you're finished here? Anything I can help with?"

"No, I'm coming out with you. Before you go, I want to ask you something," she said.

Delaney couldn't think of a better time to show Nash that she was ready for him to be more visible in her life. He had made many efforts to show her that what they shared was beautiful. She was ready to do the same.

"Okay. Ask away."

"You mentioned family weekend with Kyrie and Kennedy. How would you like to come with me as my guest? I know it's asking a lot. Unlike me, everyone on that campus will know who you are. It could get crazy. I want you to meet my kids."

"Really? You're ready for that?"

Delaney gasped when Nash quickly pulled her into an embrace. He kissed her so ardently, she almost forgot what they were talking about.

"Wow! What was that for?" she asked.

"You are letting me all the way in. You're not afraid of being my woman. Yes, being on campus would definitely be crazy, but I can't think of any place else I would like to be. I can't wait to meet these amazing kids of yours."

"Be warned. These are college kids who play sports and know all about you. I want you there, but I also want you to be prepared."

"True. I'll need to have my team reach out to the university. Visiting colleges is old news for me. It will definitely be crazy. Perhaps I can plan something with the school while I'm there; maybe a meet and greet with the players. I'm also going to make a donation to the athletic program."

"You don't have to do that."

"I don't, but I will. I wouldn't visit and not do something."

"Kyrie is going to have a heart attack. Both of them will when they find out we're together. Kyrie even asked me if I knew you. When I asked him why, he said that he saw a blog post that you had been spotted in New Orleans that same time I was there. I didn't want to lie to him. I simply said I had heard about that too. You know the brain of a kid his age. He went into a new conversation topic quickly," she joked.

"They will get to see for themselves how much I care about their mom. I want them to know it's not a passing phase for me."

Delaney looked up at him and then looked away. Nash turned her face back to him.

"I'm guilty of reading some of the social media posts about you," she admitted.

She didn't think she was snooping. Nash is just so amazing, she wanted to see more of him and what he loves doing.

He nodded.

"I assumed you had when you followed me back on Instagram. That's the one site that I manage myself. My team manages my other social media accounts. You cool?"

"You know a lot of beautiful women."

"I'm yours, Delaney. Despite anything women or the media say or claim about me, from our first meet in New Orleans, there has been no one but you. I want your kids to know that as well. I have had a reputation. That's not all that I am when it comes to relationships. I hope you can see that in our time together."

"I see it. I feel it. Yes, I know it. We are together," she acknowledged.

"We are, aren't we? We're together?"

"We are. I'm happier than I've ever been, Nash. You have a lot to do with that."

"I love you, Delaney. Don't freak out because I said that. I know it's probably fast and maybe unexpected. I wanted you to know what you mean to me."

Delaney beamed from ear to ear. She wasn't the only one. Nor was she hesitant about what it meant; not anymore.

"I love you, too. This love dropped in our laps like a ton of bricks. I'm not going to freak out hearing the words. I'm going to live in them. I'm going to love them as much as I love you."

Nash kissed her slowly and deeply and her head exploded with love. Her eyes drifted closed as her mouth opened to receive him. This time the kiss felt new and different. Now that love was living in the air and spoken from the heart, each kiss meant a little more, starting with this one. The sensation of the kiss zipped through her veins.

The kiss sweetened as they swayed together, his fingers skimming across her back, feathery like until they reached her neck where he cupped her there and whispered more words of love against her lips.

"Did I hear you say you loved her?" Calvin said from the doorway, ending their kiss.

Nash dropped his head heavily, shaking it from side to side.

"Bro, wear some louder shoes. Stop sneaking up on us," Nash kidded him. They all laughed when Calvin flipped Nash the finger.

"Marisol, you won the hundred dollars. She made a bet with me that you were in love with Delaney. I told her that there was no way you would ever declare your love. I knew I would lose the minute I met Delaney. I happily lost that bet. Now, either get a room or bring the rest of the food out. I'm starving!" Calvin yelled and left the kitchen.

"I promise he's not always this crazy. He isn't used to me being this into a woman. We can talk about next weekend later tonight."

Delaney nodded her head.

"I need to tell the kids we're coming. They should know about us before that weekend."

Nash winked and kissed her cheek. Delaney jumped when her phone buzzed in her back pocket.

"I'm following your lead. I'll take the tray out while you get that."

It was a text from Kennedy.

*"Mom, where are you? I've been calling the house."*

She texted back quickly to keep her from worrying. Sometimes Kennedy was more of a mother to her than just a daughter.

*"I'm out of town with a friend. Anything wrong?"*

*"No. I was just checking on you. A friend? What friend? A new friend? My godmother? Wait, is it a man friend?"*

*"Tomorrow, Ken. I'll tell you tomorrow. You're sure you're good?"*

*"I'm good, mom. I hope you're having a bunch of fun. You don't do that enough. I'm all set for our call with Kyrie tomorrow at noon. Love you!"*

Before she could reply, Kennedy sent a bunch of emojis that made her smile.

*"Love you too."*

She couldn't wait to tell them about Nash. She had a feeling that his presence in her life would be a welcome surprise for the kids. They will be happy for anyone who makes her happy. Nash did that ten-fold every single day. Telling her kids about them was the last stage of their love with no regrets. Nothing could stand in their way of complete happiness.

\*\*

"Drive slower!" Zonnique yelled from the back seat of the car.

"Girl, no one can see inside of the car. You know how dark the tint is. Why are you in sunglasses? You look crazy back there."

She sucked her teeth at the Jawan Douglass. She had drive four hours to meet up with him for this drive-by.

"Don't worry about how I look. You're driving too fast. I can't see anything," he yelled.

"Maybe take off those dark ass glasses. You might be able to see something. What are you looking for anyway? It's a house. It's a very nice house, but still, it's just a house. You said she's not even here. What's the big deal? You got me out here in the middle of the night playing inspector gadget."

"She's not here. She's at Nash's house. I wanted to see how she was living."

"Who? This woman who stole your man?" Jawan joked.

"That's not even funny. Nash isn't my man. He's the father of my kids; that's it."

"Whatever you say. You're going through a lot for no reason. You drove all the way here just to have me drive you through her street? Just to look at her house?"

"I want you to drive downtown too. I want to see where her business is. This house is nice. She's got money," Zonnique asserted.

"Is that what this is about? Money? You think she's after Nash's money? What? Do you think she'll take money out of your pocket now that he's involved with her? He's Nash. He's been involved with a lot of women."

Zonnique wanted to agree, but she already knew that this woman was someone different. She wasn't Nash's usual run of the mill kind of hottie. She was hot and sexy for an older woman. One thing she knew about Nash was that he had a penchant for older women. Delaney had it all.

She took in as much as she could as they passed by her house again. She wanted to tell Jawan to drive back around again. That was before she saw the curtains sway on the house across the street. Someone was checking them out.

"I know. This woman is different. No, it's not about money. Clearly, she has her own."

"Then, what is it? You came all the way here at this hour for what?" Jawan asked.

She started to answer and then stopped. The truth that she wanted to say would make her sound ridiculous. Slouching back down on the seat, she left the house in the distance. To told Jawan to take her to her next destination. She wasn't ready to explain herself. Now wasn't the time.

## 20

Nash nodded his way through the treatments for two commercials which he had less than a week to either approve or suggest changes. One was for the athletic shoe line collection endorsement deal from early in his career that stayed in place even after he stopped playing ball. The other was a sports car endorsement deal. He had recently resigned that deal for the next five years. The company had offered him his pick of a car from the new line, one worth a hundred thousand dollars. He wasn't a car hog. He had four of them even though he could only drive one at a time. His favorite was definitely his Range Rover. Instead of accepting a new car, Nash asked that the company agree to making four one hundred thousand gifts to the college of his choosing. To say that they were surprised would be an understatement. No doubt, they were used to other celebrities selecting the cars. He wasn't about that. He wanted to be sure these companies gave to the communities he supported.

New commercials for both of his deals would be hitting the airwaves in October, during the upcoming basketball season. With Zonnique out of town for yet another week, he remained in Miami to handle his business. That wasn't his original plan, but with her taking a lot of last-minute trips with her fiancé for, he was nothing if not flexible.

The best part of his post-basketball career was being able to focus on all of his business ventures while making sure Yasmine and Ashton could count on him being a huge presence in their lives. He loved playing ball and all the traveling that was involved, but nothing gave him more satisfaction than the hugs from the kids every day. He had missed them over the past weekend while he went with Delaney to FAMU. To say he had a blast would be an understatement.

"Are you going to give us your feedback or do you plan to stare at the iPad screen for another thirty minutes?"

Nash lifted his head a little, turning it to the right where Vi sat tapping her fingers on the restaurant table where his team gathered to hear his thoughts. Along with Vi, there were three executives from the shoe wear company who flew into town to meet with him when he shared that he needed to remain in Miami. Before he could offer to reschedule or to have the meeting virtually, his choice, they had agreed to meet him anywhere he chose.

One of his attorneys had flown in along with two of his publicists and four members of his marketing team who were all based out of Los Angeles. At the opposite end of the table sat Kilton. He valued his opinion when he needed someone who would be honest without worrying about their salary. The rest of the security team were sitting at another table just as a precautionary measure. Thankfully, Floridians respected his privacy and didn't swamp him for attention when he was out and about.

"Well?" Kilton chimed in.

"With the few small changes I mentioned over the past two hours, I'm good with these. Can the updates be made, especially to the music, and keep us on schedule? Also, are we still on point for the shoe commercial to play during half-time at the first Miami home game?" Nash asked.

He directed his question to Byron, who sat on the other side of the table. They had already finished eating their early morning breakfast. All were now sipping on coffee and nibbling on muffins the restaurant provided for them on a huge tray in the private dining area set aside just for them. The best thing about the location is that it was directly across the street from the recreation center where he was planning on joining some local college ball players for a pickup game. That was something he did a few times a year. He had another hour before he needed to end the meeting.

"I made a modification to the contract for you to take a look at. The team wants to be sure you're going to be at the game in person. Your percentage as one of the team owners has a stipulation about the number of games you will attend every season. They know you're still a draw for the audience even though you're not playing. Most are home games with two away games later in the season. I did that so that holidays with your children or their activity schedules won't be impacted. I made your wishes, or should I say, requirements, known. There was a collective agreement of nodding of the heads until I got that included in the contract. If you sign today, I can have these sent off to the team attorneys immediately," Byron explained.

"Sounds like everything is a go then."

"Mr. Patterson, we want to thank you for the continued partnership," one of the executives offered.

"Yes, we're excited that our working relationship will continue for the next ten years," Tovan, another executive added. "We wanted to talk to you about our idea for a new athletic wear line that we are hoping to work out an additional deal with you on. We have a team ready to work with you from the fabric selection to the colors and design. We're talking sweat suits, workout t-shirts and shorts. Most of all, the uniforms, not just for the male youth athletic gear for your academies, but for the girls, as well. I know you didn't like our original pitch for theirs. We took your advice and reached out to five WNBA players. They've agreed to partner with us. We love the idea of female athletes weighing in. Is it possible to set up a meeting sometime in early December to show you what we've come up with? I think you'll like what you see."

Finally, Nash thought. He disliked the original idea for the gear for girls because to him, they looked too masculine. His team had shown the original gear to a few select middle school girls who loved playing basketball. Their response was less than enthusiastic. When he asked for their honest opinion, they all agreed that the uniforms could have a little more flair for girls, distinguishing them more from the ones for the boys."

"That's exciting news," Nash offered.

"What about Yasmine?" Vi asked.

Nash hadn't forgotten about his daughter's constant pressure on him to allow her to get into the modeling business. She overheard him talking to his team about the advertisement of the uniforms once they agreed on what they would look like. She wanted to be one of the models. He already knew the camera loved her. He hadn't made her a promise, but he wanted to give her a chance.

"I'm leaning toward her doing it. We'll see how she does. I need to talk to Zonnique about the plan first. We talked a little about it a few months ago. When Yasmine isn't with me, she's working overtime on her mother to convince me on her behalf," he explained.

"Do you want me to set up a meeting with Zonnique when she's back in town?" Vi asked.

Nash chuckled. He didn't want discussions with Zonnique about their kids to turn into business meetings with an entire team.

"I'll handle it myself. She and Chopper are due back this weekend, I think. She knows the wedding is coming up and with the kids in the wedding, we need to connect on that. I can have that conversation with her then. Yasmine will be excited. Zonnique was a little hesitant the first time we talked about it. She didn't want her to become a target for the media simply because she's my kid. I told her that would come with the territory no matter what kinds of things Yasmine wanted to be a part of. She's signed up for cheerleading for our community youth football team. At the second meeting, after parents noticed us at the first meeting, they had so many families show up to sign up their kids along with an influx of media that focused on me and Yasmine."

Nash was still bothered by the extra attention they got. He quickly dismissed it and told Yasmine to focus on cheerleading. He allowed his security to handle those who tried to overstep to get close to him.

"You're Nashall Patterson," Kilton said. "You will forever have media following you around. That also means they will be all over your kids. You said yourself how good Yasmine is. She's serious about modeling and acting. Her thirst will only grow with the two of you doing the audio book together. Add this in and your kid is well on her way to knocking this out of the park. We'll protect her just as we protect you."

"You know what, it's early in the day. Let me see if I can get Zonnique on the phone. Let's get this settled now and have that plan in place. I don't want to have it lingering on. She's typically an early riser. I think they're an hour difference on time. Give me a minute," Nash said and left the table to make a private phone call.

He stepped outside into the hotness of the day, blocking the sun by lowering the shades that rested on the top of his head. Moving to the side, he stayed in front of the large window of the restaurant. He didn't want to give Cord a heart attack by not being able to see him. He took out his cell and was about to call Zonnique when his eyes caught someone walking out of the gym entrance to the recreation center across the street. Even with a hoodie on with the hood pulled down covering his identity, it was the oversized bodyguards that were familiar to him that told him who he was looking at.

Nash moved closer to the curb as cars whizzed by in both directions, preventing him from crossing. Instead of racing over in the middle of traffic and definitely causing his own team to jump into action, he yelled his name.

"Chopper?"

He added a questioning tone to his voice as confusion had him momentarily thinking he could be mistaken. When Chopper turned in his direction, Nash watched the muscled guys with him literally stop traffic to allow Chopper to hustle across to him.

"Hey, Nash! It's good to see you, brother. What are you doing downtown?" Chopper asked.

Nash was full on confused.

"The question is, what are you doing in town? Zonnique said she was out of town with you this week. As with the norm for a while now, I have the kids."

Nash noticed Chopper looking everywhere but at him after their handshake. Something was up. And, where was Zonnique if not with Chopper out of town? That clearly wasn't the case.

"Yeah. I don't know what to tell you. She's not with me."

Nash thought perhaps Zonnique was stepping out on him. Did he just blow up her scene?

"Okay. I'm backing up from this conversation. I don't mean to pry. It was a surprise seeing you across the street."

Chopper started to turn away, but then turned back to him. He looked troubled.

"Listen, you didn't blow anything up. This is all Zonnique. You should probably talk to her about what's going on," Chopper suggested.

Nash saw a look. He knew that look. He hadn't revealed anything about Zonnique that Chopper didn't know about. He could see it all over his face. Chopper knew exactly what was going on.

"Is there something I should know about without telling her story? I see I need to talk to her. Of course, her private life is her own. I would like to know why she lied about this week."

"Nash, this isn't the only time she's lied about being with me. Without telling her story, which you should get from her, Zonnique and I haven't been a couple in a few months. I know you're a busy man, but I guess you haven't noticed that when

233

you come by the house, I'm never there. We haven't been pictured together in a while. She hasn't been going to any of my shows. Lastly, she called off our engagement. It's all her; not me."

Nash was stunned. Those few sentences packed a huge punch to his gut.

"What? Months?"

He thought back over all of the conversations he had with Zonnique about Chopper. She talked about planning the wedding with her friends. She told him about where they were planning to go on their honeymoon. She shared that she and Chopper were thinking about having two, maybe three kids together. She even asked what he felt about that. There were so many details about their relationship that Zonnique shared, he couldn't believe he didn't realize none of it was true. He thought they were always honest with each other. He was also thinking about all of the times she told him she was out of town with Chopper in the past few months. If it was all a lie, where had she been going?

"Things hadn't been good with us for a while. I moved my homebase here because she wanted the kids to be closer to you. I understood that. I have a son and his mother is wild. She's only about the money and not my relationship with my son. I wanted to be with her and build our life. I'm on the road so much doing shows that I was willing to make our home where she wanted it to be. It wasn't until I proposed that I realized something was wrong," Chopper admitted.

"Wrong?"

"I'm going to say this and you can take from it what you want. Zonnique is usually at the house when she says she's with me out of town. It's true that used to be case. Think about all of the pictures you would see of us together. A hot topic was always how fly she was dressed. All of the blogs couldn't wait to capture what she would show up in. You may not have paid attention, but there has been nothing for a minute now. I've been quiet about it. Bloggers assume it's because of my crazy schedule that she hasn't been around. They all know she has kids by you. I assume they believe she's doing her mothering thing. She's been going through something, especially lately."

"How did I not pick up on this?"

Nash kicked himself for not paying more attention.

"You couldn't have. She's very slick. We started having issues after the engagement was announced. I hope I'm not overstepping by saying I believe the issues have a lot to do with you."

"Me?"

"Yeah. Look, I know the two of you have this great co-parenting thing on lock. I commend it. I know it can't be easy, but that works. I think she expected a different kind of reaction from you when she told you ahead of the public announcement that we were getting engaged."

Nash was confused. He's always been supportive of every move in Zonnique's life. He loved keeping the peace between them for the sake of the kids.

"Chopper, I was very supportive. From my heart I was happy for her. I want to see her happy. You did that for her. I congratulated her. I even sent you flowers and wine to mark the celebration. I came to your engagement party. I even worked with the kids on what they said at the party. There has been no negativity between us about your engagement. How can this have anything to do with me?"

Nash couldn't understand what was going on. He looked around as onlookers saw them talking and began to recognize them.

"Let's go inside and chat," Nash suggested. "Any minute, we are going to be swamped," he added.

"Good idea."

With Chopper in tow, Nash walked inside of the restaurant toward an area in the back away from all ears. He and the owner were on the best of terms, so he waved them back toward his office.

Once inside the cramped space, Nash turned to Chopper for more of an explanation.

"Nash, you really have no idea what's going on with her, do you?"

"I don't. I'm hoping you will enlighten me."

"I can't be sure because though I love Zonnique, I thought I could read her. I'm not sure that what she was offering was genuine. Don't get me wrong, we had a great time together, but there was always something holding her back from really being all-in with me. That something, I believe, is you. Have you ever given her any reason to think that there could have been more between the two of you besides having Yasmine and Ashton?" Chopper asked.

Unequivocally sure, Nash responded right away.

"Never. We started out in a relationship that turned into more of a friendship than a relationship. We were on the same page. I thought we always were."

"I don't think so. Things really turned weird after you met your woman. I don't want to share what I think she was or is thinking. Again, talk to her about that. She told me that you're in love. One thing she said to me was that she never, ever expected you to fall in love with someone. She's been through you being with this or that woman, but never like this. I spoke to her about a week ago. She asked me about my tour schedule and begged me not to say anything to you about our situation. She wanted to handle it. I tried, but whatever she's going through, it's not working for us. I played along with her allowing people, mainly you, to think we were still together. I thought it was so that she could share with you our news about the breakup. If she still hasn't done that, then there is more to this than even I thought."

Nash leaned back on the desk in the small office, crossed his arms and legs. He was dumbfounded to believe Zonnique would go through extremes in keeping the state of her relationship with Chopper a secret. She would normally tell him everything. In fact, there were times when she would share things that he thought was more than he needed to know. His only concern was for the welfare of their kids. He thought back to the previous weekend that he spent with Delaney in Tallahassee. While he was there, suddenly, Ashton got another fever. She called every couple of hours to ask what he was doing, how things were going with Delaney's kids and when would he be back. Ashton was asking for him. When he would ask to speak with Ashton, Zonnique would say he was asleep because he wasn't feeling well. By the end of the weekend, when he returned to Miami, Ashton was all better. He remembered his son saying he wasn't feeling really bad, but that his mommy said he had a fever and she gave him medicine.

His nerves kicked into high gear.

"Is she at home now?" Nash questioned.

"As far as I know of, she is. I'm not sure because I haven't spoken to her this week. I know that the last time I was out of town, she asked me to tell bloggers who asked about her that she was relaxing in our hotel suite. She needed to keep up the façade until we could issue a joint statement about the engagement being off. I decided to go with her schedule. I wanted her to do things her way. I wanted to be supportive of whatever she was going through. Looks like you and I both are pretty clueless. I don't want to keep you. I saw your group when we were walking back here. Looks like you're in a meeting. I'm sorry that she hasn't come clean with you about our relationship. I do think there is something about your relationship that's eating away at her. So much so, she hasn't been herself for a while now. If I had to pick a point when, it would have to be when you told her that you experienced love at first sight. Congratulations on that, I should add. I see the media trying to dive all into Delaney's life and finding only goodness. She's a remarkable woman. I suggest you think back to anything that has changed since you revealed your relationship to Zonnique. That's when the big change happened with her."

"Thanks, about Delaney. I'm a lucky, lucky man. And thank you for enlightening me."

"Can I say something and then be gone?" Chopper asked.

"Absolutely."

"I think Zonnique is jealous that when you say you're a lucky, lucky man, you're not talking about her. I would appreciate you not mentioning anything to her that we ran into each other or that we had this conversation."

Nash nodded and extended his hand to shake Chopper's right before he was left in the office alone with his thoughts.

He still couldn't quite grasp what Chopper was saying. He and Zonnique didn't have a personal relationship anymore. In fact, they hadn't had anything intimate or personal since Ashton was about a year old. They kept each other in the friend zone and found their own partners for anything intimate. He needed to find out what was going on in Zonnique's head without getting too involved in her personal business. He didn't want to cross a line.

He needed to get back to his meeting. His day was full before he needed to pick the kids up from school later in the day. He was taking them with him to his local office for much of the evening. He had several other late afternoon and early evening meetings. His office was near their favorite diner where they could get burgers and milkshakes. He needed the extra time to figure out how to approach Zonnique without embarrassing her with what he knew.

## 21

Delaney was happy to be working from home. Since the revelation that she was the woman of Nash's attention, a feat that other women had tried and been unsuccessful at, she had been getting requests for interviews. The Monday after the weekend with the kids, she arrived at her office to find several media outlets were trying to get in to speak with her.

The entire weekend with the kids had been nothing short of perfect. After sharing with Kennedy and Kyrie that she was in a relationship with and had fallen in love with Nashall Patterson, both had looked at her through their phone as if they'd seen a ghost. Kyrie exclaimed first. Kennedy's response was delayed. Suddenly, both kids cheered and congratulated her.

Kennedy said she knew something was up because she'd seemed happier since returning from New Orleans. They talked for over an hour with her spending a lot of that time answering their questions. She then told them that Nash was coming with her for the weekend visit and asked if either had any reservations. Both couldn't wait to meet him. They also couldn't wait to tell their friends that their mother had wooed one of the top bachelors in the country.

When that weekend arrived, Kyrie was more than happy to show Nash around. He even accompanied him to all of his on-campus appearances that he had agreed to. The crowds and the media that followed them around was massive. She loved the look on her son's face when other professional basketball and football players arrived for appearances. That was all done, thanks to Nash and his contacts. According to the students and all of the news reports, that was the best weekend, outside of homecoming, that the school had ever had.

Nash and other players had made huge donations to the athletic programs, spread equally among men and women's sports. The only not so good part of the weekend was dealing with Davis. What she regretted was not telling Davis about her relationship with Nash before she brought him with her. She thought back to their chat at her house when he happened to stop by. Davis now knew who her mystery man was. That weekend, he was weirder than usual.

Davis would normally be more engaged with the kids and her, but that weekend, he was more standoffish. Several times he was nowhere to be found. He explained that by saying he had some work calls to tend to. In all the years the kids were at school, he never let anything interrupt his time with them. She hoped it wasn't Nash that kept him away. The kids didn't notice and seemed really happy. That's all that mattered to her. Still, the looks that Davis gave her were concerning. She tried not to let him steal the joy of the weekend away. There was too much excitement to allow him to bring her down. What was most disturbing was how his eyes seemed to always be on her. Finally, she stopped looking his way. His anger at her relationship with Nash was apparent.

She dismissed anything about Davis. She was missing Nash. Lately, they've only had late evening or middle of the night conversations due to their busy schedules. The wedding was coming up in a little over a week. They had been making plans to spend some quality time together in the days after the wedding. She would be busy with Monica in the days leading up to the wedding. She had decided to take a few extra days to stay at the property where the wedding was being held. The massive luxury resort was one that Nash owned. She'd seen pictures of it. To say it was exquisite wouldn't do it justice.

Guests were treated to a two-hundred-foot-long lobby with vaulted ceilings that were hand painted. It was nestled on three hundred feet of waterfront acres. It was the perfect escape to get away to. There were rooms and bungalows that made up the resort. According to what Nash told her and what she read, there wasn't an amenity that wasn't accommodated.

Nash had his own private quarters at the main resort hotel along with his own private three-bedroom bungalow. He was loaning the bungalow to her kids while they were attending the wedding. She started to protest, but let it go. The kids were too excited. She didn't want them getting too comfortable with extra treatment because they knew him. She knew she was being hard and ridiculous. She was as excited as they were.

Nash assured her that they would enjoy some nice, quiet downtime once all of the festivities were done. By then, Monica and James would be headed off to their honeymoon, her kids would be heading back to school and Nash said that Zonnique would be taking the kids back to Miami with her.

She had been invited to the wedding having known James for as long as she has known Nash.

With the work day finally being over, she decided to stick to her plan of shutting work down at a decent hour and stepping away from it in the evenings.

Going from her home office into her kitchen to grab a quick bite to eat, she noticed the camera that overlooked the back side of her property was blinking. That meant that it had caught movement along the property and she hadn't noticed.

The gates on either side of her house were not locked. That allowed her landscaper to access the back of the property for his weekly upkeep. He wasn't scheduled to arrive until the weekend. She wondered what the camera caught. Peeping out of the window for a quick check, she did see that the gate on the left side of the house was wide open. She remembered that it was closed when she arrived home the night before. She hadn't been out of the house since then, not even to check the mail. Turning off the alarm, she went through the French doors to the large back deck and down the stairs to the brick pathway next to the pool that led to the gate. Seeing nothing, she relatched it and walked back toward the house. That's when she saw something that had been put on the deck in a box under the eight-seat patio table.

Going up on the deck, she reached for it. Perhaps someone found a package for her that had been left someplace else and found it easier to put it in the back as opposed to out front where someone could steal it. Either way, she reached and picked it up, taking it inside the house with her.

Before opening it, she checked the camera footage to see who may have dropped off the package. What she saw startled her. Whoever it was had entered her gate in the middle of the night. The person had avoided being seen by the camera. Only a black glove-covered hand reaching the box to the deck could be seen. As fast as the person had entered her property, they had exited, rushing off, not closing the gate all the way.

Finding a pair of scissors, she opened the oblong box. Inside was a single black, dead rose with a note that said, *"that man isn't for you. Stick to your own lane. He's out of your league."*

Before she could think, she dropped the note back into the box and threw it all in the trash can.

"Who could do such a thing?" she questioned out loud. Before she could think to do anything else, she called a friend and neighbor of hers who worked for the local police department. Within minutes, Corinne Dalton was at her front door.

"Are you okay?" Corinne asked, rushing in. She saw that Connie had her hand on the gun at her hip, ready to use it with if she needed to.

Delaney knew she looked shook. That was exactly how she felt. She also had an idea of who left the flower and note.

"It had to be Davis. He's been creeping me out lately driving by for now reason when he lives in Miami. He's been trying to make some kind of play for me, but I'm not interested. Recently, he learned I was seeing someone. I haven't seen him lately. That doesn't mean he hasn't been hanging around. I think my relationship set him off."

"Are you sure it couldn't be anyone else? A fan obsessed with Nash? Before you ask, yes, I saw all the media coverage and all the talk of your romance."

Delaney nodded. There weren't too many of her friends and neighbors who hadn't heard. Her own family had been blowing up her phone after they found out.

"I didn't think about that. Now, I really don't know. Davis has never done anything like this. I shouldn't have leaned right to him doing it."

"Let me tell you this while I gather the box, note and flower; you are dating a big celebrity. I mean he is *major*. He's Kobe Bryant status. He's Michael Jordan level. He was last year's bachelor of the year. Nashall Patterson has been on every woman's to-do list for years. Guess what? He announced to the world that he's in love with you. That's going to bring out all kinds of obsessed women and a few men. You need to up your security. You said the back gate was open?"

"Yes. I have never locked it before."

"You need to do that now."

"How could anyone find me?"

"You are a business woman. Besides that, the internet has made it easy to find anyone. If there is an electronic foot print, it's unavoidable. The point now is to protect yourself. The minute you showed up on Nash's arm, everybody did everything to find out more about you. Finding where you live was easy. That's just how the internet works these days."

Delaney shifted uncomfortably.

"Corrine, there is more. I don't think this was the first time. Before the public announcement about Nash and me, I spent a few days with him in Miami. When I returned home and Nash headed back home after dropping me off, that next morning, I found about a dozen rotten eggs thrown about in my back yard. My cameras caught the eggs being thrown over the privacy fence, but it's so high that who was doing it couldn't be seen. I thought perhaps it was a few kids with nothing else to do. Do you think it's connected?" she asked.

"I don't know. Anything else strange?" Connie asked.

Delaney was hesitant. She didn't want to make something out of their being nothing.

"I just..." she started.

"Tell me," Connie pushed.

"I went to the gym one evening. When I came out, there was this long key scratch on the passenger side of my car. It wasn't too deep, but it was there. I got it fixed immediately. I do have pictures that were taken for the insurance company. There have been other little things. None of them stood out until now. I haven't been paying close attention."

"You need to start doing that, especially if you're out at night alone."

"This is all crazy."

"To be safe, have your security company reposition your cameras and maybe add a few more. Russell and I had to do that to our home. As a cop, kids often play pranks. We wanted to catch them. We haven't had any problems now that all of our new cameras are more visible. We don't have many problems in this quiet community. I think this is targeted specifically to you. I'll get these tested, but I doubt we'll find much. Keep your eyes open and call me at any time if you see or hear anything suspicious."

"I will. Thanks for coming so quickly. I would have dialed 9-1-1, but I didn't want to take away from real emergencies."

Corrine laughed. "You have a copy on the block. That's better than any call to 9-1-1. I'll be in touch if we find anything. Be more aware. If need be, you call 9-1-1 anyway. This could be the beginnings of you being harassed. I want to see this nipped sooner rather than later."

Delaney walked Corrine to the door and locked it behind her immediately. She felt a cold chill in the air. Could someone really be targeting her? Could it be Davis? Could he be this jealous? These days, she didn't put anything past anyone.

She felt violated. Who would do this? So much was adding up now. There was also something else she hadn't told Corrine about. She'd been getting emails of a creepy nature. She assumed everybody got spam here and there. Thinking back over what she'd read in the emails, they were more than that.

Her first thought had been Davis for that too. Then she didn't think that he would do the egg thing. She didn't know. All she knew was that she was afraid. She decided to call Nash earlier than they had planned. She wanted to know what he thought. Surely, as a celebrity, he's had to deal with all kinds of weirdos.

## 22

Nash couldn't sit still. Kilton had been driving him home from a business meeting when he needed more space to breathe. Hearing what sounded like terror in Delaney's voice had his heart beating fiercely in his chest. To hear that someone was purposely terrorizing her had him on edge. He felt at fault. This was the last thing he wanted with their relationship going public. He should have known the crazies would surface. He dealt with his easily. He hated that this was happening to the woman he loved.

Once Kilton found a spot where he could get out, he stepped out of the truck and paced like a madman. His woman was hurting and he was hours away from her.

"Baby, are you okay? You're not hurt or anything, right? No one touched you or harmed you?" he asked with angst.

Nash didn't want to show her this kind of anger, but he was ready to hurt someone for her.

"Nash, I'm fine. I can hear how upset you are. Calm down, please. I didn't call to tell you so that you would be this upset; this worried."

"I am. Baby, I love you. Don't ask me to not be worried about you; about this. Someone is doing things to you on purpose? This could be my fault!" he exclaimed.

"No, no. Don't do that. We don't know that."

"I'm on my way. Kilton and I will be there faster than the speed of light. Are you sure you don't know who is doing this? You have seen anyone? Emails aren't giving you a clue?"

Delaney tried to get a word in but Nash wouldn't let her speak. He was too upset after she told him what happened with the eggs and now with the flower and note. He thought it was a result of their relationship. Truth was, she had no idea.

"No, nothing."

"I never should have pushed you for us to go public. I'm sorry I did that. We were doing fine when no one knew but us. Now look. This could have been worse. It could still get worse. I'm coming to Tampa!" Nash declared.

"Baby, no. Don't you dare get on the road at this hour. Where are Ashton and Yasmine? Aren't they with you this week?" she asked, pleading with him to listen to her.

"Yes, they are. The sitter is with them. I'm coming from a meeting. She's always on-call. I won't be able to sleep with you there alone."

"I'll be fine, I promise. I just put in a request for my security company to come out for an upgrade. There is an opening this evening. I'm waiting on them now. I have a friend from my office who is coming over right now to sit with me. I don't want you worrying about me."

"Being hours away from you, especially after those two incidents makes me nervous. Your friend from the police department is going to be looking out for you?"

"Yes. She and her husband are both cops. She lives a few houses down on the other side of the street. I initially thought it was Davis. I'm sure I'm wrong there."

"Your ex-husband? Why would you think that."

Delaney just realized she never told Nash about the various messages and encounters with Davis.

"I should have told you already that he's been trying to weave himself back into my life. He pretty much told me that he wants to be a family with me and the kids again."

"Oh."

"I love you, Nash. When I said it, I meant it. That also means I'm not in love with anyone else. Nor am I looking or willing to give anyone else a chance. I love what we have. Davis could have sent the black rose and the note. I don't think that was him with the eggs. I know that he was angry after the weekend in Tallahassee. He called a few times talking about our age difference and how you and I can't possibly have anything in common. He even said I was getting revenge on him for when he messed around while we were married, which I no longer care about. We're divorced and I'm done. Monday, he sent me an email saying he deserved a second chance after all of our years together. There was more to it but that was pretty much the message. I told him that he didn't have a chance."

"Are you sure you're done with that part of your life?" Nash asked her.

Delaney knew she had no doubt.

"I'm done, done. He didn't just mess around on me. He made an unforgivable error. Nash, Davis has a son. This son was conceived during my marriage. When I found out, that's when I filed for divorce. That was the main reason, but there were others too. He was having an affair with a woman in his office here. That's why he eventually switched to the Miami office. My kids still don't know that they have a little brother. I told Davis to tell them and he still hasn't. That kind of betrayal, as far as I'm concerned, is indefensible. Sometimes, a relationship can come back from an affair, but not really one that produced a child. He's around Ashton's age, I think. I'm not too sure. I don't really care. When I say I'm done, that's the truth. When he tried to say I was dating you out of revenge, I have no idea what he was talking about. I dismissed it. I don't have enough energy for revenge against another living soul; just against myself for the time I wasted not being happy my way. As far as my security, I know I need to be more aware. With us being together and who you are, I should have known to up my security anyway."

"Baby, I'm so sorry. I didn't mean for my life to be dropped at your door, if that's what this is."

"Stop apologizing. We don't know who or what this is. I will see you next week for the wedding. Until then, I promise I will be safe. I wanted you to know about it."

"As long as you're sure. After you're home and the alarm is on each evening, call me. I won't sleep unless I know you're safe. I can have a friend check out your system. He is ex-military and can make sure your system is the top of the line. Before you say no, let me do that for you. I want you to be and feel safe. I also want to know that you're safe when we're not together."

"If you want to do that, I'm not going to push back on it. I want to know that my security system is the best. When my kids are home, I need to know that I don't have to worry about their safety. Thank you for suggesting it."

"Anything for you. I'll have him on a plane tonight."

"Wait, your friend doesn't live here?" she asked.

"No. He's in Los Angeles. His name is Adonis Duquette. He's currently doing some security work for a politician."

"You're going to fly him here tonight?"

"I am. He did some work for a few other high-profile celebrities. If I call him, he'll come. I need him to make sure you're safe. Have your company fix you up for tonight. Adonis, we call him A.D., will be at your house in the morning. I can't wait until you're in West Palm Beach for the wedding. I won't do away with my worrying until I have you in my arms."

"I can't wait. I think I'm going to grab a bite to eat before my security company gets here. Then I'm going to take a much-desired hot bath for about an hour."

"You're killing me, baby. Can I join you by video? Can I watch? I need something to hold me over until next week."

Delaney laughed at the idea.

"Only if you're as naked as I am. I want to be able to see you and watch your reaction to what I now know I'll be doing in that tub. Deal?" she asked.

"Like I said, anything for you. Call me when you're ready. If you need me, call me. I've got some friends in Tampa who can be at your house in minutes if I ask them to. I'm always nearby if you need me, even if I'm not. Got it?" he asked.

"I got it. I love you."

"I love you, too. See you shortly," Nash said and kissed her loudly through the phone before ending their call.

Nash didn't stop pacing because the call had ended. Now that the call was over, his temper raged out of control.

"Dammit!" he yelled.

"Is Delaney good?" Kilton asked, getting out of the truck.

"Man, she better be or I'm going to jail. Some kook is coming for my woman."

"And you think this is about you and her? Actually you?" Kilton asked.

"What else could it be? This didn't start until recently. She's also getting creepy emails. Someone is trying to warn her away from me. She thought it could have been her ex-husband, but this sound more like some the messages I get. I expect it. I don't want that for her. She's not prepared for the lunatics."

"True. The difference is she has you and she has me. Looks like she'll also have A.D."

Nash dialed his phone.

"Damn right she does. I'm calling him now."

"Nash!"

Adonis answered on the first ring.

"Brother! How are things in Los Angeles?" Nash asked. "Oh, Kilton is here with me too."

"Tell that fool I said what's up. I thought he was coming this way last week."

"He was. I needed him for a last-minute business trip. He's telling me to tell you he'll be out there in a few weeks."

"Tell him I'm looking forward to it. I have some new security equipment I think he'll want to invest in."

"I'll relay that. Listen, I hope you aren't too busy. I need a major favor. It's about the protection of my woman," Nash rushed out.

"Ah, the woman. You told me she's it for you. I love hearing that. I'm still out here making work my woman. What's up? What can I help you with?"

"This is the tough part. I need you here in Florida; in Tampa to be exact. She's having some problems that may be a result of our relationship. I need her home security system upgraded to the best there is. I trust you and only you with that."

"Does she have a system now?"

"She does. I don't know what it is. They're doing a check on it this evening. That's not good enough for me. She lives four hours from me. I want to know she and her kids are safe when they're home. I'm really worried. Someone was actually on her property. You know I'm going bat-shit crazy. I want to drive like crazy from here to Tampa. I promised her I wouldn't. I did get her to agree to having you check out her property and do whatever you feel is the best in security without it being too overwhelming."

"Man, I'm sorry to hear that. I know you're worried."

"That I am. How fast can I get you here? I know you're a busy man. I need you as soon as you can break free."

"Nash, that's a given. I'm on the first flight out. I can get my team to take over in my absence. I can't begin to tell you what growing up as friends in New Orleans has meant to me. You know I have your back."

"I appreciate you, man. I'll secure a private jet for you tonight. Is that good?"

"I'm already packing. Text me the details. I'll check into a hotel. Make sure your lady knows to expect me first thing in the morning. I'll bring everything I'm sure I'll need. I'll make some calls to get that in order. I'm on my way, brother. Don't you worry about her. I'll check things out tonight. Tell her don't be creeped out if she sees me checking out her house late tonight. If you send me her cell number, I'll text to let her know it's me on her block. In the morning, I'll have her more secure than the White House."

"I knew I could count on you. Let's catch up soon on all that's been going on with you. I heard about your latest case."

"Yeah, it's a tough one. There's a lot more that you don't know about. I'll bring you up to speed soon. Text me everything you know. I'm on it like a second skin."

"I'm making arrangements right now. Call me when you land. I don't care what the hour is. I'll have a rental Navigator truck waiting for you. I know that's your preference."

Adonis laughed out loud.

"You know me so well!"

"That's because we're brothers."

Nash ended the call and exhaled.

"Feeling better about all of this now?" Kilton asked as they got back in the truck.

"I will once A.D. touches down in Tampa. Whoever is doing this to her had better make sure I never find out their identity."

"No jail time for you," Kilton joked.

"For her and my kids, if I had to, I would."

"I know you would. Let's not let things get to that point."

"I'm going to have someone on the outside look into this on a quiet tip. I'll never be able to focus again if I have to deal with Delaney being at risk; not now, not ever. I love that woman like crazy. You know that."

"I know you do. She also knows you do. You're taking care of her. Start with that before you start getting murderous tendencies. Besides, whatever and whoever needs to be handled, I got you."

**

255

In the quiet of her home, Delaney leaned against her kitchen counter and let go of the frustrated breath she had been holding in. Was her world spiraling around her and she had no clue as to who was behind it? Could it be Davis? Should she approach him about it? If not him, who could it be? Who else wanted her to stay away from Nash? Could it be as simple as a fan who was jealous? She didn't know.

Chicken salad on a bed of lettuce and a glass of wine was all she could focus on right now. Upping her security would help her feel more secure. Nothing would be right until she found out who was taunting her. Nothing.

**

"She was still seeing him. She must think this is a joke. Maybe this new email will do the trick. It's time I upped my game. Nash wasn't the man for her. It's time she knew that."

The sound of keys being typed on the laptop rang out in the night air.

"It's time to take the kid gloves off."

## 23

Delaney rushed into the bridal party suite ahead of Monica; both were excited about the next chapters of their lives.

"I'm a married woman now!" Monica shouted and danced around after Delaney closed the door behind them. The rest of the bridal party were probably still partying in the ballroom where the lavish five-course meal had been served. Tonight, was a party to be remembered.

After four hours of dancing and celebrating, James gave Monica the signal that they needed to get ready for their late-night honeymoon departure to Tulum, a place she'd always wanted to visit in Mexico. They were about to have two amazing weeks celebrating and loving on each other. Delaney couldn't be happier for her. She laughed when Monica flew by her dancing as if she was flying high on a cloud in her white gown with a diamond covered bodice and flowing train.

"You haven't danced your shoes off yet?" Delaney asked as she chased behind Monica trying to undo the ties in the back of the dress to help her get it off.

"I can't keep still. I'm happy!" she cheered.

"I get that. You're going to have one very unhappy husband if we don't get you out of this dress and into your travel outfit. What did you do with it? When we left the suite earlier, it was hanging up on this rack? What about everything else you selected to take with you? That was all here too," Delaney questioned, pointing to the long white clothing rack that had been filled with clothes earlier. Everything from sexy outfits to even sexier lingerie had been on it.

"Oh, the woman Nash hired to make sure not a single thing went wrong this entire weekend said she would pack it all up for me. If you look in the bedroom, there should be several suit cases."

"Good. That will make getting you ready easier."

"The only thing left out on the bed are the clothes for the trip. I cannot wait to get there. And, speaking of Nash, my goodness that brother can wear a tuxedo. I would ask if you noticed but the two of you couldn't keep your eyes or your hands off of each other."

Delaney hid the big smile on her face as she entered the bedroom to check for everything Monica would need.

"I see everything. Let's get your dress off. You know that man is hot for you and ready to get you to himself in Mexico."

"Hmph. Don't you dare act like I didn't ask you about Nash. Well? I know we didn't have a lot of alone time once you arrived two days ago. With the entire wedding party here, there wasn't much time for just me and you. How did things go with Davis' family? I saw you talking to his parents."

"Oh, I'm cook with them. They wanted to know how I was doing. They also wanted me to know that they heard about me and Nash. I told them I was happy. I believe they're happy for me."

"I looked at Davis while you were talking to his parents. He is some kind of mad at you. I've never seen him this jealous before."

"That's because he knows he can't do anything to get me back. I'm over it and him."

"Well, I'm glad you're here now. It's been a crazy, mad dash since I got here last week. Can you believe this place? The décor is incredible. The transformation the event planner made to accommodate what me and James wanted was nothing short of amazing. Everything in gray, silver and white. It was all so lovely. Now, back to Nash. Again, well?"

When Delaney stopped moving and found Monica glaring at her with her arms folded across her chest, she knew she wasn't going to be able to escape the conversation about Nash.

"Yes, I saw him. There was no way to miss him. Whew! When I tell you…"

"What? When you tell me what? You like to keep me hanging on. You and Nash have been hot and heavy since August. It wasn't until I saw how he looked at you all evening that I realized that this thing between you is not just a fling. You said you were in love and I see that. Nash is love? James still can't believe it. He said he didn't think Nash would ever find a woman to love. This isn't just about sexing each other up all the damn time, which I know you do. This is much more. Do the kids know? Three months and your love is like a fairytale. I love it."

"Of course, they know. You saw him with me when we visited them at school. You were there."

"I'm not talking about if they know about you and Nash. I'm talking about if they know that you're in love with him and, that he's in love with you. I also remember the two of you all touchy and feely that weekend at FAMU. I'm sorry that I feel so out of touch with what's going on in your life."

"You know it's okay. This is a big time in your life. These past few months were meant to be all about you. My love life can wait when it comes to our talks. Besides, you've already said it. I'm in love with him. Can you believe that? I still find it crazy and unexpected. Don't get me wrong – I'm loving every minute of it."

"You're happy?"

"Happier than I ever thought I'd be. I've never put more miles on my car or trusted my team at work to do their jobs more, allowing me to not spend all day and night in the office. I'm living like never before."

"That good, huh?" Monica asked as she stepped out of her wedding gown. Delaney quickly carried it to the garment bag, the only thing hanging on the rack. She would hold on to it until Monica returned from her honeymoon.

"Oh, yes. It's not just the great sex either; it's more than that. We have fun. I even talked him into my favorite activity recently."

"Roller skating? You took Nash roller skating?" Monica snickered.

"Yes, and he surprised me by being a great skater. I also found out that he loves aquariums, so we did that on a date."

"So, this is not just a bunch of knocking boots non-stop. I know Davis is my cousin, but we've talked about how unsatisfied you were in that realm. I take it Nash is knocking it out the park?"

"Really? That's what we're calling it now?" Delaney jested.

"I didn't want to get vulgar and downright nasty about it since he isn't just a booty call. You've had a few of those since your divorce. I didn't see any signs of falling in love with any of them. I want to be as respectful as I can. I hope you're not letting Davis and his behavior affect you."

"I will say that where you see the love looks from Nash toward me, Davis has spent the entire day glaring at Nash. I told you how he acted a fool when he first found out. He literally asked me what was I doing with that baby ball player."

"Jealous," Monica said flippantly.

"Exactly. After what he did, he shouldn't say anything."

"How young was she?"

Delaney dropped her head down, shaking it quick from side to side.

"At that time? Twenty-three."

"And now he's all shook up over you and Nash? It's because he knows it's not some fling. He sees the two of you together. When Vivian came over to give me and James a hug during the reception, she whispered to me that she couldn't take her eyes off of the way Nash was looking at you when you walked down the aisle. Everyone has been talking about the way he lit up and never shifted his gaze away from you."

"Can I tell you that I felt that gaze, honey. It melted every part of me. He looks at me like that all the time. It may be a different gaze, but the intensity is always the same. I feel it when he touches me and kisses me. I don't throw Nash in Davis' face, but I'm also not going to shy away from enjoying a man I love and who loves me because Davis can't handle it. I think he really thought I would take him back."

"I guess you filing for divorce wasn't a big enough clue that you never would? Do you still think he left that black flower and note at your house?"

"I don't know what to think. Someone created a fake social media account and tried to troll me about my relationship with Nash. That came after the flower, rotten egg, email thing. That's the latest. I don't see Davis doing that. In that case, someone else is really pissed off that he's with me. As of right now, I still don't have a clue. There have been no more sightings of anyone randomly showing up at my house. The new security system that was installed is quite visible from all sides of my house. The locks on the gates now have codes that only the kids and I have. Nash's friend from Los Angeles took my old system completely out and installed a new one. I love it. He even installed monitors in my office. I can also watch my cameras when I'm at work or just out and about."

"Ah, the joys of dating one of the most powerful men in the country."

Monica was right, but she could deal with it. She's now more aware.

"Are you almost ready?" Delaney hollered, catching sight of Monica rushing back and forth across the door in the bedroom where she was finally changing into a beautiful cream colored mini-dress that she'd bought for her.

"What do you think?" Monica asked while posing in the doorway.

"Beautiful. James is going to lose his mind when he sees you in that."

"What are you and Nash getting into tonight?"

"Nothing. I'm hanging with the kids. We're going to do something fun and then have a late dinner. They're heading back to school tomorrow."

"I think the kids want to explore the night-life. I was talking to Kyrie. He was saying he wanted to ask Nash about some places to hang out while they were here for one night. I guess they decided not to?"

Delaney didn't know about that. Sometimes, she could be absentminded when it came to remembering her kids were adults.

"I didn't think about that."

"Let them kids do their thing. Maybe you should go out on the town with your man tonight. I know you're the ultimate mother hen, but they'll be fine."

"I know. I don't want them to think I'm focusing more on Nash than on them. Work already takes up so much of my time. I want them to know that they are still my number one priority."

"You think they don't know that? Do you have any idea how happy they are that you're happy with Nash? I've heard an earful from both of my godchildren."

"You're right. I'll text them to tell them to go ahead and have fun."

"And Nash?"

"I'll stop by his suite when we're done here."

"You're not sharing a suite with him?"

"I am planning on it. I was struggling with how it would be for his kids and mine."

"Honey, you are thinking too hard on this. Just relax and enjoy yourself. You and Nash are two grown ass people. If you want to ride that man from room to room, do that. You both know how to do that without your kids being in earshot. I wish you would relax and just go with it."

"He asked me to go away with him to Bali for two weeks in December."

"See? That's what I'm talking about. Just do it. That man wants you to have all of his love. Think about how busy he is and yet, he makes sure you and his kids get equal time. James said he's cut back on working around the clock. You met an amazing man while preparing for my wedding. There is no better time to get and fall in love."

Delaney didn't need to be told to love Nash. The excitement she felt whenever they were together was unmatched to any feeling she'd ever experienced. When they danced together at the wedding, she had to control her facial expressions each time he whispered nice and naughty sentiments in her ear. She wouldn't dare tell anyone that when they both disappeared for about fifteen minutes, Nash had taken her to a small room at the far end of the hallway from the ballroom, placed her up on a table in that room, spread her legs and planted his head in place to send her body and mind to paradise. His words of continuing that encounter later still resonated with her. Monica was right, it was her time.

"You're right. Are we about done? I need to see a man about making room for me in his suite. I don't know what I'm hiding from. No more after today though. I need to go to my suite, get my things and find my way to his. His kids were going back with Zonnique after the wedding."

Delaney turned around after checking that she'd picked up or packed up everything and found Monica looking at her with a weird look on her face.

"Laney, don't think that I'm being paranoid, but I caught her looking at you and Nash when you were dancing. If you thought Davis was throwing daggers with his eyes, Zonnique was hurling swords. She was scowling at the two of you. I wish you could have seen her face. Are you sure she's supportive of you and Nash? I know you said she's been kind and sweet and all that, but still."

"I told you she's engaged to someone. She may have been tired or something. I know she's been doing a lot of traveling with him. Maybe she wasn't looking at us. I was surprised her fiancé wasn't with her at the wedding. He may be on his concert tour."

"If you say so. I saw something else, but I won't poke the bear. I'm ready to go so that you can get to your man."

"Wait until he sees what I packed for him."

"Then let me get to my *husband* so that you can get to your man!"

**

Secretly, Nash's money was being put to good use. The man Byron connected him with was the best at what he does. What people may think about him but not know is that, though he was thankful to have had the career that has afforded him a good life financially, he would give up every part of it for his family. Since the day he fell in love, that included Delaney and now her kids also. That's why after sending the kids off with their nanny to get them packed up and ready to go home with Zonnique, he found himself slipping out of the wedding reception in his all-black tuxedo with gray accessories to take a call he'd been waiting on for the past few days. From the last text he received while dancing with Delaney, he waited until she was occupied with helping Monica get dressed to leave for her honeymoon to step away to take the call.

Zonnique, the nanny and the kids had been gone for about an hour, right after Ashton yawned for the fifth time before falling asleep in his arms. Yasmine, who was also bushed, had settled for laying her head on his leg from her position in the seat next to him. She had also fallen asleep. He held them that way until Zonnique walked up to him. They had accomplished their tasks of flower girl and ring-bearer like champs. He would see them in a few days.

Stepping into one of the smaller meeting rooms, he dialed Ivan Page, the private detective who was once a military intelligence officer. Byron had once dated Ivan's niece and they were still close, even though the relationship didn't work out.

Ivan did a lot of work for Byron's law firm when it came to checking into people. He had hired Ivan to do what he could to find out who had been harassing Delaney, pretty much scaring the wits out of her. He knew she tried to hold a straight face with him as if she wasn't bothered by the situation. He wasn't buying it. Someone was trying to scare her away from him.

After talking with his friend, A.D., he called Byron who recommended Ivan. Within minutes after his call with Byron, Ivan had called him. He wanted Ivan to investigate quietly and find out who was doing it. The latest had been some social media posts that Delaney had sent him a few days before she arrived in West Palm Beach. The accounts, from what he could see, were new accounts without an actual person behind it. For him, that would be hard to dive into, but not for Ivan.

During his first check into everything, Ivan was able to get his hands on the items that had been left at Delaney's house that the police now had. He didn't even ask how he got those. Ivan had been planning to test them for fingerprints or anything else he could find out. Since Delaney arrived for the wedding, she had ventured out to do some shopping. She came out of the store to find a note on her windshield with a vulgar curse word scribbled on it. That had really frightened her. Following that, he pushed Ivan to do more and find more. When he got the text with the smiley face, he knew Ivan had found something.

"I'm hoping the smiley face means you have something good to tell or show me," he said quickly.

"I don't know how you'll take this. It's actually good and bad news. I want to ease into this so be patient with me," Ivan said.

Nash sat down at one of the long tables in the quiet, darkened room. He tried to will his patience to be still.

"I'm going to try. Do what you do. Let's hear it."

"First, let me start by answering your first question from our initial conversation. You said Delaney thought her ex-husband may have sent the black flower with the note. I can tell you that's not true. It's not him at all. He has been driving through her neighborhood a few times and yours as well, in Miami. Of course, you live in a gated community with around the clock security. He didn't get further than driving by the gate. I've talked to a few close friends of his who agreed to keep our conversations a secret because they aren't really as big of a fan of his as he thinks. They all said the same thing. He's not obsessed with Delaney, but he does love her and he wants her back. He's a slick guy, but he's not a dangerous man. He wants her back, for sure. Trust, that he's not a threat; at least not at this point. He's angry, but not losing his mind over the two of you being together. It's merely a case of him being extremely jealous. I was told he has finally come to the realization that you have swept her off of her feet and she's enjoying the ride."

"Okay, so we can take him out of the equation, if you think we should. I think Delaney was still questioning if it could be him. She'll be happy to know that it's not. I'm happy because he is the father of her children. That could be tricky."

"I do. I've had him watched. No real issues there other than he wants her. No disrespect, but your woman is beautiful. I see why he would want her back."

"True. She's mine, though. What's next."

Nash was confident in that.

"The flower gave me nothing, but the note did give me something interesting. There were no finger prints, which is pretty diabolical once we get to the nitty-gritty of it all. Lady luck was on your side this weekend with Delaney being in West Palm Beach with you. Our home visitor decided to make another visit to her home in all black like some ninja. His name is Jawan."

"Jawan? I don't know a Jawan."

"You wouldn't, but someone close to you does."

Nash was already on edge. Ivan was prolonging the inevitable.

"Who?"

"Zonnique. Your children's mother."

Impossible, Nash said in his head.

"What are you saying? Zonnique has something to do with what's been happening to Delaney?"

"Yes. Not just at her house. The online accounts that have been trolling her all link back to Zonnique."

"You're sure about that?"

"I wouldn't tell you if I wasn't sure. I know who both ladies are to you. I had this information confirmed and then confirmed again. It's definitely leading back to Zonnique.

Without involving the authorities, yet, my guy and I had a little chat with Jawan after we snatched him up as he tried to slither up to Delaney's garage. He actually had a can of spray paint on him. Who knows what he was going to do. I will say, it took him seconds to tell us the full story. He's a friend of Zonnique. She asked him and another guy to scare Delaney away from you. I asked him to prove it. I told him I had the flower and the note. He said he could give me proof that Zonnique wrote it. She had originally written down Delaney's address on a piece of paper. When she came to town, she gave it to him so that he could drive her through the street. He still had it in his wallet. The penmanship matched. Am I missing something about Zonnique that you didn't share?" Ivan inquired.

"Zonnique? Again, you're sure?"

"Nash, why would this guy just pull her hat out of the air? Trust me, it's her. Remember I said, those social media and email accounts that have been terrorizing Delaney lead back to Zonnique's IP address. It's her."

"I don't understand why she would do this?"

"You've seen no signs of anything? Sounds like she doesn't want you and Delaney together. You need to talk to her before the authorities get involved."

"Thanks for this information. I'm glad you told me before the authorities got involved. I don't want her arrested. I do need her to know that I know it's her. Damn. This is crazy!"

"Do you want to hear the rest of what this guy had to say?"

Nash was done. He wanted to hear it all but only from Zonnique. If she was the mastermind behind all that had been happening to Delaney, he needed an explanation. His greatest fear would be Delaney's reaction. She could think that this was too much for her and walk away. He couldn't lose her. This wasn't some out of control fan. This was the mother of his children. He was speechless.

"No. I'm going to get what I need directly from Zonnique. It's clear her embracing my relationship with Delaney wasn't authentic. She's been lying about being happy for me. Why, I don't know, but I will find out. You did great, swift work, Ivan. I appreciate it."

"You know how to reach me if you need me again. I have everything if you plan to turn anything over to the authorities. Delaney's case is still an open on. At first, the original officer was going to keep things off the books. She decided to file an official report to be sure Delaney was protected. I have the records of everything that was reported to have happened to her. You may want to get your eyes on that. My opinion? Zonnique needs some serious help. The few emails and social media posts that you told me Delaney received was only a drop in the bucket. The emails from Zonnique were threatening at a dangerous level."

"Delaney didn't tell me that."

"Sounds like you need to talk to them both. I'm sure she didn't want you to worry any more than you already are. Good luck, Nash. I'll email you everything I have including photos."

Nash put his phone in his pocket and headed for Delaney's room first. Zonnique and the kids should be on their way home. He decided to wait until he was back in Miami to confront her. He needed to figure out how to tell Delaney that her stalker wasn't her ex-husband or some fan of his. It was Zonnique, the person he last suspected. His conversation with Chopper came back to him. He tried to warn him that Zonnique was going through something. He spoke that there may have been more to her than being the mother of his children. He didn't listen. When he had the chance to talk with her, he would listen. He wanted to know why.

## 24

"Miss Zonnique, I don't think you're supposed to be here. I could get in trouble and lose my job."

Zonnique wave Amelia off. The nanny losing her job was the least of her concerns. She was fighting for her sanity at this point. She was fighting for a man she thought would one day come to his senses and realize they were supposed to be together. She couldn't fathom why Nash refused to be jealous of her relationship with Chopper. She had laid it on thick just for him. He wouldn't bit.

"Your job is not what's important here," she shouted back.

Rushing around Nash's four-bedroom, five-bath owner's suite at his lavish West Palm Beach resort, preparing for his return to his room was all that she cared about.

As she moved about tossing rose petals in every room, Zonnique counted all of the battery-operated candles she'd placed on the table in the kitchen before deciding exactly where she wanted each cone to be.

"Mr. Nash told me I was to let you in his suite so that you could get Yasmine and Ashton's things. He was expecting you to return back home to Miami with them. He has a car waiting for your ride back. He didn't say anything about you staying or decorating his living quarters like this."

Zonnique was sick of hearing the sound of Amelia's voice. She was in charge now, not the nanny. She had been patient enough. Seeing Nash with Delaney in his arms had sent her over the top. She was about to pull out all of her tricks. She never has before, but now, she had to. He wasn't leaving her with much choice.

"Your one and only concern is for my children, not with what I'm doing. Did you put their pajamas on before they fell asleep?"

"Yes, but that was so that they could wear them in the car going back to Miami tonight. Those were his instructions to me; not this. What is it that you're doing?" Amelia queried.

Amelia's words meant nothing to her. Ignoring her would mean she could accomplish her task. She couldn't allow anything to make her stray from her purpose. Tonight, her only purpose was showing Nash that they were the power couple, not him and Delaney. She hated that some woman who refuses to stick with enticing men of her own age would swoop in and steal him away. Delaney didn't just steal Nash, but she stole his heart. That was more dangerous than the many women he's bedded over the years. She wasn't jealous of any of them. Delaney was different. Nash was in love with her. That had been her nightmare for a long time.

"I'm going to show Nash that he loves me; that he wants me and not Delaney. He can't love her. There is no way he can love her after only a few months. Can you believe that? I've been waiting around for *years* for him to finish hopping from bed to bed. I've been waiting for him to be ready for a serious relationship. I gave him two kids. I've been a great friend to him for years. How can he pass me over for that woman?"

"Miss Zonnique? Are you okay? This doesn't sound like you?"

Hearing Amelia still talking to her was getting on Zonnique's last nerve. She had things to do. Why was Amelia trying to get in her way? She never liked the woman anyway. What woman spent more time with someone else's kids than her own? Where were Amelia's kids when she was looking after Ashton and Yasmine? She wished she was with them now and not trying to stir up trouble for her.

The moment she passed by the floor to ceiling, black leather encased mirror in Nash's bedroom, Zonnique saw herself. What she saw had to be the reason Amelia had asked her if she was okay. Her blond wig was messy, making her look like a mad woman. Hair was pointing in all directions. What she saw looking back at her was a big difference from the perfectly put together woman in her designer Pink Chiffon, Strapless celebrity gown that she'd worn to the wedding. She remembered the countless number of eyes that rested on her throughout the wedding and reception. What she hated was feeling like she had to compete with Delaney for Nash's attention. She could easily admit that Delaney looked hot in her silver, form-fitting, off the shoulder with a slit all the way up her thigh, silky gown. Her stomach turned every time she caught Nash practically foaming at the mouth whenever his eyes landed on Delaney. How could he be so deeply in love with her already?

Trying to fix her hair in the mirror, she saw that her makeup could use some refreshing. She'd already changed out of her dress and into a see-through nightie that would surely get Nash's attention back on her. Her breasts were large, firm and sat high even after having two children. She was smelling good and feeling good. If she could just get pregnant again by him, she could work her magic to make him fall in love with her. Her pregnant with the kids had brought them together. Not in the permanent way that she'd secretly hoped, but it did keep them connected. She was the only woman for him. Looking over her shoulder in the mirror, she spotted Amelia looking terrified.

Zonnique turned around sharply and walked up to her.

"Can you stop following me around? Why aren't you in your room that connects to the kids' rooms? I don't need you for tonight. Now, go!" she demanded.

When Amelia didn't flinch or move, her rage grew. She'd already spent months tampering her anger over Nash and Delaney and now standing before her was a defiant nanny.

"Mr. Nash was..."

"I don't care what he said, does, whatever. He's not here right now. If I even see you thinking about calling or texting him, you'll never get another job anywhere! Do you understand me? I'm tired of everyone telling me what to do or what they're going to do. Why can't you just do what I ask? If Nash comes to his senses and realizes that I am the only woman for him, I will make sure he triples your salary. I bet that will go a long way to helping you out with your family. That husband of yours who can barely keep a paying job will appreciate the extra money."

"This isn't just about the money. Mr. Nash trusts me. I always follow his instructions. He won't like what you've done to his home here. Flowers all over the floor and you here. He will be very mad."

"Well, he deserves to be mad. I'm sick of walking around quietly waiting and waiting for him to see me. I've been in the wings a long time."

"What about Chopper? You are getting married?"

"No, I'm not. I never was. Don't you love your husband? Don't you love how he loves you? I want that. I want that so much. Truth is, I only want it from Nash. I love him. I've always loved him and only him. How could he be this blind and not see it. Ugh, but he loves someone else."

Zonnique walked in circles around the bedroom. She looked over at the bed to where Nash had probably made love to Delaney more than once. Had she been in this suite? Walking over to the bed, she turned her back to it and allowed her body to freefall on it. This is where she belonged. Why couldn't Nash see that? She can't lose him. She can't let his heart go to another woman.

"I understand how you feel. I'm sorry that you are hurting. I've been in Mr. Nash's employ since Yasmine was born. I know he cares about you. This isn't you. You can't force him to love you. Let me draw you a hot bath in your suite. I think that might help you think clearer. We need to get out of Mr. Nash's bedroom before he returns."

Zonnique saw Amelia moving toward her and she crawled to the other side of the bed.

"This is going to be my bedroom with him soon. He won't be able to resist me once he sees me. I need to fix my hair and makeup. Then I'll be perfect for him. Go check on the kids."

With her voice calmer, Zonnique stood on the other side of the bed, walked around it and out of the bedroom door. As she headed back toward the main room, she turned her head expecting to see Amelia following behind her to continue tormenting her thoughts and interrupting her plan. Nothing was going to do that.

On the kitchen island, she saw the bottle of wine that was chilling in a bucket of ice along with two wine glasses she took from the pantry. She had already placed her bag of tricks in the bedroom. It may have been years since they'd had sex, but she was ready for the high-voltage level of bedroom activities she was sure he still enjoyed. She was putting it all out for him. It was her time. She needed to get the strawberries she'd bought from her room that had been delivered earlier in the day. She grabbed the bag and tossed them in his fridge. She now needed to dress it up and take them and the wine into the bedroom to get ready for Nash's return.

Before she made it halfway to the kitchen, there was a slight knock at the door. Before she could get to it, the door opened and on the other side wasn't Nash as she had hoped, even though she wasn't quite ready for him. Her anger rose higher when Delaney walked in, uninvited.

Their eyes connected and each looked at the other as if they were determining who was in the wrong. Zonnique watched Delaney's eyes take in her outfit, which didn't leave anything to the imagination. All of her womanly parts were clear and visible through the sheer material. She looked like she belonged here. Delaney was an interference that she needed to disappear. Nash was, no doubt, on his way.

"Zonnique?" Delaney asked.

When she didn't move from the doorway, Zonnique whipped her wild hair around, placed her hands on her hips and made sure she didn't look like a visitor.

"What are you doing here?" Delaney asked.

As her surprise guest looked around, probably for Nash, Zonnique knew her only option was to put on a show. She'd seen enough reality television shows to know how to play this masterfully. Nash was hers. Nothing else had worked on her. It looks like she was going to have to confront Delaney face-to-face.

"What are *you* doing here? We aren't expecting any visitors," she said smugly.

"We?"

Zonnique sashayed toward Delaney who had yet to close the door. Several things stood out. Delaney had a large rollaway suitcase in one hand. In the other was the card key she used to open the door to the suite. Nash must have given it to her. She was expecting that.

"Yes. Nash and me. I'm sorry you had to find out this way. I will talk with Nash about telling you how things are going to be from now on. I can't continue to be his little secret," she incoherently let the words roll off of her tongue. She didn't know all that she was saying or contemplating saying next. She didn't care. As long as Delaney left her be, she would use everything in her imaginary arsenal.

"What are you talking about? Where is Nash?"

"Delaney, maybe you should leave. This isn't a good time, as you can see. We have plans for tonight."

"We?"

The look on her face gave Zonnique a sense of satisfaction that she never thought she'd feel facing the woman who had slipped in and stole her man. Seeing someone's expectations fly out of the window was exhilarating.

"Look at me. Does this answer any questions you may have? Okay, since you insist on answers. Here it is. Nash and

I are going to be married. Yes, you heard me correctly. See, being here at the wedding has helped him see the light. He loves me. I'm sorry that you got caught up in the middle of our years of going back and forth with each other. I've always been in the picture. We plan on making it permanent. Look at this room. Do you see all of these flowers he had placed around just for me? See all the rose petals? See that wine on the counter? I'm just as surprised as you are. He told me to come to the room and get ready for him. I think he went in search to tell you that he doesn't love you, but that he loves me. He wants us to be a family; me, him and the kids. We even talked about having more kids. Did you know he wants more children? I don't think you'd be able to give that to him. How old are you again?"

She was about to continue on, but the hurt on Delaney's face said all she needed see. Weeks of taunting her and this was all it took. She should have thought about doing this earlier. Her expression spoke volumes. Then Delaney's expression changed to anger, not just hurt.

"You're lying!"

"Am I? How did I get here? Why am I dressed like this? This is Nash's suite. He had to let me in."

"But, but..."

"But what? Oh, you thought him saying he was in love with you is new? Oh, I get it; he told you that he'd never said that to another woman before. Yeah, he does that. He's ready to settle down. He's doing it with me, not you. You got so caught up in him and that good-good. He put it on you, huh? Yeah, he does that too. He's working with a lot, right? Mmm, I know how you could get addicted to what he's swinging. It's never about love with any other woman but me. Did you think you were the only one? Never. Nash has never been faithful to any woman."

"You're getting married? You're engaged to Chopper."

Zonnique snapped her fingers for good measure.

"You did think that, huh? Nash knew I was never going to do that. Chopper knew it too. I ended that when Nash started coming to his senses. He didn't tell you? I guess you have been in the dark a long time. I'm sure he didn't want you to find out this way. You should leave before you embarrass yourself any more than you already are. Aren't there men in your own age range that you can play house with? I will say, he surprised me with you. He typically goes for the much younger crowd, not that I can't see the appeal. You are definitely sexy, bossy, powerful – all those qualities he loves in a woman. I'll be those for him now, thank you very much. It's time your little trysts ended. I've had enough of him playing around on me. I'll take care of all of his needs from this point forward."

"You and Nash deserve each other. I don't have time for this kind of childish mess," Delaney said and turned around.

Before she could think of what to do next, Zonnique was ready to put the nail in the coffin of whatever Nash and Delaney had going on.

"Oh, you don't have to leave. The show will be starting soon if you'd like to watch."

When Delaney's head turned back in her direction, Zonnique unzipped the nightie she had on and let it fall to the floor, leaving her standing in the middle of the room stark naked.

"Nash was never going to give up all of this; not even for you."

"I don't have time for this."

"You're right. Neither do I. I've had enough of letting Nash have his fun. That's over and done with. So is whatever you had going with him. You can leave the room key. You won't need it anymore."

Zonnique ducked when Delaney threw the card key. She couldn't help but laugh. She'd finally won.

**

Delaney grabbed her suitcase and left. She'd had enough of being humiliated. As soon as the door closed, she raced toward the elevator with the only thing on her mind being to get out of West Palm Beach. She didn't know what was going on, but she couldn't handle what it looked like.

"Delaney?"

She heard her name being called by the one person who could explain what she had just seen, but even for him, she didn't stop. She moved past one large marble pillar after another, forgetting that the closest elevator was in the other direction from where Nash was calling her name. She would have to race around to the other side to get to the other elevator. She didn't care. She needed to be far away from him and Zonnique. She didn't know what kind of games they were playing with her, but she wasn't here for any of it.

"Delaney!"

He called her name again, racing after her. Catching up to her in no time at all she moved her arm away when she felt him reaching for her. Keeping her back to him, she tried to hold back the tears, but they continued to fall.

"Don't touch me. Don't ever touch me again!" she yelled and then stopped. Though the only suites on this level, where they currently were, belonged to Nash, the marble pillars and railings overlooked the lower-level floors where others may hear them. She didn't need any more embarrassment.

"Whoa – what's wrong? Why are you running away from me?"

Unable to hide her anguish any longer, Delaney turned around sharply and faced him.

"Ask Zonnique. It appears she has all the answers."

"Zonnique? What answers? What were the questions?"

"Nash, Are you serious, right now? All of a sudden you don't know who she is?"

"Delaney, calm down and tell me what's going on?"

"Have you been playing me? I mean, I know you young, rich guys think you can do anything and treat people, especially women, any kind of way but I thought you were different. I was vulnerable and open with you. How could you?" she yelled even louder this time.

What she didn't care about was being heard. Behind Nash, she could see Zonnique exit his suite and take up residence in the hall. At least she had on a robe this time. When her eyes darted behind him, Nash turned his head quickly in that direction before looking back at her. As if he didn't get a grasp on what he saw behind him, he turned his head back around again.

"Zonnique? What the hell?" he questioned loudly.

"Whatever the two of you have going on, leave me out of it. Tricks are for kids and I'm far from that. I thought you were too."

"Delaney, what are you talking about?" he pleaded reaching for her again. She again moved out of his grasp.

"Talk... to... Zonnique," she stressed.

Nash again looked between the two women. He didn't know what he was seeing. To begin with, he needed to know why Zonnique was dressed in a robe coming out of his suite. Why was she still here and not on her way home?

It was clear he needed a moment to figure out what he was seeing. With Delaney fiery mad at him and now walking away, he stood and waited for his head to clear. And then he knew. Everything that he'd been finding out about Zonnique, first from Chopper and then from Ivan were all coming to the surface. Zonnique had done something and Delaney was the casualty. He could talk to Delaney until he was blue in the face and it wouldn't matter. He first had to deal with Zonnique. If he was to have any kind of future with Delaney, he had to first confront his past before he could move forward. There was a lot that needed to be reconciled. Delaney needed a little space and he would give her that. He couldn't chase after her without knowing what he needed to explain to her. The answers he needed were going to be found with Zonnique.

Regretting that what he really wanted was to go after Delaney and prove to her that his love for her was real, he let her race off. He, instead, turned and locked eyes with Zonnique. Where she had been smiling, it dissipated once she saw his face. Whatever she was expecting would happen, his face told a different story. The time to iron all of this out had come. He knew it was time for them to have a conversation about whatever she's been cooking up.

Zonnique had hurt the woman he loved. How could he have missed all that she'd changed into? His steps to his suite were slow. He knew the woman in front of him. She was thinking that what had once turned his head in her direction would work again. Not this time. Not now that he was in love.

His love for Delaney would never go away. Whatever he had to do to show her that she was all he wanted and needed in a woman, he would do it.

First, Zonnique had some questions he needed answering. He met her at the door.

# 25

### *Two Weeks Later*

Delaney tried sleep a few times and yet, it was close to two in the morning and her mind was still racing. She should have gone home hours ago, but being in her office gave her refuge from the outside world. If she worked her fingers to the bone before, she really had gone above and beyond that in the past two weeks. She was still struggling with her encounter with Zonnique. The fact that she hadn't talked to Nash in two weeks told her a lot about their relationship. Perhaps Zonnique had been right. She also admitted to herself that it was her fault that she and Nash hadn't spoken or seen each other in the two weeks.

After going back to her room that fateful night at the resort, she didn't leave and head back to Tampa as she was planning to do in the heat of her anger. Instead, she stayed the night in her room. She finally left when Kennedy and Kyrie left to head back to school the next day. She wanted to see them off. The one person she craved seeing, but didn't was Nash.

She'd gotten several texts from him telling her that he loved her and only her. She didn't respond. She also hadn't responded when he called, texted and sent her flowers over the past two weeks. The situation was still too raw for her. If he was serious, he would have made seeing her a priority and not just sentiments through texts, calls and flowers.

That night after rushing away from him and Zonnique, she secluded herself in her own suite, choosing the quietness of being alone with her thoughts. She couldn't stop picturing Nash in bed with Zonnique. Seeing her standing in his suite like that proclaiming that she and Nash were together had crushed her. She was stupid enough to believe that the kind of love she longed for would come her way. How could she have been so wrong about what they were sharing?

Standing from the comfortable couch in her office that was large enough that she could comfortably sleep on it if she could just get her mind to rest, she walked over to the large window that overlooked downtown Tampa.

Earlier in the day, for a Saturday morning, the office had been bustling with staff. Everyone, along with her leadership team, were working long hours on the launch of the new company software that would make her firm even more competitive in the information systems world. They were also working on bids for additional contracts with deadlines that were approaching. Work was all she could focus on. Her personal life was in shambles. It was too bad she didn't have anyone she would like to confide in.

Delaney knew she was lying to herself. She had many friends, some as close as sisters. What she couldn't handle would be the scrutiny or snickers of friends who deep down probably thought she had no business with Nash to begin with. Were they talking behind her back about how she was playing cougar with a man too young for her anyway?

She hadn't told anyone that she and Nash were broken up. When the kids asked about him, she played it off that they were both too busy to connect lately. When Kyrie mentioned that Nash had called him a few times to connect about going to a basketball game so that he could meet the players on the Miami Heat team, she wondered why Nash didn't mention the end of the relationship. Nash was contractually obligated to go to a number of games. He didn't, however have to take Kyrie with him. She was happy that despite what they were going through, Nash had kept his promise. Kyrie was excited about the game coming up the Sunday after Thanksgiving. Soon, she would have to explain everything to Monica, the only person she knew she could talk to. She and James were due home from their extended honeymoon in a few days. Her plan was to take a drive to New Orleans. The conversation needed to happen in person.

The busy Tampa streets were full of cars and bright lights. People were going about their lives, happy and probably in love, the way she had been before Zonnique killed her vibe with her revelation.

In the still of the night, for the first time, she thought back to that night. The wedding had been perfect. Even in a crowded room of over three hundred guests, she and Nash seemed to always find each other's eyes. The love she thought they shared was evident to anyone who looked at them. How could she have been so wrong? What had she missed? At least she didn't have to deal with any additional nasty emails or social media posts. That seems to have ended.

She couldn't stop wondering how she could have let things get so off-kilter that she didn't see the signs. After Davis' long-term cheating, she should have been able to see what was in front of her face. How could Nash and Zonnique not have something going on? Wasn't it true that men loved going back and tapping the mother of their children? Isn't that what people called it? She missed all of the signals. How could a man love her so deeply, so passionately, so lovingly the way Nash did with her and still play her for a fool? Perhaps Zonnique had been right – she should stick to dating men her own age. She did that and even that hadn't worked out for her. She met Nash and he turned out to be all she wanted in a man, not just needed.

Turning, she took in the expanse of her office. This isn't what she wanted her life to be. She had made promises to herself after her divorce from Davis. She was going to get everything out of life that it had to offer. She was going to lead with her heart and not follow what was expected of her. Work – this, this was expected of her. Working until she was exhausted was expected of her. Letting work control her every waking hour was expected of her. She was doing what she said she would not do ever again.

She had been spending all of her days and too many of her nights here in this office. She didn't want to go back to this. The middle of the night between Saturday and Sunday and she was sleeping in her office. She was back to missing out on life again because she fell in love but love didn't love her back the way she wanted.

Her office phone pinging shattered the quiet of the night. It wasn't a call. It was the sound the phone made when security in the lobby was trying to reach her. Why would the security team in the building lobby contact her at this hour? They knew she was here. Usually, they left her alone, especially when she spent the night. She reached for it quickly thinking something must be wrong.

"Yes?" she said with caution.

"It's Phillip."

"Hi, Phillip."

"I'm sorry to disturb you, Ms. Monroe. We've tried calling and texting your cell phone but you didn't answer."

Delaney forgot that she'd turned her phone off and plugged it in. She wasn't expecting any calls.

"Sorry about that. My cell is off. Is anything wrong?" she asked.

"No, not wrong, but you do have a visitor."

"A what? Who would be here at this hour?" she questioned.

"Besides you?" Phillip asked.

Delaney then felt stupid. She should be home and she knew it.

"Yes, besides me."

"It's Mr. Patterson; Nashall Patterson is here. We didn't want to just send him up even though we assumed you must have known he was coming at this hour. What should we do?"

"He's here?"

Delaney stumbled over to her desk chair, sat down and stared down at her desk phone. Her heart was racing and her hands were shaking. What was Nash doing here at this hour? How did he know where she was? Her car was in the garage, which was not accessible at this hour. She raced over to her window and looked down. She saw a large black truck sitting in front of her building with the hazard lights on. Was that him?

"Um, Phillip, yes, you can let him up. He doesn't need to be accompanied. Just key the elevator for him, please."

"I sure will."

Delaney pushed the speaker button to end the call and stood up so fast that she hit her knee on the edge of her desk. She covered her mouth to calm the scream she wanted to let out. She needed to calm down. Nash was here. Was she ready to see him or hear him tell her that what they shared was a lie? Zonnique had told her enough. Hearing it from Nash would break her for sure. Still, it was the middle of the night, he was in Tampa and had found her at the one place she didn't want to be. She stood and turned the overhead light on, lighting it fully as if it were the middle of the day and not the middle of the night. Seconds later, she heard the elevator ding and looked to where he would exit.

Moving to stand at the entrance to her office, she didn't bother checking her hair or her makeup or even her clothing. He was getting her as she was, no filters.

Watching him walk toward her took her back to the first time he visited her at the office. She had an excitement that could barely be contained. She still had that same feeling. Even with what happened, she still wanted him; she still loved him. Was she simply doomed to be mistreated?

"Hi."

Nash standing before her saying one word was all it took for her to feel the magnitude of how much she missed him.

"Hi," she said back. She wanted to sound harsh, but with him standing before her like something out of a dream, she couldn't.

Neither of them moved toward each other. Nash stood a few inches away from her. She finally moved to let him come in, pointing him to the sofa.

After he sat, she moved to lean against her desk. She crossed her arms and waited.

"Are you going to ask how I knew you were here?"

"No."

The coldness in her voice shocked her. Their interactions had always been loving, even from the start. She missed him, but she wasn't feeling extra loving.

"How have you been?"

"Fine."

"One-word answers. Okay, I'll take that. At least you didn't have Phillip and his team throw me out."

"I thought about it," she lied.

"No, you didn't. That is not you. I don't care how angry you are with me."

"You didn't come all the way here, unless you were already in Tampa, just to idle chat with me. Why are you here?"

"For you."

"What?"

"You asked why I'm here. My answer is, I'm here for you."

"Don't play with me, Nash. I'm not in the mood for any more games. You've had your fun at my expense."

When he leaned back, her eyes perused all of him from the way his black sweat suit looked on him to the sexy way he now sat with his legs crossed with one hand on his knee with the other splayed across his arm.

"Is that what you believe?"

"Isn't it the truth? I heard it first-hand from Zonnique that night. I'll never forget her words of how the two of you had been...well, I don't need to say it out loud. It hurt enough to hear her say it."

"Do you believe I love you? I mean, do you really, truly, from your heart believe that I love you?"

"Nash, I don't know what to believe. She stripped down naked in front of me. She told me that the two of you were making plans to be together. She was in your suite, naked, flowers everywhere, petals all over the floor, wine chilling on ice."

"Delaney, please, answer my question. I don't care what Zonnique did that night. I need to hear your answer to my question. When I told you that I was in love with you, not just the first time but the many, many times after that, as of today, do you think I was lying to you for some reason?"

"I don't know what you were doing."

"Delaney, seriously. What I'm asking is not that hard."

"Yes, I believe you were telling me the truth. At least, that's what my heart believed."

"But no more?"

"I don't know. I haven't talked to you in two weeks."

"Baby, I've tried to reach out to you, but there was a lot going on. I tried to stay connected the best way I could with all that has been happening."

"Do I even want to know?"

"Yes, you do. You want to know because I love you. You want to know because that's the kind of relationship we have; yes, I said have. You want to know because we care what each other are thinking and going through. I also don't plan on leaving here until you do know. First off, I love you. Nothing about those words or my actions with you around those words have changed; nothing."

"But Zonnique," she uttered.

"She's got some problems; the biggest being lying. She's been doing a lot of that for quite some time. I had no idea of everything that has occurred. Before I go into that, it's important that I know that you will hear me out. Most of all, that you believe that I am so in love with you that I would never, ever play childish games with your heart. It's me you should be listening to when it comes to that. I was not lying to you when I said I've never said those words to another woman before. That was the honest to goodness truth."

"Zonnique?"

"I have never been, nor am I now, in love with Zonnique. She is the mother to my most precious gifts. I love the friendship we shared for years. No, I have never been in love with her; not like I am with you. I couldn't make up how I feel about you. Didn't you taste it in my kiss? Didn't you feel it every time I entered your body, kissing it all over, loving you the way you desire? The way I could never get enough of? I get it. Zonnique said some things that made you question my love, but you didn't even give me the benefit of the doubt that my love for you was real."

Delaney exhaled, letting go of the tension her body had been concealing for the past few weeks.

"She's the mother of your children. She said..."

"Zonnique told a story based on the life she wanted that was living in her head only."

"She lied? Why would she do that? Why would she go to that extreme? It was so sudden. I don't get that."

"I didn't either at the time. Will you listen to me explain what I know? If when I'm done, you think I'm lying, then I will leave. I won't like it, but I will. There is no other woman I want to love that isn't you. If you can hold on to that for now, we'll come back to it."

Delaney relaxed against the desk.

"Okay."

"Come sit with me, please? You don't have to be that far away. Were you asleep?"

Delaney sat down on the other end of the chair, afraid to have any part of them touching each other. She was too week in her resolve when it came to him.

"I wasn't, though I should have been. I should be at home and not in the office. This is where I come when I can't sleep. There is something about the bright lights of the city that I love. Besides, I was working late."

"I understand."

"How did you know I would be here?"

"Because, sweetheart, you are a lot like me. I turn to work when I'm troubled. I know that you do the same thing. I admit that I did go by your house first. I also tried calling and texting for the past few hours. I thought you were still ignoring me. I'm not complaining because I understand. I apologize for not coming by sooner. I would have but my family life took a hit with Zonnique."

"Is she okay?"

Nash smiled at her with all of his pearly whites.

"See? Even after what she said to you and tried to make you believe, you still care. That's the woman I know you are. That's the woman I am unconditionally in love with. Zonnique will be fine. There were some things happening with her that I didn't recognize. I don't know how I missed it but I did."

"She lied?"

"Yes. I don't know exactly what she told you but I can assume it was wild and crazy based on what I saw when I entered my suite. I stood there shocked for a minute at what my eyes settled on, especially her. She and the kids were supposed to be on their way back to Miami. I gave Amelia instructions to get the kids dressed for their ride home. I assumed they would sleep in the limousine. Instead, they were in their rooms at the resort asleep. Until I saw her in the hall, I had no idea they were still there. She went into a tangent of how long she's waited around for me to see her; to want her; to love her. I had no idea."

"She's been faking her happiness over our relationship?"

"She's been doing that about everything it seems."

Nash's eyes dropped to the floor and then he looked over at her, turning his body so that they were directly facing each other.

"Why?"

"I didn't know she expected and wanted more from me. I thought we were at a comfortable place called friendship even though we share kids. That weekend, I had planned to really talk to you about some other things that had come to light around Zonnique."

"Like?"

"She was behind what was happening at your house. Not her directly, but she had someone try to scare you away from me. She was never threatened by any of the women I'd been seeing over the years; that is, until I fell in love with you. My heart was yours from the minute I met you. I told her that. I didn't realize that her sentiments of support were fake. She hid that well."

"But, she is engaged to Chopper. This is all so crazy."

"Yes, it is. I had a talk with him recently and discovered that they were no longer together. He, in his own way, tried to warn me that Zonnique was struggling mentally. He allowed her to convince him to play along with the engagement even though they have already split up. She never wanted him. She only wanted to make me jealous enough that I would ask her to leave him and be with me. When I met you, she was afraid of what I felt for you."

"Oh, my goodness."

"Exactly. That night she went over the edge. When I talked to her after you ran off, I saw something in her eyes that I'd never seen before; it was desperation. She was fighting for a love that was one-sided. I won't go too far into the weeds with all of this. I came to see you because I needed to explain why I didn't come for you that night or haven't in the past two weeks."

"I'm sorry I didn't wait around to let you explain."

"You couldn't have known. If it were me and I had to deal with the same type of thing with you and your ex-husband or any other man, I can't say that I wouldn't have reacted just as you did. I admit that I'm cocky enough to believe that despite what that night appeared to be, I would not lose you behind it. What we share isn't something that people find every day. Our coupling is perfect."

"What happened to Zonnique? Are the kids, okay?"

Delaney felt ashamed that she immediately went to Nash being a liar. Being with Davis for so long had her rush to judgement with Nash. She shouldn't have done that. She reached over and took one of his hands in hers and caressed the backside of it.

"Zonnique is getting the help she needs. The kids are okay, but that night, they saw a side of her that I hope they never have to see again. She went completely off on me. I had to call Kilton and the team to come to my room – no other details, if that's okay," he said.

"No details are needed."

"Okay. Well, the kids were asleep in their room. Amelia was there too. She got so out of control, loud, screaming, crying, then loving, then hollering. The number of emotions were insurmountable. Her makeup was running because she was crying so hard. It was pretty bad. Then the kids started crying and ran down to us. Zonnique had dropped the robe and was pacing around naked as a jay bird. They were afraid and ran to her. That's the only thing that calmed her down. Hearing them cry because they didn't know what was wrong with her was hard. It took all of my strength to pick them up and take them back up to their room after Kilton arrived with one of my female cousins. I snuggled with the kids until they fell back to sleep. When I went back downstairs, Zonnique was laid out in the floor crying. She was back in her robe. Someone had also put a blanket over her. I picked her up and just held her until she calmed down. I don't know how much time had passed. When she came around, she was her usual, pleasant self. We saw many forms of Zonnique that night."

"This is sad."

"It is. We did a chance to really talk after she calmed down. With everyone in the room, I told her I knew about her and Chopper. I also told her that I knew she was the one terrorizing you on line. I let her know I was aware of the guy she sent to leave the note and flower at your house. Though I wanted to run to you and explain, she is the mother of my children and she needed my help."

"Nash, you don't have to explain that to me. Knowing you as I do, I wouldn't have expected anything else. I didn't know she had issues. I understand what you needed to do."

"Thank you. I needed to get her taken care of. That night, I called her parents. I sent a jet to pick them up and fly them in immediately. I told them to meet me at the hospital where I took her and stayed until they arrived. For the past two weeks, she's been getting the inpatient care that she needs. What I didn't know, until her parents shared it with me, is that Zonnique had some issues when she was younger. This isn't her first time in a hospital. Thankfully, her treatments are working. She has a long road, but she's getting help."

"The kids are fine?"

"Yes. They needed me with them around the clock. They were confused, especially not being able to see her since that night. I put everything on the back burner to tend to my children. There is something that frightened me that I've learned since she's been hospitalized. She had faked a few of Ashton's illnesses. She did that to get my attention. She was medicating him with cold medicine even though he wasn't sick. To her, he was. I can't explain it. All I can say is that she needs a lot of help."

Delaney covered her mouth and put a hand over her heart. Her heart was with him and the kids. She couldn't imagine any of this.

"It's good that she has all of you around her."

"Her parents have been in Miami since that night. They have been staying at her house and helping with the kids. Zonnique is better; they are better and now, I'm here to hopefully work on me and you being better. I know it's been two weeks, but how I feel about you is the same. I don't hold anything against you and your reaction that night. I get it. I only hope that you know I would never lie to you, disrespect you or mess around on you. I love you, Delaney. I'm hoping you are still willing to trust me with your heart. My love is genuine."

Delaney wanted to respond but she couldn't. Her heart was overwhelmed with what he must have been dealing with for the past few weeks. She was angry at herself for not being there for him; for not being the shoulder for him to lean on. She moved quickly and slid on to his lap. When he held her close, she wrapped her arms around his neck and held on. When he snuggled into her, she knew this moment was needed. He needed her arms. He needed her love.

"I love you. I'm sorry I leaped to what I saw instead of what I knew. Deep down, I knew your love for me was real. In the moment, it was my go-to response. It matters to me that she gets the help she needs. I would never have thought that she was the one coming for me."

"Me either. I didn't find that out until after the wedding. I went by your room to talk to you about it, but you weren't there. That's when I went to my room and saw you in the hall. I didn't know what had happened. I sent you messages, texts, flowers, so that you would know that I was thinking about you."

"It's okay. You did what you needed to do. I love you for that."

Nash kissed her on the cheek. She moved her arms slightly when he sought out her mouth. The kiss had been a long time coming. She needed it. The way his mouth loved hers, it was clear to her that he needed her touch as well.

He continued kissing her until they both needed to come up for air. She smiled when his lips curved up into an intimately seductive smile.

"No more sleeping in your office, baby. You work too hard. I know what this company means to you, but it will be no good if you spend this much time here. These past two weeks have shown me that my businesses will continue on even if I'm not focused on them all the time. Please tell me this is your last time spending the night in the office."

"I promise. In fact, I'm ready to get out of here. Do you need to head back to Miami?"

Delaney knew that she'd been without him for two weeks. No way was she willing to spend another night without being in his arms.

"No. I came here to get my woman. I wasn't sure how things would turn out. I wanted to be free to come see you and explain. Zonnique's parents pretty much threw me out of Miami and pushed me here. I guess they were sick of seeing me heartbroken over you. I missed you like crazy."

"You're here now."

"I am and all I want to do is spend some time with you catching up with your last two weeks and making up for how much I have missed all of you. From your lips to just holding your hand and holding you in my arms; I've missed it all. I can't say I'm a lot of fun right now. I didn't drive here but I'm tired as hell."

"Do you want to come over to my house? I promise to let you get all of the rest you want and need."

Nash nuzzled her neck.

"I have a better idea. I booked a room at the Marriott here in downtown. Why don't we go there, get some sleep and let me wake with you right by my side. Are you free to let me spoil you tomorrow? I don't want to leave that hotel suite for anything. I can order us breakfast, lunch, dinner and snacks whenever you want them. I know I need to get back to the kids in a few days, so if you will allow me to take up all of your free time, just let me love you. If I have learned anything recently, it's that family is everything. The people I love are everything. You are everything to me. You and me; nothing and no one else at least for a few days."

"I like the sound of that. I didn't have any plans for tomorrow. If I take my laptop and can work from the hotel room, I can squeeze out more days. If I need to be here, I can slip in and then get back to you. I don't have any clothes with me."

Nash leaned back and looked her up and down.

"You won't need them. I'm serious. I miss this body. All this lusciousness will not need to be covered up unless it's with my body."

"You're serious?" she asked.

"Damn right I am. We're okay, right? I mean, not just for this moment or the next few days. I'm talking going forward, we're good?"

"Yes, we are. I'm glad you came to explain everything. I hope Zonnique will be okay. I've missed Yasmine and Ashton."

"They've missed you too. They've been asking for you."

"If you're okay with me calling them — I'd like to talk to them tomorrow."

"Of course. They will be excited to talk to you. "How are Kennedy and Kyrie doing?"

"They're good. I talked to them this morning."

"I talked to Kyrie a few times. They don't seem to hate me behind what happened."

"I didn't tell them."

"You didn't?"

"No. I didn't know what to say. I needed time to work that out. Then I decided to say nothing. Kyrie was so excited when he called me about the basketball game you're taking him to after Thanksgiving."

"I made him a promise way before any of this happened."

"I know. Thanks for not backing down from that."

"I would never do that. I promised you that I would love you and I meant it. I also promise to love all on you but in the morning. I haven't slept good in a minute."

"Sleep definitely needs to be in the agenda. I tried to sleep and couldn't. In your arms I'm ready to go right to sleep. Love me in the morning?" she asked.

"Of course, baby. Haven't you discovered that I love, love, love morning sex?"

"What do you do when we're not together?" she quipped.

"Let's get to my hotel and let me tell you about it. I want to be sure I get all the pity sex and love I can from my woman. I love you. Never doubt that under any circumstances. People will write stories and spread gossip for clout. Don't fall for anything you read or hear. Always come to me first, baby. I will always give you the truth and my heart. Deal?"

"Deal. Thanks for loving me. I could not have dreamed you up or the fact that I would love you so much."

"You did dream of me. Remember the man from your dreams? Never forget that it was me all along. When you said you couldn't see his face? Now, you can see it as often as you like. You will never need to wish for or dream of your perfect fantasy guy. I'm here for all of that."

"I think back on those dreams and you're right; it was you all along. I had to meet you and only you for that fantasy to become a reality."

"I'm glad I'm a part of it all. We're united. Nothing and no one can stop this love thing we have."

"Is going to Bali in December still on the table? I know you have a lot going on. I also know that in the midst of it all, you need a break. Going away can be good for us. I don't want to take our love for granted. I want all of you."

Delaney meant every word. Nash coming to her to share his truth was exactly what they needed in order to keep their love on track. Now, she needed to do her part and be there for him as much as she can.

"Yes, yes and yes again. I would love to put everything on hold for us to get away. I don't know what will happen with Zonnique. I'll let her family deal with that. They know how to reach me. Her parents have already said that they will stay in Miami for as long as it takes. They're retired, so they already plan to stay through the end of the year. These past few weeks have been a lot. We need that trip to slow it all down."

"I'm for that. Let's get out of here and slow this night down with some sleep. I'll go to my house and get some clothes tomorrow. Tonight, I only need a hot bath and your body wrapped around mine."

"I'm for that. Thanks for being understanding. I couldn't come to you until I was sure we could get back to building our love with the attention it needs. I love you baby! That's forever," Nash declared.

"Ditto, baby. Ditto."

# Epilogue

*Thanksgiving*
*One Year Later*

Nash let out an exhaustive breath.

"This will go down as the best Thanksgiving dinner in the history of dinners."

Delaney agreed and nodded her head where it rested on Nash's t-shirt covered chest. The Miami house was quiet. The food was all put away. They were finally stealing a quiet moment together.

"I'm with you on that. Can you believe how quiet this place finally is? It's been full of people all day. If I wasn't so tired, I'd stay up all night just to enjoy the silence."

Delaney was too tired to even admit how tired she was. None of that mattered now. She was exactly where she wanted to be.

"Where is everybody?" Nash asked.

"Well, James and Monica are visiting friends. They're going back to their hotel tonight but will see us tomorrow."

"Oh, right. I forgot they had a few other stops to make."

"So did my kids. I'm glad they finally made it before dinner was over."

"Did they enjoy having dinner with their father?"

Delaney nodded again.

"They did. Kennedy said he cooked a huge feast. Davis does love to cook. She and Kyrie surprised me by calling it a night early. I assumed since they were here in Miami that they'd be out in the night life. With this being their last year in undergrad, they have been hitting the books hard. Yasmine wanted to sleep in the room you put Kennedy in."

"They are joined at the hip. Yasmine watched the front door all evening waiting for Kennedy to get here. I love how they have bonded."

"Me too. Kyrie put Ashton down and then went to bed himself. Everyone else left and went home or to their hotels. We'll have another houseful of people tomorrow for brunch. I'm glad you had the idea to have Thanksgiving here at your house. Did the kids get to talk with Zonnique? I know you called her a few times but didn't get an answer."

Nash wasn't happy that it took a couple of hours for Zonnique to call and talk to the kids. He had been concerned until he called her parents to find out what was going on. Back in January, after everything had gone down after James and Monica's wedding, Zonnique decided to move back home with her parents. She promised to continue her treatment. She wanted to be closer to family. That meant being away from the kids. It was clear to everyone that for a while, she needed a life with no responsibility other than to take care of herself. He now had the kids full-time.

"Yes, she called right before we sat down for dinner. She's still getting used to a new medication that makes her sleep a lot. She didn't hear her phone. Her mother told her I called. The kids loved talking to her. I'm going to take them to see her for the Christmas break. They're excited."

"Are you planning to stay there a few days?" she asked.

"No. I'm going to come right back. I'll let them have their time with her. She only gets to see them on Facetime. They both understand that she has to get better. I think having the kids for two weeks will help her. What about you? Do you have plans during that time?"

"I asked about your schedule because I was thinking of planning a trip to the cabin in Georgia for the two of us. Two weeks of just us."

"Just us?" he asked.

"Yes. My kids are going to Jamaica for break. It will be their last trip before graduation."

"Are you sad about the time after graduation? Kennedy is moving to Washington, D.C. to attend Georgetown University Law School. Kyrie is moving to Los Angeles to attend UCLA for graduate school."

"Uh, don't remind me. I'm going to miss them. I see a lot of frequent flyer miles in my future. I'm happy for them. This will be the first time that they won't be at the same school. David and I have talked about splitting our time to make sure we get visits in-person with both kids."

"You'll be in that house by yourself."

"True. We're only four hours away."

"We don't have to be."

Delaney sat up and turned the volume down on the television.

"Come again?" she questioned.

"Hear me out. I'm over the four-hour distance between us. We tear up the road to see each other. I want us to move in together. I know it's a lot. That would mean my kids being under one roof with us. That in itself can be a lot. It's been on my mind. I want you with me. I don't want to uproot your life, especially your business. I'm thinking the kids and I can move to Tampa. I'm thinking of looking at properties there; definitely something on the water. I may even build. I want us to be together. I know it's a lot to think about. I'm hoping you'll think about it," he said.

Nash waited for all of the emotions he saw on Delaney's face to pass. He could see her wheels turning.

"Yes."

"Wait, what? Did you say yes to thinking about it or yes, you would like for us to move in together?"

"Yes, to us moving in together. I don't have an issue with that at all. You're right. We spend a lot of time on the road going back and forth to visit each other. We've been together over a year. This relationship is everything I could ask for. I'm so crazy happy. I love you. I want to be where you are. Having Ashton and Yasmine with us is a bonus. You know how much I love them."

Delaney felt her entire body being lifted into the air.

"Music, baby. Pure music to my ears."

Nash kept walking with her in his arms.

"Where are we going?" she asked.

"To bed to seal this deal. The house is quiet. Their rooms are upstairs while ours is down here. I need some lovin' to wrap this all up. Besides, tomorrow, we need to start making some plans. We need to either find a house or build one. It has to have enough room so that Kennedy and Kyrie will always have a home with us. We're going to have a wonderful life."

"You know what – that's the best and sweetest revenge on life. We are living it with love, on purpose."

# New novels from Cheryl Barton – Coming Soon!

*Three's a Crowd*
The Sullivans of Montana, Book 4

Preorder now at
https://www.amazon.com/dp/B0B44FB7GH

Businessman Shelton Sullivan was clear that as a kid, he loved life growing up on the Sullivan Ranch wrangling cattle and riding horses. As a man, he prefers big city life, wrangling expensive suits and most of all, riding sexy women. He was blindsided when a woman penetrated the wall of steel that surrounded, what some said was his black heart, when it came to being in love; he preferred lust.

Deputy Sheriff McKenna Gibson needed a fresh start in a new city. Escaping a life that was crafted for her had become old and dull. Sizzling, spicy encounters with Bozeman's most eligible bachelor was exactly what she needed to help her forget the secrets she was hoping to leave behind in her old life as a military wife.

Without warning, Shelton found himself swept up into McKenna's amorous sensualities that very much matched his own dalliances. Their steamy, seductive encounters led to even more explicit and erotic romps until Shelton's world crashed down like a Montana boulder. McKenna is injured in the line of duty and his world is rocked off of its axis when her military husband blew up the love he thought was blossoming from the one time he decided to let down his guard.

Is Shelton willing to forgive and forget and turn away from the red-hot stirring in his chest at the thought of her?

## *Leaks, Lies, Lust and Love*

The Brothers of Chi-Town, Book 7

Coming in 2023 at www.cherylbarton.net

Carlos Kincaid is an irresistible, rugged loner who has always been that good guy who finishes last when it comes to women. Just when he is getting his life on track, his Achilles' heel shows up by the name of Everly Robinson. Along with her came memories of their inexhaustible, hot, steamy, lust-filled nights between the sheets.

Everly chose the wrong man one time too many in her life. Now, she's on the run from a dangerous man and in desperate need of help. With nothing but the clothes on her back, she returns to the only man she trusts. Carlos was also the only man she's ever loved despite toying with his heart and leaving him for his best friend.

Carlos is frustrated that old feelings could lead him back into the arms of the woman he needed to hate in order to forgive. He couldn't tell if her story was filled with lies or truths. Unfortunately for him, Everly is still the only woman he wants more than his next breath. Is he willing to risk his heart and his life for a woman who once betrayed him and his love for her?

# *The Sweetest Temptation*

Preorder now available at www.cherylbarton.net

As a teenager, Gabrielle Mann fell in love with strikingly handsome Adonis Duqette, an older, close family friend. He was the sweetest of temptations who helped her save face in front of her friends. He then broke her heart by rejecting her declaration of love.

Adonis is his given name; A.D. is what his friends call him. As a special forces operative, he was simply known as, Jaguar. When the Mann family is in need, Adonis drops everything to provide protection for Gabrielle, no longer a teenager, but a sexy, vibrant, damn-near irresistible woman. He once had no problem resisting his desire for her. Being back in her life, he was about to risk it all for the woman he had begrudgingly left behind.

Gabrielle's star-studded career as Hollywood's next "IT" girl is derailed when an unknown assailant targets her political family. Adonis reappears in her life to her chagrin. He once told her to forget about him and she did. Now he's back, looking hotter and hunkier than any man should legally be. While he's trying to save her life, she's trying to save her heart from the one man she vowed to never love again. Gabrielle is about to learn that some things are easier said than done.

# *An Unexpected Destiny*

### Sister Act, Book 1
### Available Now!

www.cherylbarton.net

Destiny Lockhart's high school crush, Lincoln Cole, is again front and center in her life. She last saw him fifteen years ago when she threw him out of her bedroom after their one night together following the senior prom. That night had been her most embarrassing moment, leaving her feeling ashamed and undesirable.

There was no way entertainment mogul Lincoln Cole could ever forget the shy, yet beautiful butterfly that was Destiny from his years as a high school football star. The now feisty, sexy and self-confident executive who dripped in vibrant, dazzling appeal reminded him that they were never meant to only have a one-night-stand. They were always destined for forever.

# *For You, I Will*

Sister Act, Book 2
Available Now!

www.cherylbarton.net

Kasey Young discovered that a man would do anything to keep her in his grips, even if it's her ex-husband. She lived her life his way for years until she'd had enough and filed for divorce. He wants to insert himself back into her life with an ultimatum; take him back or lose custody of their kids. Kasey found herself between a rock and a hard place needing the help of a man she barely knew, but who stirred up deep carnal desires that had been lying dormant.

Attorney Darren Braxton stepped up to the plate to help Kasey with her child custody case as a favor for a friend. What he hadn't planned on was the hedonistic lust for a woman who could cause him to lose all he's gained because he can't say no to her. He did the one thing he could think of to save them both; he married her.

## *On The Right Track*
The Sullivans of Montana, Book 2
Available Now!
www.cherylbarton.net

Professional racecar driver, Dayton Sullivan, is the youngest of the Sullivan cowboys out of Bozeman, Montana. He's found himself in a bit of a jam when he falls in love with Kima McDonald, the daughter of a man who could be responsible for the death of Kima's mother.

Dayton and Kima run off to the Sullivan Ranch in order to escape the life she's being told she has to live to support her father's illegal schemes. It's discovered that her father has debts that can only be settled if he can get Dayton back on the race track and Kima married to a man she doesn't love.

Can their love sustain them through the ups and downs they'll face against her sinister father?

# *It Should Have Been You*

Now Available on Kindle Unlimited
www.cherylbarton.net

Karma:

Dr. Clayton Myers was never a believer in karma, but he did believe in fate. Both would soon collide and expose a secret that would impact the perfect life and relationship with the only woman he ever loved, but not the only woman he took to his bed. That revelation would put his life on a path he accepted while never forgetting what could have been.

Disappointment:

Dr. Donna Spencer had experienced one of the darkest days of her life at the hands of the man who made a promise of forever. She took the hit to her heart and realized nothing good lasts forever.

Fate:

After years of no contact, Clayton and Donna's paths would cross again, forcing them to face the past where their love resided, while wondering what should have been and if they could find their way back to love again.

## *The Power of Seduction*

Now Available on Kindle Unlimited

www.cherylbarton.net

Bakery owner Raquel Hastings assumed her relationship was perfect in every way, both in and out of the bedroom where she had enjoyed the most tempting, titillating, and out-of-this-world sensual romps between the sheets with sexy engineer, Preston Sharpe, a man who knows his way around a woman's body. That was until he took a job in another country which left her only with memories and intoxicating desires to be loved like that again. Her world had been turned upside down until the day he returned with a plan to turn her world right side up.

Preston's alluring visions of Raquel haunted him at night, alone in his bed in a foreign country without the woman he loved. With the chance to return home and to her loving arms, he dreamed of once again sharing nights of satiating passion that only two hearts meant for each other could share. He knew he had to ready his game of seduction if he were ever going to again have Raquel back in his life and in his bed. This time, his plan was to make it last forever with the hope that Raquel could forgive him and give their love another chance.

Read it for free on Kindle Unlimited!

https://www.amazon.com/dp/B09LSLFG6D

Make sure you check out book 1, of "The Brothers of Chi-Town", I Can't Let Go – now available for download and in paperback at www.cherylbarton.net

## *I Can't Let Go*

Carter Garrison vowed to love, honor and cherish his wife, Sienna, forsaking all others, something he forgot to do during a weekend of fun, bad company and poor judgement.

Sienna Garrison never dreamed her college sweetheart, Carter, whom she pledged her life to, would break her heart and when he did, she moved out and moved on - or tried to.

What better occasion is there than a friend's wedding to stir up old feelings and memories of love, intense passion and nights of sensual titillation. Gazes from across a room after almost two years apart revealed depths of love that had never died.

Seeing Sienna again reminded Carter of what he'd lost and he vowed to never let go by doing whatever he could to get his wife back even if it included begging and pleading. Is Sienna ready to forgive and take a chance on life again with the only man she'd ever really loved?

When Carter brings on the charm and turns up the heat, no woman is immune, especially Sienna.

Don't forget to snag your copy of book 2,
Swagger and Baggage, in "The Brothers of Chi-Town"
series – now available at www.cherylbarton.net

## *Swagger and Baggage*

It's not a coincidence that casino owner, Torrence Allen, ran into his college sweetheart, Reese Michaels again; it's fate. As his memories unfold, he had tried everything to keep her in his life and his bed back then and failed at both. She wasn't ready for him then, but he hopes she is ready for him now.

Reese Michaels never thought she'd see Torrence again. Their split in college was dramatic and hurtful and still, no man had been able to win her heart. She considered herself the permanent third wheel to friends who had found love and marriage.

Torrence's swagger has always won women over, but it's his baggage that's causing his life to spiral out of control. He messed up and found himself without the woman he has always loved.

## *About the Author*

Cheryl Barton lives in Maryland and in her spare time she loves to read espionage, crime and romance novels, cook, watch Sci-fi movies, spend time with family and friends and enjoy Maryland steamed crabs. Cheryl is celebrating over 30 years as a government employee and loves writing romance novels when she's not working.

Cheryl is the author of over forty romance novels, four inspirational novels and is proud of six book compilation projects with several other incredible women.

Cheryl was a 2019 Finalist for the Emma Award given by Romance Slam Jam and a 2018 Finalist for the Literary Trailblazer of the Year award by the Indie Author Legacy Award. Cheryl is a member of the Contemporary Romance Writers where she currently serves on the board as the secretary.

### Connect with Cheryl Barton

www.cherylbarton.net
www.crbarton.com
www.amazon.com/author/cherylbarton

Instagram: @cherylbartonbooks
Twitter: @cbartonbooks
Facebook: @cherylbartonbooks
YouTube: https://www.youtube.com/@cherylbarton